"Madison Smartt Bell writes with the urgency of someone who just received a dire prognosis. And *Behind the Moon* will remind you that you are alive."

—JONATHAN SAFRAN FOER, author of *Here I Am*

"*Behind the Moon* would have caught my attention simply because it was written by Madison Smartt Bell—a writer whose voice I always trust. I would have expected another precise detailed chronicle like *All Souls Rising*, one of my favorite novels. But this is not at all the voice I know—this is a unique and startling descent into a completely different kind of narrative. Yes, a fever dream but couched in the voice of a deft and careful writer who knows how to steer us into the lives of characters in trouble. We shift from the feverish imagination of Julie in her hospital bed to the plainly matter-of-fact accounts of the boys who chased her into the cave where she slipped and fell into a dream of cave paintings and the all too close terror of a black-headed bear. Between fever dreams and stone-hard reality, Madison Smartt Bell has crafted a powerful examination of what is and what might be. It is simply wonderful."

—DOROTHY ALLISON, author of *Bastard out of Carolina*

"This new novel by Madison Smartt Bell is disarmingly good. The patience, the deliberate strokes, the understated tension and the inevitability of it all is pure Bell and yet he shows up here with a completely different voice. I love these characters. I love the writing. *Behind the Moon* is a brilliant work."

—PERCIVAL EVERETT, author of *Half an Inch of Water*

"Bell gives us this fast-paced, spiritually inspired dream-story, full of heart and hope and danger. It's adventure at its finest: a spiked drink, a desert cave, a gunshot, a mother looking for her child. Buckle in: you are headed for a terrific ride."

—DEB OLIN UNFERTH, author of *Wait Till You See Me Dance*

"*Behind the Moon* is a visceral, full-body primal experience; terrifying, seductive, Madison Smart Bell at his best."

—A.M. HOMES, author of *May We Be Forgiven*

"*Behind the Moon* is a thrilling and uncannily powerful story by one of the best living American fiction writers. I couldn't put it down."

—JOHN MCMANUS, author of *Fox Tooth Heart*

"Madison Smartt Bell is one of the great American masters. His prose scintillates with particularity and hints at divinity. I read *Behind the Moon* in one sitting and was moved by Julie's inchoate spiritual longing as well as her mother Marissa's primal drive. This book has a pre-religious power, read it and be inspired."

—DARCEY STEINKE, author of *Sister Golden Hair: A Novel*

"With spare but lyrical prose, Madison Smartt Bell tells a harrowing story with propulsive drama. A haunting and hypnotic read."

—HEIDI W. DURROW, author of *The Girl Who Fell From the Sky*

"Madison Smartt Bell's *Behind the Moon* is a fever dream, indeed. Modern medicine has conceived no antidote for such an atmospheric, rewarding entanglement of lyrical genius. Mr. Bell writes like a scrimshaw's angel, as he's been doing, luckily for us, nigh four decades."

—GEORGE SINGLETON, author of *Calloustown*

"In his latest work, Madison Smartt Bell secures his position as one of the country's most innovative, inventive and accomplished writers. Part horror story, part dream, part meditation, *Behind the Moon* creates its own meta-Gothic category. The story turns the usual teenaged drama of sex and drugs on its head and then spins it into a four-dimensional God's eye woven with mystical, spiritual and maternal threads. From the heart-racing opening to the eye-opening end, you won't be able to put this book down."

—JESSICA ANYA BLAU, author of *The Trouble with Lexie*

"Madison Smartt Bell is a master of structure with tremendous range, which is on full display in *Behind the Moon*. This cinematic novel is a rare combination of smart literary novel and compelling page-turner, at once menacing and sweeping, dark and transportive, eloquent and hallucinatory."

—MICHAEL KIMBALL, author of *Big Ray*

"Taking readers to places both spiritual and shot through with adventure, Madison Smartt Bell's new novel renders the many ways in which longing can take form, with both disastrous and redemptive consequences."

—CHANTEL ACEVEDO, author of *The Distant Marvels*

BEHIND THE MOON

BEHIND THE MOON

A fever dream by
Madison Smartt Bell

City Lights Books | San Francisco

Cover and book design by Linda Ronan
Original calligraphy by Miles Mermer

Thanks to Hillary Louise Johnson for being the first to get
the point and for the germ of a design plan, to Linda Ronan
for making this fantastic design happen, to Stacey Lewis for
making them look, and to Elaine Katzenberger for being a
wise, good, patient and insightful editor.

Library of Congress Cataloging-in-Publication Data
Names: Bell, Madison Smartt, author.
Title: Behind the moon / Madison Smartt Bell.
Description: San Francisco : City Lights Publishers, 2017.
Identifiers: LCCN 2016057672 (print) | LCCN 2017004677 (ebook) | ISBN
9780872867369 (softcover) | ISBN 9780872867444 (hardcover) | ISBN
9780872867376
Subjects: LCSH: Coma—Patients—Fiction. | Teenage girls—Fiction. |
Shamanism—Fiction. | Magic realism (Literature) | Psychological fiction.
| BISAC: FICTION / Literary. | FICTION / Visionary & Metaphysical. |
FICTION / Psychological. | FICTION / Occult & Supernatural. | GSAFD:
Occult fiction.
Classification:LCC PS3552.E517 B44 2017 (print) | LCC PS3552.E517 (ebook) |
DDC 813/.54—dc23
LC record available at https://lccn.loc.gov/2016057672

City Lights Books are published at the City Lights Bookstore
261 Columbus Avenue, San Francisco, CA 94133
www.citylights.com

For Celia,
who tried her best
to help me make it better

"The dreamer enters the unknown world. . . . The dreamer, in the course of such journeys, meets other beings and speaks with them. She may sometimes meet other dreamers, in the form of energy. She is able to make speedy departures and returns between the known world and the unknown world, which always gives the impression of being outside time."

—Mimerose Beaubrun, *Nan Domi*

"Understandably enough, they would have believed that caves led to that subterranean tier of the cosmos. The walls, ceilings, and floors of the caves were therefore little more than a thin membrane between themselves and the creatures and happenings of the underworld. The caves were awesome, liminal places in which to be."

—Jean Clottes and David Lewis-Williams,
The Shamans of Prehistory

"The acoustics magnify every sound, and it takes the brain a few minutes to accept the totality of the darkness—your sight keeps grasping for a hold. Whatever the art means, you understand, at that moment, that its vessel is both a womb and a sepulchre."

—Judith Thurman, "First Impressions: What does the world's oldest art say about us?"

1

The eye was on her first—the first thing she knew. A brown eye with sickles of a yellow gleam around the edges of the iris, attentive, indifferent—did it even see her? She could not see any part of herself, only the eye that seemed to regard her, with a kind of warmth, she felt, but she was still wondering if it saw her at all and not at all sure that she wanted it to.

She couldn't feel her body in the dark, and she thought of being frightened by that, but it was just a thought, not fear itself. She remembered that not long before she had been truly frightened, but she didn't remember anything more than the sensation. Where did the light come from in which she saw the bear? It was so, so dark at the bottom of the . . . Of the shaft. A sort of shaft, maybe; she had fallen into it.

Maybe. She didn't remember that, either. There was no pain. Now the bear's head organized itself around the golden-brown eye, there the dark muzzle, damp nostrils, a hint of white teeth and red tongue . . . another eye, but this one hidden under the heavy, hairy bone of the brow, and turned a little into the stone, as if it had not yet come out of the stone.

Maybe it was only a   a trick of a few deft lines, streaks of hematite and ochre, that made the bear appear in her mind. Cunningly stroked across a natural contour of the rock. Yet she could feel the warm ebb and flow of the bear's breath across her face (it was that near), could hear the grumbling of its breath. The big shoulder and the high, humped back of a grizzly coming toward her, as if through a fissure of the rock.

Emerging, as if the stone was water. A grizzly!—she should have been afraid.

But this, this creature was older than any grizzly, by hundreds—no, thousands of years. And the eye was like her own, she knew, and she was seeing with the same eye that saw her.

2

A bright white light bore down on her, piercing, like a laser or a diamond.

Julie, Julie . . .

The voice hauled on her, dragged at her. She knew it. Did she, had she loved it once upon a time?

Julie . . . What happened? Julie . . .

The voice wanted her to come out of the cave. She would not come.

3

In the yellowish gleam of her mind's eye she saw herself
among them, five of them on three motorcycles raising red
dust as they came across the desert floor toward the rock shelters. She would have liked to ride with Jamal but he had the
smallest, lightest bike—hardly more than a scooter really, and
Marko had urged her up behind him, while Karyn and Sonny
rode together, and Marko roared out in the lead. Julie sat with
her legs uneasily forked around the squat muscles of Marko's
back, and now and then he looked over his shoulder at her
in a greedy way she didn't like, but she liked the rush of air
in her face and the way her long black hair streamed in the
wind, from under the band of the turned-around ball-cap she
was wearing—none of them had helmets.

To savor the speed she closed her eyes. A picture appeared: a tousle-headed little girl in a calico dress, riding
behind her father on a bicycle, reaching out for something—
rambler roses twined through pickets of a fence the bicycle
passed; in this daydream it was springtime. The little girl could
never quite get her fingers to touch a rose, but whenever she
reached, the rear wheel of the bicycle wobbled, and the father,
unaware of the cause, bent more sternly into his pedaling.

"Don't do that." Marko's voice, cutting through the snarl
of the engine. "You'll dump us."

Julie started out of her reverie. Had she, herself, reached
out her hand? There was nothing nearby. They were crossing

a long wide flat of the desert and the nearest hillocks of paint-ed sand looked halfway to the horizon.

Sonny pulled level with them, the drone of his engine beating with Marko's. Karyn's face smooshed out against his leather back, her mouth a little open, moist, like a sleeping mouth that breathed against a pillow. Sonny shrugged his near shoulder, rolled the throttle with a faint smile. He pulled ahead, and Marko tilted in to the right of his tailpipe. In the roar of the bigger engines Julie couldn't catch any hint of Jamal's smaller one. She tried to look back to see where he was, but she couldn't turn her head far enough without unbalancing the ride.

Now they were coming into the long shadow of the cliffs where the rock shelters were. Marko swung the heavy bike in a long curve that brought them out into the sunlight again, beside a boulder, where Sonny had stopped. He put his heel down and cut the motor. In the quick shock of silence Julie thought she heard the cry of a hawk overhead and she looked up, blinking into the sun, which was still high. There would be several hours of daylight yet, and she thought it must be three, or three-thirty—buzzers would be ringing to let her out of school, if she hadn't skipped.

Karyn, who might have been thinking a similar thought, gave her a complicit smile as she swung her leg clear of the saddle of Sonny's bike. Hastily, Julie scrambled down herself. Her legs felt rubbery from the long, shuddering ride. She took a few backward steps away from the others and turned to look in the direction they'd come from. With a distant, crickety sound, Jamal's smaller bike persisted toward them, leading a plume of the reddish dust. His hair in a cloud around the triangle of his face. Sunlight winked from a yellow lens of his wraparounds.

"Rice-burner," Sonny said, and turned to spit Skoal Bandit juice in the sand.

Marko winked at Sonny, then pulled the bandanna from

his head and used it to wipe grit from his face. "That's a spaghetti-burner, dude," he said and grinned aslant at Julie, pushing back the inky waves of his hair. "He'll get here some day, won't he?" Marko said. White teeth.

4

Now the light of the eye was extinguished, and she saw instead a pattern of dots, in umber and ochre, splayed over a hump of the stone, dividing into two bands like a tree trunk forking, like branches of a stream. The pattern swirled and scattered, and then for a time there was just darkness.

She could feel an object in her hand, a cool and smoothly contoured rectangle; it must be her phone. If she turned it on, there would be light. If it turned on.

Away on the surface, in the rose-colored dusk, the moon had appeared before the sun quite set, a wafer frayed on the edges like lace and pale to near transparency, against the deepening blue of the sky. Jamal said one of those weird things that charmed her: *I wonder what it's like behind the moon.*

5

The bikes ticked slightly as they cooled, there beside the boulder. Jamal had pushed up his yellow sunglasses to investigate his saddle bags. Karyn frowned into the screen of her phone, blinked at the bright images emerging and dissolving. Sonny ran his blunt fingers down her spine into her waistband, and Karyn elbowed him and wriggled away.

"Of course no signal," Sonny said. "What else did we come here for?"

Marko pulled a clear bottle full of a bright violet liquid from his inside jacket pocket and tossed it Sonny, who had to stoop to catch it. Bad throw. Straightening, Sonny uncapped the bottle and passed it to Karyn, who took a gulp without looking, still fidgeting with her phone. Once she had registered the taste she pushed the phone into her tight front pocket and reached for the bottle again. Then Sonny offered the bottle to Julie. Julie shook her head.

"It's okay," she said. "I've got water."

"You need your vitamins," Marko said. She could feel him looking at her—she didn't look back. Jamal was laying out the components of a small dome tent on the sand beside his silvery-blue Vespa. Julie watched him, his long fingers shaking out the sectioned poles so that the elastic cords snapped them together at full length. She picked up one of the poles and flexed the fiberglass.

"Here," Jamal said. "You thread it this way."

Marko bent over his heavy black-and-silver Harley,

unloading from the leather saddlebags: trail mix and MREs, a much, much bigger tent kit, a small vinyl case that he unzipped to reveal a sleek little video palm-corder.

"Whoa," said Karyn. "Cool camera! Where'd you get that?"

"Ultimo." For a moment, Marko caught her in the camera's steely eye. Julie watched Karyn, playing up, shifting the rounded weights of her body, tossing her honey-streaked hair back and exposing the white line of her throat.

"Okay, lemme see," Karyn said, reaching for the camera. Marko held it away from her, making her reach across his body, then let her have it.

"Jeez," Karyn said. "High rez, huh?" Her fingernail jabbed at the tiny buttons. "Look how you can zoom in on that. Look, Julie, I can see all down in my pores."

Gross Julie thought, but she was helping Jamal with the tent, capturing the poles at the corners so he could slip the floor pins into them. The tent took shape as its own small world, a free-standing hemisphere, and for some reason Julie pictured the other half that would make it whole, existing somehow like a reflection beneath the sand.

Jamal stood back, resting his knuckles on his narrow hips, and in the next moment a gust of wind caught the tent and whirled it end over end across the sand toward the horizon. Jamal stood frozen for a beat before he took off after it, and Julie started after him, but the wind was faster than both of them; they would never have caught the tent if it hadn't died down.

Jamal seized the poles where they crossed at the top, then doubled over, winded by the two-hundred-yard dash. Julie trotted up, gasping herself, and laid one hand on the curve of a tent pole. Back by the boulder, under the cliff, the others were capering and slapping their knees, their faces twisting with inaudible laughter.

"Shit," Jamal said, running a finger along a four-inch tear in the netting of one of the side windows.

"No biggie," Julie said. "There's no bugs out here anyway. Too dry."

Jamal looked at her thoughtfully, then nodded, as if they'd made a deal. Then he picked up the tent like a briefcase and started back toward the cliff.

"Need help?" said Julie.

Jamal shrugged. "It doesn't weigh anything." But then the wind gusted up again, and Julie had to catch the other side of the tent to steady it.

"Stakes won't hold in this loose sand," Sonny said, when they had come back.

"Tell me about it," said Jamal. "We'll have to get rocks and weight it down."

"What, inside?" Julie said.

"Of course, inside," Jamal said. "Hold this a minute."

Jamal's tent would barely hold two people, and that was without any rocks inside it. There were only two tents. Julie had not thought about how that part would work out, and she decided not to think about it now, holding the tent in place while Jamal looked for rocks.

6

She could feel a cool, metallic object in her hand; it must be her phone. If she could turn it on, there would be light.

The screen shed a pale luminescence toward her, a pale glowing rectangle, like light caught in a mirror. It contained no image and no word. At first it seemed that she looked down into it, holding it cupped in the palm of her hand, but in the dark of the cave there seemed to be no gravity, and this cup of light might just as well have been beside her, or above, impossibly distant, like that frayed wafer of daylight moon, faint in the washed colors of the evening sky.

7

"Rice-burner." Sonny smirked, turned his head sideways to spit Skoal Bandit juice in the sand.

Jamal straightened from the tent he was assembling, rested his light knuckles on the black waistband of his jeans. "You dissing my *machine*, yo?"

"No, man," Sonny said. "I wouldn't do that." He turned to offer Julie the garnet-colored bottle. "Here you go, girl. Cut the dust."

Jamal stooped over the parts of his tent. Karyn was mugging for Marko's camera, striking a series of runway poses—chin up, wrist cocked to the ear, giggling into it, *ooh la la*. A slight heaviness in her movement made Julie wonder if Karyn might have had a shot or so before they started. Not that she'd mind a buzz herself, but then she wasn't a complete idiot: dehydration was an issue out here, and Julie had one liter of water for herself. She didn't quite know what the others had brought.

Marko ducked and weaved like a paparazzo, pursuing Karen with the camera's metallic eye, as Julie took a small sip from the red glowing bottle. There was no bite of vodka or gin. Just vitamin water, something like that—but a sicklier sweet than usual. She took a larger swallow and handed the bottle back to Sonny. Karyn was play-fighting Marko for the camera, *gimme gimme lemme see*, and Marko held it high over her head, making her stretch for it. Her T-shirt hem rode high and the gold of her navel-stud winked in the sun.

"Damn, don't break it," Marko said. He let her have the camera. Karyn gathered it toward her cleavage, wiping her dirty-blond hair from her face as she peered into the camera's bright screen. Her chipped black fingernails clicked on the camera's tiny buttons. "Look it, Julie," Karyn said. "You can practically zoom right down your own throat."

"Gross," Julie said, absently; she was admiring the tent, which Jamal had just finished assembling: a silver-gray hemisphere sealed into the sand. Something in the shape of it appealed to her. Something about the way her image of it trembled around the edges. Sonny cracked a beer and gave it to her—where had he found that? The foam was acrid in her mouth, connecting with a bitter aftertaste from the vitamin water she'd had a few minutes before. She took a larger gulp to wash it out.

Two slightly sweating, soft vinyl coolers had appeared beside the pair of Harleys. Sonny pulled out two more beers and dragged the coolers into the shade.

"Don't be dumping that ice," Marko said.

"Huh," said Sonny, "I ain't drinking it, not out of there."

"We can cook with it," Marko said. "We got a pack of freeze-dried stuff."

"Are we Boy Scouts or what?" Sonny said, and Karyn laughed, elbowed him, let her blond head roll back against the warm stone of the boulder.

Jamal fired up his little stone pipe and sent it round among the others. Julie took the weakest possible hit, then left the circle before the bowl could come to her again. She didn't want to get too high too early. Maybe at night, when the stars came out, when sleep would be soon to come. The business of the tents would all be sorted out by then, but she didn't want to think about it now. There was a voice in her head that said *be careful,* and she especially didn't want voices to start splitting off and talking to her from somewhere else.

The shadow cast by the cliff wall had grown to about six feet long, and Julie walked into it, feeling perhaps she might disappear. She sat down cross-legged in a niche of the vertically channeled stone. From here the orb of the tent seemed like an object of contemplation, like some meteorite that had embedded itself in the desert floor, and she imagined the other half of the sphere it described, twinning with it beneath the sand. There was a kind of aura around it. The stone behind her was still radiating warmth, like the walls of an oven, from the sun that had been shining on it for most of the day.

Trippy weed Jamal had—she reminded herself to go slow with that, lifting her arms and setting her palms together in a mudra above her head. As her palms touched she felt a spreading warmth below her navel, much stronger than she'd ever been able to get in her half-hearted attempts to practice yoga. A tingle across the smooth-shaved skin of her bare armpits. The tent rippled as a light breeze shivered over it.

Jamal was studying her from behind his yellow lenses, in that way that made her feel no one else could see her, even though the others were all there. On his cat-shaped, sallow face, the buggy glasses made him look like pictures of a space alien, sometimes.

"The Jule in the lotus," Jamal said; funny, but it wasn't a joke.

The wind came up and snatched the tent, which flew away across the plain of sand, sometimes skating on its flat bottom, sometimes rolling end over end. The others were laughing, watching Jamal caper after the tent—every time he almost caught it the wind would pull it just out of his reach. Julie was running like you can run in dreams, with a deep, springing, effortless movement, breathing as evenly as in sleep. That was trippy weed for sure. They captured the tent at last and held it still between them. Rippling in the remains of the breeze, the silvery fabric glimmered like snakeskin, and Julie still felt that warmth in her belly, spreading like the onset of happiness.

8

The pattern of dots billowed toward her, stretching and pocketing over the same roll in the wall that had formed the shoulder and hump of the bear. Or maybe she had moved somehow and was now in a different part of the cave. She didn't know how she could have moved, because she couldn't feel her body, although she remembered that not long ago she had felt the cool curve of her cell phone, fitting into the cupped palm of her hand.

She watched the pattern; it seemed important somehow to grasp it. A pattern in four dimensions; in her mind she heard those words, like a voice-over in a movie. But she was seeing it only in three. Umber, ochre, now a near-scarlet red, and there were three spirals swirling around each other—a triple helix, the dots drawing toward each other but never quite touching, as if a magnetic energy held them together, held them a certain distance apart.

For a moment she was inside the swirling particles, as if she was standing under rain.

9

She followed Jamal up the ledge that led to the first rock shelter. He climbed magnetically, as if he had suckers on his fingers and toes, and his head looked outsized on his slim body, maybe because of its big cloud of hair. Where the ledge leveled out to a wider shelf there was a vast overhang, three stories high, with a few trails of vine hanging from its upper lip. Because the overhang blocked the setting sun, it was suddenly almost cold. Julie wrapped her arms around herself. She'd left her jacket with the bikes.

On the inside wall there were tags spray-painted by other kids who'd come out from town, fat cushiony three-D letters smushed together like marshmallows crushed in the bag. Jamal pulled a plastic trash bag from his pocket and methodically began to scour up beer cans. After a moment Julie shook off her chill and helped him. There were chip bags and candy wrappers, too.

"Now what?" Jamal opened a crooked smile, hefting the three-quarters-full bag.

Julie shrugged and walked to the outside edge. Away below and to the left, Sonny and Marko were anchoring poles for an umbrella tent—it would be big as a room in a regular house when they were done. Karyn had scrambled to the top of the boulder and lay on her back on an Indian blanket, her white forearm shielding her eyes from the red rays of the declining sun. Julie pictured the turbulence that would follow if she or Jamal dropped the trash bag.

"Nah," Jamal said. "The bikes won't carry it. We'll be doing well to come out with what we brought in."

Julie turned toward the inner wall. At one end of the puffy chain of tagging, there was a narrow, dark slit in the rock. "In there?"

Jamal shook his head. "You ever think how you can't throw anything away? I mean, you can throw it. But it doesn't go away."

Now Julie was conscious of herself shrugging. "I guess so," she said, which seemed equally hapless. Still carrying the bag by its closed throat, Jamal walked toward the rock shelter wall.

"Wiggers," he said, shaking his head as he read the tags, left to right, stopping where the opening pierced the stone. Julie stood a step behind him.

"You ever go in there?" she said.

"No thanks," said Jamal. "I don't like tight places."

Julie looked into the gap in the stone. It seemed flat black, as if painted on the surface like the tags, as if after all there was no interior. She would have had to stoop just a little and turn sideways to get into it. Jamal was almost a head taller, but so skinny he might have folded himself up so he would also fit.

He set the bag down and touched her shoulder with a fingertip; the touch felt faintly electric through the cotton of her shirt.

"Come on," Jamal said. "Let's go find the sun."

10

Seeming somehow to know her way, despite the utter darkness, she moved a little distance along the passage, then turned back. It wasn't so completely dark after all because there was the light of the phone screen, behind her now; its bluish-white, unnatural luminescence spreading from the cupped hand of the girl where she lay. Then the light went out. But the battery would not have died yet. The screen had shut down to conserve the battery.

She thought of turning the phone on again, and yes, a thumb must have pressed a button, for the light reappeared, and now she could see how the body lay where it had fallen, half on its back and half on its side, knees drawn up, the pale face turned sideways, eyes closed now. On the rock where the head rested there was a darkness flowing, more beyond the fan of Julie's dark hair. Yes, surely this was Julie's body, but she was not inside that body now.

Would the blood smell attract the bear? But the bear was an illusion, it was painted on the wall, and then there was something else painted there, or not, something she saw now or had seen, a swirl of bright specks in spirals, like a cyclone or the image of a broad-bladed, fleshy leaf that bulged and rippled in the rising wind.

The light of the screen shut down again; she turned away from it and continued along the passage, careful not to brush the wall on either side. She seemed to know where the walls were, although she couldn't see them. The freshness and sense of movement in the air was receding behind her. Ahead of her the black atmosphere felt increasingly heavy and close, but it was important that she continue to move deeper into the cave.

11

Ascending more gradually now, the ledge wrapped around the cliff wall to the north. At a narrow place where Julie hesitated, Jamal reached back to help her along, and then they had come out into the warmth of sunlight. Jamal let go of her wrist and turned toward the lowering sun, raising one hand to shade his eyes, inside the yellow goggles. On this side of the cliff the horizontally striped stone hills were densely grouped together, with shallow, dry canyons snaking between them. The first phase of the sunset picked the landscape out in bands of turquoise and rose.

"Wow," said Julie, "We could be on the moon."

"Except—" Jamal pointed to the horizon. A glint of reflection from a car window as the vehicle turned a loop in a band of blacktop. It was too far away to hear the motor, and when the car turned out of sight Julie couldn't even pick out the thread of highway any more. The whole desert valley resonated with an airy silence.

Then squeaking, like a hamster in distress, and it grew louder, but there couldn't be a hamster in mid-air. From below the lip of the ledge where they stood the beating wings of a hawk came into view, flogging the air as it flew to perch on a crag a dozen yards away.

Julie pulled out her phone to take a picture, but felt Jamal's warm palm, this time on her forearm.

"Don't," Jamal said. "Just. . . . Watch it."

The hawk tightened its talons, and the squeaking

abruptly stopped. Julie didn't know if she wanted to watch, and she wanted to ask what the hawk had caught, but how would Jamal know better than she? It couldn't be a hamster of course, and it was bigger than a mouse, and furry. A prairie dog. Did they have those here? She watched the hard bright eye of the hawk as the curved beak dipped, cut and penetrated, then raised a quivering strip of bleeding meat. There was something dreadful about it and yet—

"They're not cruel," Jamal said, as if he'd read the half-formed notion from her mind. "They're just not on our program."

12

"You ever think how you can't throw anything away? I mean, you can throw it." Jamal shook his head. "But it doesn't go away."

Still carrying the bag of litter by its closed throat, Jamal walked toward the rock shelter wall. With a faint clatter of beer cans he set the bag down and raised a crooked forefinger as he scanned the painted tags from left to right.

"Freakin' wiggers," he said. Julie didn't quite know what he meant by that. Jamal was scanning left to right; then his head stopped moving.

"What?" Julie asked.

"Yeah," Jamal said. "Come here. You can only see him at just the right angle—depends on the light."

Julie put her head near his and then she saw it, an image shallowly etched in the stone, just to the left of the dark opening that led who knows where. A round, shapeless body like a small child might draw, stick legs running, an antlered head. If not for the head, the petroglyph reminded her of paramecia she had watched through a microscope in ninth-grade biology class. Jamal had been one of her lab partners then, and they had taken turns lowering their heads to the black ring of the microscope's upper lens.

"Who did this?" she said.

"Brulé." Jamal's voice went guttural as he said it.

"What's that mean?"

"Burnt Indian," Jamal said. "No, but they didn't do it.

I'm just blowing smoke. These things are way older than those guys."

Julie felt her bare arms stippling up in goose flesh. It was cool here in the shadow of the rock shelter, and a current of colder air seemed to come out of the slit in the stone wall. Jamal crouched over his heels, a finger tracing.

"There's more down here, I think. There were. But you can't see much of them now, under the tags."

"That's awful," Julie said.

Jamal squinted up at her. "What?" She saw his gray eyes floating in the yellow bubbles of his lenses.

Julie shrugged. "Kids tagging all over . . . something like that."

"Yeah . . . I don't know." Jamal straightened and took a backward step, still looking at the wall. "Something else'll come along and cover all this up too, don't you think?"

Julie looked down, to her knee level. On the stone was spray-painted the letters KAOS, in the lurid red and purple colors of a bruise. A tag for a gang Marko and Sonny had belonged to in high school, it was probably four or five years old. There was indeed something under it too, the pattern Jamal's fingertip had followed. Her eye could not make out what it was. Jamal caught her right hand with his left, pulling out her forefinger as if it were a pencil. As he guided her finger over the stone she felt that she was beginning to read the image, but the glimmer of understanding spooked her for some reason. She giggled to disguise the feeling, pulled her hand away from Jamal and took a long step back from the wall.

A butterfly lit on the peak of the A in KAOS. Its wings stirred the air, an iridescent, heavenly blue. Julie shivered as the butterfly flew.

"Hey, you're getting too cold," Jamal said. He threw an arm over her shoulder, bumping her clumsily into his ribs. "Come on, let's go find the sun."

13

The hawk finished eating, shrugged its feathers into a ruff around its neck. Its head pushed back and it shrieked once before it flew. The sharp, harsh sound thrust out of the open beak like a blade. It seemed to linger once the hawk had flown, its cross-shaped shadow briefly stroking over the turning of the canyon below the ledge. Julie shuddered.

"It bother you?"

She turned to find Jamal's face nearer to hers than she had expected, his own nose a bit hawkish really, but he had taken off his wraparounds and his pale gray eyes looked warm.

"I don't know," Julie said, not knowing if she wanted him to come nearer; if he did come nearer their faces would touch. At the base of her neck she felt the faint warmth of the setting sun. To the left of Jamal's curly head was the frail lace round of the daylight moon. Julie turned away, toward where the—whatever it had been when the hawk had caught it wasn't much of anything now. A pattern of bones hanging loose in the remains of sinew, a stain of red fluid spread over the stone.

"Have you heard the bear tape?" Julie's back was still to Jamal.

"What? —what are you talking about?"

Julie looked at him now. She had made him uncomfortable. "Don't you know?"

"That's no reason why *you* should." Jamal had put the yellow wraparounds back on. "What's making you think about it, anyway?"

"That, I guess," Julie tossed her head, a little sulkily, at what the hawk had left. "Don't tell me if you don't want to, then."

"Don't be like that—" Jamal cut himself off. He leaned on his elbows, let his head drop back, till his longish dark curls grazed the stone they were sitting on. The white-dusty moon and the reddening sun were at opposite ends of the sky, with the space between them curved like a rainbow.

Jamal sat up and shook his head, as if to dissipate the sourness of their last exchange. "I'll tell you if you want to know," he said. "I guess it's even dumber not to."

"It's just—"

Jamal took off his glasses, and looked at her again with that warmth.

"Karyn talks about it?"

"*Karyn?*"

She could see the widening whites of Jamal's eyes. "I mean she talks about Sonny and Marko talking about it."

"Right," said Jamal. "I guess that figures." He looked away, up toward the moon, then quickly back at her.

"Well so there was this guy, you might have heard, who got a notion he could live with grizzly bears. A long way from here, off on the edge of the world, I guess. Somewhere you needed a ski-plane to get there. A nut-job, this guy, if I have to say it. Anyway he kept going up to wherever it was to hang with the bears, whatever, and he would shoot video of all this. Him and his bear buddies. And he talked this girl, a girlfriend, I guess, into going up there with him for a couple of weeks. . . ."

Jamal dropped his head between his knees. "That's the part I really don't get . . . why the girl played into this. She was good-looking, and she seemed plenty smart, so why she'd go off in the boonies with this loser lunatic—"

"You've seen this?"

Jamal picked up his head and looked at Julie. "You can rent it if you want. Some director got hold of the nut-job's video and turned it into a docu-drama. But the part you're talking about's not in that. . . ."

"The part I'm—"

Jamal began to hurry the story, words rattling together like cars on a speeding train. "It went wrong one day with the bears, it seems, and—the bears ate them. Both of them. All gone. Then a few days later a plane came in to take them out and all they found was bones. And the camera. That's the part you heard about. There's no picture I guess, or not much picture, because the nut-job dropped the camera and it's just getting pawed around in the weeds, but you can hear them. You can hear them screaming and you can hear the bears—"

Julie's stomach shrunk to a cold wavy kernel. "You've heard this?"

"*Hell* no, and I don't want to hear it. I don't want to hear anything about it. I wouldn't have told you if you didn't ask."

"So it's *my* fault." Julie flared up. "Because I asked."

"I'm sorry." Jamal turned half toward her, put his hand on her shoulder again. The touch calmed her. "It's not like I *wanted* to talk about it but it seemed better to tell you than make some big mystery about it—which is what Sonny and Marko do, and then it gets a hold on you, just because you *don't* know. . . ." Jamal looked off across the peaks and canyons, turned candy colors by the light of the setting sun. "Sometimes I wonder if that's what hooked the girl in, some mysterious mojo the guy made up for her about his bears."

"And Ultimo has this thing, this tape."

"I don't know what Ultimo's got," Jamal snapped. "Sorry. . . ." He squeezed her shoulder, let it go. "Sonny and Marko say Ultimo says if it exists somebody wants to buy it, and as long as somebody'll buy it somebody will sell it. So maybe Ultimo sells copies of the thing, like some kind of snuff-film or whatever. . . ."

"You know him? Ultimo?" Julie felt the syllables of the name between her tongue and her teeth, with a faint illicit thrill.

"If I see him coming, I know who he is." Jamal laughed briefly. "Then I get on the other side of the street."

He looked again at the rodent remains smeared over the rock. "Okay, you're right. It *is* like the hawk."

"What do you mean," Julie asked.

"Like the bears, you know, they were just being bears. It wasn't the bears. It was the people."

14

There was light again, but not moon or phone light. Instead it was a warm, reddish light, from a fire or torch. It played over the wall of the passage on her right side, but she couldn't see the source of it on her left, because she didn't look in that direction, and because she knew that in fact her eyes were closed; she was seeing what she saw in some other way.

The passage opened into a wider space. She felt that to be so from a change of the air. The warm light had vanished, and the darkness was complete. All directions disappeared, but she kept moving, without hesitation, as if there was a path she could follow, one she knew.

15

Jamal propped his elbows on the stone, leaned and let his head fall back. The mop of dark hair brushed the stone behind him. Julie studied the wedge of his Adam's apple, thrusting up. There was a little cut just under his jawline, from shaving probably. Jamal's beard was as heavy as Marko's although the rest of him was not. The yellow wraparounds, and the angle of the light, made his face look stony, mask-like. He rolled forward suddenly and caught her looking.

The sun had struck into the horizon, shattering like the red yolk of an egg, spilling crimson and violet bands across a cloud bank to the west. In this intense light the colored stone layers of the sand-castle mountains were picked out with a jewel-like clarity. As the red line on the horizon compressed, it grew painfully bright, which was maybe why Jamal still wore his sunglasses, now. Behind his head was the papery moon, gathering ghostly light from the sky as the sun faded. Jamal not moved any nearer to her but she felt a pressure, not necessarily unpleasant, between his face and hers. What did he mean? How would it be to be with Jamal, behind the moon?

It was cooler, and she shivered and wondered if he'd reach for her; maybe he was wondering the same. But instead he slipped his narrow hand into his windbreaker and came out again with the black stone pipe. He packed the bowl and turned the stem toward her, one eyebrow arching.

Julie didn't know why she should be so skittish about a little herb tonight. She wasn't usually. *Be careful*—the voice

41

that seemed to come from some distant adult, one of the tiresome kind. Didn't Julie know very well what she was doing? They'd planned the escapade with thorough care, so that that Julie's mom believed that she was spending the night with Karyn, and Karyn's parents believed the reverse was true, and in case they stayed out more than one night they had a back-up plan for that as well, except there was no phone reception here, but they could ride somewhere to where there was. The idea of the tents popped into Julie's head again, this time like a word problem in math. *Julie, Jamal, Sonny, Karyn and Marko have two tents. Tent A has a volume of X and tent B has a volume of Y. If Y >X, how do the five people divide into the two tents?*

If Julie liked the idea of sharing Jamal's little cozy tent with him, then she didn't know what she was doing so well after all, because this was the first time she'd let this interest appear to her so openly. It wouldn't be so cozy anyway, now that the tent was half full of rocks to weight it down. Julie knew Karyn was doing it with Sonny and had been for months (Karyn, without exactly ever talking about it, had let her know in a dozen little ways . . .) but that tent solution didn't solve Marko's position. So she and Karyn might share the smaller tent, lumpy with rocks as it would be, but this seemed like a solution to offer the parents if they'd dared tell the parents they were going off to camp in the desert with the boys; it couldn't be the real solution. Besides, the idea of Jamal in a tent with Sonny and Marko seemed weird and wrong, like putting two different species of animal in the same cage.

These thoughts ran through her in a rapid blur, in the time it took to wave away the pipe. Jamal snapped his lighter over the bowl, drew the flame down, held it. With his exhale, which was nearly smokeless, he said, "You sure?"

Julie shook her head again. "Your weed's too trippy."

Jamal took his wraparounds off and looked at her a little strangely. It wasn't the look that would lead him to say something like *the Jule in the lotus.* It was more like he was inspecting around the edges of her eyes. He looked like he was going to say something but he didn't.

"What," Julie said. "What?"

"Nothing." Jamal put his glasses back on, looked down at the stone space inside his crossed ankles. The stitching on his left boot strap had come loose on the inside. "You didn't drink any of that pink stuff, did you?"

"What, Sonny's bottle? No, I brought water." A shock of understanding struck her, like a slap. "Wait a minute, are they trying to *dose* us?"

Jamal raised his head, but not all the way. He said, "It's just molly."

"*Just molly!*" Julie had jumped to her feet. An unpleasant giddiness swarmed in her head.

Jamal got up and reached one hand toward her; Julie backed away from it. The vermilion sunset band had burned itself out below the horizon, and what light remained was turning dove-gray.

"Karyn's okay with it," Jamal said, unhappily. "She's done it before."

Karyn's okay with it. Julie could feel the words in her mouth, as if she'd spit them back at him, sharp and incredulous. But a new kind of problem, with a few different variables, was beginning to shape itself in her mind. She said nothing, only whirled away, rushing back around the ledges the way she had come, aware of Jamal scrambling along behind her, calling to her not to run like that she could fall—

16

Julie kicked Jamal's sack of cans out of her way as she tore past it. Kicked it into Jamal's way possibly, for Jamal was coming along behind her, calling to her, but in a strangled whisper, to stop. To *talk* to him. And she knew that certainly Jamal could have overtaken her on the ledges if he'd wanted to, that he'd decided to try persuasion instead, even when persuasion wasn't working.

On the eastern side of the cliffs it was quite dark now, the last stains of sunset blocked by the mountain, the wispy moon too frail to throw much light. Behind her she heard Jamal, catching his foot in the bag of old cans, stopping to free himself and throttling a curse. The reddish desert across which they'd biked in the afternoon was now diffused in a pale, internal glow. Against it Jamal's little tent sat dully, or no, it had the faintest surface sheen, gathered from the light of the silver stars beginning to appear. The larger tent had a light within it, concentrated and surprisingly bright; like a will-of-the-wisp caught between the fabric walls, it kept moving along the inner surfaces, casting dark, large, eerie shadows, but Julie couldn't make out what they signified. It seemed to her she could hear the whole tent purring like a large contented animal, but maybe that was the effect of Jamal's pipe.

She dropped to the level sand and walked toward the big tent softly. Jamal was hissing from the edge of the cliff, beckoning her to come back to him, but he seemed to want not to make too much noise, maybe because of whatever was going on in the tent, and so Julie herself was careful to be quiet, setting each of her red high-tops down like a cat's paw on the sand. Something tingling, a soft expansion in her throat (if it was fear or excitement she didn't really know) was making it slightly hard for her to breathe. The same sensation prickled below her navel. How were you supposed to knock on a tent, anyway? She could hear Jamal now, padding up behind her over the cooling sand, not wanting to call to her because—

So she wouldn't call to the people inside. She caught hold of a big black zipper at the top of the curving tent door.

17

In the darkness there was a sound of drumming, warm broad hands slapping loose skins (skin maybe still growing on some animal's hollow flank, not yet stretched over the dug-out wooden round of a drum). With the drumming the light returned, warm like torchlight, though there were no torches nor torchbearers to be seen, as if the hands that drummed were fanning flames. Like a river of pulsing fire away and down to her left, illuminating the gallery wall to the right of her and above . . . and the gallery was big, enormously hollow, like the halls of cathedrals in other countries maybe, that she might have seen in photos, on TV.

On the right wall and spreading up onto the ceiling above were bison, such a stampede of bison as she had never seen (even if she was really only seeing them projected on the lids of her closed eyes), magnificent in umber and ocher, humping their weighty shoulders out of the natural curve of the rock, bigger too, it seemed to her, than the ordinary buffalo still to be found here and about on the ranches or even ground up and packaged in the meat counters of the groceries around where Julie lived her daylight life. Among them too were antlers, not deer, she thought, but elk. And they looked at her in the same way as the bear had done before (where had the bear gone, then?). The eye of each animal person was upon her, like it knew her. Even though there were so many of them in this procession, which seemed at times perfectly orderly, as if every animal knew and followed the same purpose, and at other times seemed completely anarchic, as though all of them were caught up in a flood.

As the light faded, the panorama fractured into the pattern of brightly branching dots she'd seen before, though now and then from the vortex she could still pick out a horn, an antler or a clear bright eye. She moved beside the stream, her bare heels (what had happened to her shoes?) sinking into heel prints made by others long ago in what had once been clay. She was hurrying, before the light failed entirely, toward another narrow opening at the lower end of this great hall, into which the animal persons also seemed to swirl, and she felt somehow certain that on the other side of the slit portal there would be a human being, its head sprouted with horns.

18

Jamal took his wraparounds off and looked at her a little strangely, like he was inspecting around the edges of her eyes. His own gray eyes looked knowing, and a little hard. He seemed like he was going to say something but he didn't.

"What," Julie said. "What?"

"Nothing." Jamal put his glasses back on, looked down at the stone space inside his crossed ankles. With one hand he fidgeted with the brass ring on his left boot strap, where the stitching had come loose on the inside. "How much did you drink out of Sonny's bottle?"

"What, that vitamin water?" Julie shrugged. "Just a taste. I was thinking it might be spiked but it wasn't."

"Not with—oh. . . ." Jamal ripped the ring completely free of the loosened strap and twirled it around his finger. The brusque destructiveness wasn't like him, and that upset Julie more at first than whatever it was he wasn't telling. That peculiar warmth and softness in her belly when they'd chased and captured the tent was still there, or it had always been there and she was now again aware of it. And with it a sort of crenellation around the edges of her vision. When she turned her head to stare at Jamal, the early stars drew lingering pale lines, like jet-trails, across the darkening sky.

"Did they dose us?" Julie heard her voice go all cracked and screechy—maybe this too was the effect of a drug, if it wasn't suspicion making her feel it. She was on her feet with her white hands balled into fists on her hips. "Jamal—what was in that bottle?"

"I don't . . . don't know anything for sure." Jamal had also gotten to his feet, fidgeting with his sunglasses and the brass ring torn from his boot, but somehow he wouldn't look at her with his bare eyes.

"What do you think, then? God damn it!" Julie felt some of her mother's bitchiness coming out of her mouth, didn't care.

"Molly, maybe." Jamal looked away toward the horizon, where the last red line of sunset was like a razor cut. "I don't know anything really, Julie—they might've candy-flipped it."

"Candy— Jamal, talk English."

"They'll cut it sometimes, you know, with acid. . . ." Jamal looked at her straight on now; the subject had gone abstract for him and so now he could explain it. For a second she thought she saw a little snail-shaped op-art graphic vibrating on the side of his face that was in shadow. "Or really the idea is to cut the acid with some X—less chance of a bad trip that way, they say."

"Who the hell is *they?*" Julie shouted at him. "Some stoner committee advisory *board?* Or is it just Sonny and Marko? *Marko!*" Her voice had climbed at the end, as if she was calling Marko, but that was something she definitely did not want to do . . . and Jamal seemed to have the same thought. He took a step toward her, one hand outstretched, as if that would calm her—Jamal's long-fingered, slender, rather beautiful hand, delicate and assured as the hand of a musician (though she'd never seen Jamal play any instrument), and it seemed almost a golden color against the rock floor below, which was taking on a milky bluish tinge as the light continued to fade.

"I'll stay with you," Jamal said, in that soothing voice— she remembered Jamal was good with animals. Once when they were walking a dry creek bed in town a big stray dog had approached them, growling, hackles up, but Jamal had been cool then, calmed the dog, eluded it, sent it on a different way from them.

"You didn't take much, whatever it is," Jamal was saying. "I'll walk you through it, it'll be okay. There's no reason to think it'll go bad on you anyway. And I'll be here if—"

"Karyn." Julie snapped, feeling droplets flying wild from her lips with the name—she was getting that far out of control. "We just leave her there to drink the whole dose then, and be with those two *Neanderthals*—"

Jamal's hand swirled down to his waistband, like a falling leaf. He'd tucked his wraparounds in the collar of his shirt; the ring from his boot hung from the index of finger his other hand.

"Karyn's okay with it." He hesitated. "It's not her first time."

There was something hidden behind the words, inside them. For a moment Julie seemed to see his head break open like the hollow moon's cracked crystal, and there inside was the hidden thing, purling like a feather of dark smoke. Jamal was blocking her way back to the tents and the others, perhaps just by chance, but she dodged past him before he could react and began to run over the ledges. She could hear him skittering along behind her, calling out, but in a hoarse stage-whisper—*Julie, come on, don't run like that! You're gonna fall and break your neck*—

19

She drew the black tab of the zipper down. The tent flap furled outward with a slow liquid motion, the thickness of a banana peel opening, but she didn't want to think about a banana, she didn't know why. A sick, excited feeling gripped her by the belly and the throat, but she was hung up on the movement of the tent flap to the point that she couldn't yet see past it. It reminded her of that curious, fleshy broad-bladed leaf form—but she was seeing that in the cave, not now, not here. The inside of the tent was big as a regular room, high enough that Marko could stand erect inside it, a piercingly bright light cupped in his hand.

Here was the will-of-the-wisp light she had seen from outside the tent, diffused and softened by the fabric of the walls, circling and probing toward the center she realized now, though the light was so bright she couldn't really see past it, only Marko's heavy dark silhouette surrounding it.

"Julie." Marko's voice was reassuring, or trying to be. "We were hoping you'd come."

White teeth. His hand cupping the camera dropped, so that the bright point of light that had blinded her softened as it pooled across the tent floor, and she could see Karyn moving out from under Sonny's shadowy weight, raising herself partway up from the rumpled Indian blanket. Pushed down from her shoulders and pushed up from her waist, her top was a wrinkled band around her ribcage, which somehow made her seem more abjectly naked than if she'd been completely bare. Her glazed eyes, a glistening on her cheek—she wiped at it with the back of her free hand.

"Come on in," Marko said. "We're just getting started."

His hand with the camera rose toward Julie again, maybe an unconscious side effect of his welcoming gesture. The image of Karyn disappeared in the glare, and Julie understood that the light that had been used on Karyn was now intended to be used on her.

20

Sometimes she got eye wiggles when she was rolling, but that was different, a lot different from seeing stuff that wasn't there at all, like those swirling paisley patterns she'd seen on the side of Jamal's face before she ran away from him on the ledges. Now it was iridescent snakeskin patterns on the tent flap when she pulled the fat tab of the zipper down and the flap peeled from its toothy track. Flipping something, candy flipping. Jamal said. She wanted to go deeper into the rolling feeling, warmth and openness, cuddlesome closeness. The tent flap furling downward was a triangle that inverted the triangle that wanted to pull her forward by the nubs of her breasts and the bottom of her belly—then too the dizzy fascination of watching that happen, the tent flap unfurling itself slowly, looking at it from some other place, like when you were watching something secret, forbidden. Even what Karyn was doing drew her on, and it didn't even matter that there were more than two. No worse, no different, than joining a rolling kitten pile. It was the light on the camera that pushed her back, its sharpness piercing like a scalpel, making her not see not understand so much as feel, way down in the base of her brain, that Karyn was being done, not doing.

White teeth. "Come on in—we're just getting started."

The light stabbed at her, pushed her back. She took two backward steps from the door of the tent before she turned and ran.

21

When she turned from the blaze of white light in the tent door, Jamal was there behind her, spot-lit, his skinny arms outstretched and his face blanched to a featureless pallor by the blast of illumination. Had he herded her, manipulated her into this place?

"You—" she said, "You—" The blur of his face resolved as she came nearer, but she couldn't think what to put behind that *You*—accusation, endearment, curse? The light went out suddenly, and for a second or two Julie couldn't see anything at all, then forms begin to pick themselves out of the darkness, blue-black sky outlining the cliff, the silvery shapes of the bikes where they were parked. And nearer, Jamal's spidery silhouette, an arm reaching toward her, and she thrust out her hand, to deflect him, or to grasp—she didn't really know which. Their fingertips barely brushed as she rushed by, and that contact tingled, shimmered like a *déjà vu*. Go, Jamal hissed—she was already past him now.

Jamal had turned back toward the tent. "Just let her go, Marko." And Julie was thinking that he meant her to escape from the situation altogether, but how? She didn't even know how to start Jamal's little scooter, the only one of the three bikes she might have been strong enough to manage, and it could never outrun the Harleys anyway, and they were out on the empty desert with nowhere to hide, unless she went up the same way on the ledges around to the other side of the cliff, where the hawk had been that afternoon—

"Too late," Marko's voice was reasonably calm, a reasonable tone stretched over strain. "She's in this far, look it, she's got to come all the way."

Julie turned back. Jamal had rooted himself in the sand, knees bent and his feet set apart. Marko crouched in the mouth of the tent, holding a flashlight now, with a softer beam than the spot on the camera, the light stain fading as it spread across the sand behind Jamal's boots.

"Julie's not in this." Jamal said. "She never was."

"If that's how you feel," Marko said, "you dumb-ass sand-nigger, all you had to do was keep her away."

Then Marko's attention moved to her, though Julie wasn't sure that he could see her where she hesitated, high on the balls of her feet, a little beyond where the pool of flashlight failed. "Come back, Jule—we're not gonna hurtcha! It's all. . . . It feels *good*, once you get into it, y'know, like Karyn is."

Something in that scared Julie a lot more than she had been scared before and the *run* impulse was shooting up her legs, erupting in her spine, and still somehow she was frozen in place, transfixed by Marko's wolverine eyes, if he could actually even see her, when Jamal was blocking most of the light. Then Marko suddenly charged up out of his crouch, raising the flashlight like a club, and it was one of those six-D-cell maglites like the cops used, too, but Jamal went down on one knee and as Marko rushed him he tossed a palm's worth of sand into Marko's face, and that broke the momentum. Marko dropped the light and covered his eye-sockets with both hands, calling out blindly, *you stinking camel-fucker, I'll kill you when I catch you, you—*

Julie ran. All she could hear was Karyn screaming, the two-note scream that switched itself on at ball-games or car wrecks or concerts or if Karyn saw a snake— it just kept on going like a siren or a car alarm till something shut it off. She reached the cliff and scrambled up the ledges, tripping and crouching, using her hands. Her eyes had recovered from the spotlight blast, and now she could see well enough in the feathery light of the moon, but she supposed the others could see her too.

55

22

Once, Julie had been riding up an escalator while Jamal (was it Jamal?) was riding down. She didn't know him then, not really, but the same impulse struck them both at the same time, so that they reached their hands across the gap between the up stairs and the down. Their fingertips brushed with a feathery tingle, for one light instant before the machinery carried them each away on a separate orbit. As if some other life had swung just close enough to hers for that faint touch, then veered off. She didn't look back after they had passed. The escalators ran in a well of glass walls, and the afternoon sun came pouring through, bathing everyone in a flood of golden light.

The herd of animal persons swirled into the opening at the end of the great hall, which she was now approaching— she was guided by a force she felt inside her, though that force was not her own. Her bare feet fit securely into heel prints that led her through the portal now. The horned being she'd expected to see was not there. She touched the back of her own head with her fingers, and saw again the image of Julie at the bottom of the shaft, lying in the bluish-white glow of her cell-phone screen. Where had the animal persons gone? She had seen them all streaming through the opening into this small round chamber, but now they were nowhere to be found. Her vision fractured, and the pattern of dots streamed in a spiral—she thought that the dots must be the eyes of the animal persons, which had lost their bodies but were still regarding her.

Then they were gone, and her vision steadied. On the curving wall before her she did see a series of little horned heads—no, they were handprints, negative images, a black paint surrounding the pallor of the stone, so that the hands seemed to glow a little, like the phosphorescent plastic stars stuck to the ceiling above her bed at home. One print seemed to attract her hand magnetically, the left one, and when she laid it there it fit so perfectly there was no line around it. Her left hand disappeared entirely into darkness as complete as the velvet black of a starless sky; it sank a little way into soft stone.

23

She ran for the bikes before she realized that she had no way to start one up, and the Harleys were too heavy for her to handle anyway. The big tent had gone dark now, and from its shadow came the shrill two notes of Karyn's repetitious scream, and the low grumble of Sonny's voice, trying to shut her up. Marko lunged toward her, a silent bulky shadow, and Julie dodged behind his Harley. Her jacket still lay across the saddle where she had left it in the heat of the afternoon. Black vinyl, torn and cheap; she couldn't afford leather. As Marko rounded the bike and came at her again, she snatched it up by one sleeve and lashed the chrome studs into his face. She had no strength, and the jacket no weight to make any real impression on Marko, but maybe a stud had caught him in the eye. He fell back against his bike, one hand rising to his cheekbone, and the bike collapsed under him. Marko dropped with it to the sand, air oofing out of him as his tailbone slammed down.

Julie ran for the cliff and scrambled up the ledges, tripping and crouching, using her hands. The jacket encumbered her but for some reason she didn't want to let it go. She stopped long enough to tie it around her waist by the sleeves. Someone was climbing up after her, though, but not Marko, not yet. He was still struggling to get his bike upright in the loose sand.

Julie stopped, winded, on the ledge below the first rock shelter. The pale moon sailed through the sky like a paper coracle. Karyn's scream had subsided to a whistling gasp. Sonny stood with her outside the big tent; he had wrapped the Indian blanket around her and draped his arm across her shoulders, almost tenderly.

There was someone climbing toward her—she heard scrabbling on the rocks . . . though still not Marko; she could see that he had just left his bike and was trotting toward the bottom of the cliff. Jamal, then. Was he speaking to her, calling her name in a low voice? Or was it only a sense that his mind was trying to reach hers. . . . It had gotten chilly quickly, now that night had fallen in the desert. Julie shrugged into the vinyl jacket. A couple of the studs had pulled partway loose when she'd whipped the thing into the Marko's face. It was secondhand, the sleeves too long, and when she wrapped her arms around herself the studded cuffs dangled like ties on a strait-jacket.

Did you know? She was thinking. *Did you know this whole sick program all along?* She remembered the math problem about the tents, but that seemed foolishly remote now, like some concern she might have had as a little girl. *Because if you knew they were planning to dose us, then how could you not know all the rest?*

She hugged herself tighter through the vinyl, crumpling slightly over the dizzy swirl in her belly that this thinking gave her, wishing the jacket were armor so she could disappear completely inside of it. And after all it was totally too awful to think that Jamal could have been in on the whole thing from the start, with Marko, with Sonny. And what had Karyn known that Julie didn't?? —no, she couldn't, wouldn't believe that.

There had to be another way to tell herself the story. Jamal would tell it to her another way. Marko was out of sight now, somewhere under the edge of the ledge she was standing on, so he must be climbing, and she could see that Sonny had left Karyn, who stood wrapped in the blanket in front of the tent, perhaps still whimpering; from the angle of her elbow Julie thought she might have covered her mouth with one hand.

Sonny and Marko would both be coming after them now. After her. She thought of following the ledges around to the place where they had watched the hawk feeding, where the stone hills rolled to the horizon. Somewhere back there was the ribbon of road where they'd seen the car pass in the sunset, but it might be miles and miles away.

Jamal's slender hands appeared on the ledge, and with a long smooth movement he pulled himself up.

Julie . . .

What! She turned from him, toward the distant moon.

Look . . . He floated one hand in her direction, as if he wanted to come nearer, but he didn't. *I didn't—all I— when I saw that bottle I had a thought. And when I saw the camera—even then I thought well, if—I thought I could just take you a—*

And she still couldn't tell if these scraps of words were spoken, or if it was just the pressure of a thought trying to fumble its way across the rift that had been opened by what had happened. What was happening still. Certainly his voice was much louder, clearer, when now he turned around quick as a cat and shouted down to Marko, "Don't try to come up here."

Jamal kicked a couple of loose stones over the ledge, and Marko shouted, not even a curse, and she heard him next in a lower tone, "Listen to me you little shit—she can't just come in and go out like that. Once you're in, you're *in.*"

When Marko's hand came over the ledge, Jamal stomped it with his boot-heel and the hand jerked away, but then Marko's head and shoulders rose over the rim. Jamal kicked him in the face, but Marko snatched his support leg, and Jamal fell over backwards, landing hard. As Marko came up onto the ledge Jamal got up quickly, and he booted the sack of cans he'd collected to tangle Marko's feet, and Marko did stumble—"You little *shit!*" he cried. His nose was bleeding where Jamal had kicked him, but he didn't seem much bothered by it. Jamal put himself in Marko's way, and Marko batted him

aside like a fly, a mosquito—Jamal flew back and fell rolling
into a cranny of the rock shelter, and Julie had no time to
wonder if he was hurt, hurt bad or not, because now there
was nothing between her and Marko.

24

Her hand absorbed into the stone, her whole forearm sinking in, as if into a pool of warm, black oil. She turned her head to press her cheek against the stone. Under her palm was a hot, scratchy something, like a pelt, and she could feel a rough breath lifting and relaxing it. The warmth and surprise of this other breath jolted all the way back to her shoulder, and she wanted to pull away but she couldn't, and after all she didn't really want to—she needed to go forward, to go through. The left side of her face lowered into the wall, like sinking into her pillow while she was slowly absorbed into sleep, and she thought that now her left eye must be just where the eye of the bear had been, before. Now she must be eye to eye with the bear. Except instead she was inside him. Beyond the infinite thickness of the stone her forearm suddenly pushed through, so she could move it freely now, turning it from the elbow, feeling the heaviness of the bone and paw-pad where her hand had been. From her fingertips sprouted the black curving claws of the bear.

25

When Marko's hand came over the ledge Jamal stomped it with his boot-heel, twisting his foot to grind down on it with the metal tap he used to scuff pavement when he put a boot down from his bike. The hand jerked away, but then Marko's head and shoulders rose up over the rim. Jamal kicked him in the face, but Marko snatched Jamal's other leg, and Jamal went over backwards, all unstrung and landing so roughly that his head snapped hard against the rock, but maybe the cushion of his thick hair had protected it, and as Marko came over the ledge Jamal got up quickly and with the side of his foot he swiped the sack of cans he'd collected into Marko's path, and Marko's feet did tangle on the trash bag—"You little *shit*!" he cried.

Jamal took one backward step, reaching around to the back of his waistband to pull something out from under the hem of his windbreaker. Julie didn't get a good look because of the quickness of the movement and the uncertain moonlight, but whatever it was changed Marko's tone.

"Oh no," Marko said. "You're not gonna shoot me."

Julie was looking at Jamal's back, since he had put himself directly between her and Marko, and over his shoulder she could see Marko holding both of his hands palm-out, leaning a little into his palms; he seemed to lean into an invisible wall. She was aware of the narrow, dark slit at the back of the rock shelter just behind her, as if it had already opened to enclose her, as if she had already moved into the close, tight mouth of the cave.

"Are you sure?" Jamal asked. Was his voice slightly trembling? It was steady when he spoke again. "How bad do you really want to find out?"

"Jamal," Marko said, staying just where he was. "It gets so much worse."

26

Once

across the gap

a feathery

tingle,

a separate orbit.

well

glass walls,

gold light

flood

anomOnanimal

swirl into the opening coming

nearer—

force she felt inside her,

not her.

The horned being

streaming into this small round

nowhere to be found.

fractured

braid SEWofD

ADP bright points

a spiral—eyes

AD I9I PJ U

awomOnanimal

still regarding her.

—no, they were handprints, negative images, a black gum surrounding the pallor of the stone, so that the hands seemed to glow a little, like the shining of the stars. A certain print seemed to attract her hand magnetically, the left one, and when she laid it there it fit so perfectly there was no edge around it. Her left hand disappeared entirely into darkness, complete as the velvet black of a starless sky; it sank a little way into soft stone.

She lay . . . no, she was standing, but gravity had changed direction, so she felt as if she were lying at her ease and comfortably supported by the wall, and against her cheek she felt a soft rise and fall, as if she'd laid her head upon a living, breathing breast . . .

On the other side of the stone's vast thickness Julie felt her forearm come free, turning and groping in emptiness, the mystery beyond the stone.

She couldn't understand how she had said it or how she'd understood what she had said. But she felt a small hand, no larger then her own (but stronger), taking hold of hers. The palm was leathery and warm, with more hair on the back of it than on hers. The other hand began to pull her through the stone.

27

As Marko came over the ledge Jamal got up quickly and scraped the rattling sack of cans to tangle Marko's feet.

"You little *shit!*" cried Marko. With his heel he kicked the trash bag behind him, out over the ledge. A moment of silence, then a clatter when it landed somewhere down below.

Jamal took one backward step, reaching under the hem of his windbreaker to draw the pistol from the bottom of his spine. The chrome of it glimmered weakly in the moonlight. It looked small.

"What is this, a fucking cap gun?" Marko said. "You're not gonna shoot me."

Julie was looking at Jamal's back, since he had put himself exactly between her and Marko, and over his shoulder she saw Marko halt and hold both his hands palm-out, leaning a little into his palms, like he was pushing against an invisible wall. At any moment the tilt would bring him lunging forward, through Jamal, toward her.

"Are you sure?" Jamal said. He lowered the barrel, using both hands; the shot, though tinny, splintered rock at Marko's feet. Marko looked down as if dumbstruck, then backed a couple of steps away.

"Hold on," he said, as Sonny pulled himself over the ledge behind him, and came from a crouch upright.

"Jamal," said Sonny. "Don't—" He turned slightly and caught Marko by the elbow. "Man, it's not worth it. Let's just go."

28

"What is this, a fucking cap gun?" Marko said. "Nah, Jamal—you're not gonna shoot me."

"What would you bet on it?" Jamal raised his left hand to support the pistol, bending his knees slightly; his upper body framed a triangle, with the barrel at the point. Marko kept on leaning forward, as if pushing against an invisible wall, and then he broke through it, roaring, lunging through Jamal toward Julie—the gun made two inconsequential pops and Jamal skipped aside, since Marko wasn't stopping. Julie edged away, but slowly, like she was pulling her feet out of paste. Behind her she felt the slit of the cave's opening, as if it had already taken her in.

Marko fell face-down at Julie's feet. Fluid seeped out from his torso, spreading on the stone beneath him, slow as maple syrup in the moonlight. Julie clapped both hands over her mouth, to clamp off screams and the urge to puke. Where was Karyn? She wished she'd really spent the night at Karyn's. She wished they both were still ten years old, whispering and scattering cracker crumbs beneath the sheets of a shared bed.

Then Sonny pulled himself over the ledge.

"Jamal," he said, as he brought himself from a crouch to his feet. "What did you do?"

"What would you do?" Jamal raised the gun barrel bolt upright, pointing at the moon, and for a moment Julie wondered if he'd turn it on himself. Sonny's eyes went from Jamal to the blood that purled from Marko's body, then back to Jamal again.

"Jesus," Sonny said. "It looks like a goddamn starter pistol."

"Not much knockdown to it," Jamal said. "But it'll kill you just the same." He aimed the pistol at Sonny, bracing it as he had before. "Three shots left."

29

Let me come out of this rock.

    She couldn't understand how she had said it or how she'd understood what she had said. Through joined hands she and she were balanced on a cusp and the wall of stone was no more than the finest membrane between them. For a moment they spun around in a slow orbit on the axis of the hand clasp. Then Julie felt herself pushing through, or the membrane was shaping itself to accommodate her, like a glove turning itself outside in. Or herself, with the other hand inverting to fit itself perfectly over her own, the whole other skin stretching over her flesh, her bones, her re-forming body.

    Now the stone wall was behind her and she stood on the ledge before the rock shelter, her face in the wind, looking out through astonished eyes of the other, into another world.

30

Jamal threw himself in Marko's way, and Marko backhanded him aside, swatting him off like a mosquito—Jamal flew off, tumbling as he landed, rolling into a crack of the rock shelter. Julie had no time to wonder if he was hurt, hurt badly or not, because now there was nothing between her and Marko, and nowhere to go but the cave.

She had to stoop, turning sideways to get into it. The edges of rock pressed into her clammily, and she thought, with a half-hysterical hiccup, of spiders, snakes—but Marko was roaring outside the opening, thrusting his heavy arm and stubby fingers after her. She *had to*—had to go further in. And what if her life ended just like this, like a kernel stuck in the whorls of a nut? The passage tightened as it turned, stone scraping the vinyl between her shoulder blades; she heard a couple more studs tear free and patter down.

Then something gave, or softened rather. The texture of the passage changed, still pressing her on all sides but rubbery now, as warm as flesh, and pulsing. Tripping, tripping—her heart tripped in her mouth—she could hope the whole thing was just a weird trip, if they had cut the molly with acid, like Jamal had said.

If she hadn't drunk that water. If she had. Her head thrust tighter and tighter into the clasping walls of the passage, then finally, dizzyingly, broke free. She was falling into a cool breezy space, with no direction and no gravity, as if she were falling asleep.

31

Marissa woke as intended to the sound of the unearthly chant: *qui sedes ad dexteram Patris, miserere nobis.* She sat up on her prayer mat, hands folded across her heart, breathing as she had been taught, sharp intakes of air through the nostrils, pulled down to the bottom of her belly, then harshly expelled. The rushing sound of her breath flowed in and out between the long sustains of the singing. Ten breaths brought her alert. What had been the dream she was just dreaming?—but she was not meant go toward that now.

Quoniam tu solus sanctus. Tu solus Dominus.

Breathing normally now, forgetting even that she breathed, she lowered her hands from her heart and let them lie palms open on her inner thighs, in the cross of her legs on the prayer mat. Her palms were full of heart warmth, as if they cupped warm fluid in the dark. The darkness was not total, though. A weak light flickered in a high corner, partially obscured, casting a horned shadow across the floor and the far wall where it broke on the black felt that sealed the window. She brought her mind to bear on the First Sin, that of the Angels.

— . . . wanting to recall and understand all this in order to make me more ashamed and confound me more, bringing into comparison with the one sin of the Angels my so many sins, and reflecting, while they, for one sin, were cast into Hell, how often I have deserved it for so many. . . .

In doing so,, she concentrated on a point of warmth halfway between her navel and her vulva, as though blowing softly on a coal—this practice belonged to a different discipline yet she believed it might aid this one.

Qui tollis peccata mundi, miserere nobis

. . . the sin of the Angels, how they, being created in grace, not wanting to help themselves with their liberty to reverence and obey their Creator and Lord, and thus they were changed from grace to malice, and hurled from Heaven to Hell; and so then . . .

qui tollis peccata mundi, suscipe deprecationem nostrum

But here Marissa's mind got stuck on the word *hurled*, which somehow attached itself to a weakness in her meditation, whispering itself into meaninglessness, tawdry as the hidden iPod on which she'd looped a Gregorian *Qui Sedes*, setting its timer to rouse her from her idle dreams at midnight, false as the yellow Christmas bulb tucked on top of her tall corner cupboard, which **hurled** the shape of its fineals across the room like horns. Mocked by her own monkey mind she trembled in frustration, **hurled** back and repulsed from the meditation even as she continued hopelessly to struggle

to move the feelings more with the will.

The music stopped, but she didn't notice, and the light was gone too, something had changed, monkey mind was fussing over these changes but she managed to smother it quickly and completely, turning her being into the new thing, whatever it was, or rather, being snatched into it by three points, the one below her navel and the two aching points of her breasts. Across total darkness curved a sliver of light like a shooting star, going down and down, hurled down. O, O, O, she thought, with unutterable sorrow, She is lost. Back in her room, which somehow her being had departed, her hands were fluttering in her lap. Far away in the other realm, among its splintering materials. Lost to me. To herself. Not to herself.

The spark went down a long way into darkness, but it did not go out.

32

Peggy Keenan flipped the top of a box of Winston Lights and shoved it across the mesh table toward her. Marissa shook her head, pushed the pack away, watched Peggy draw a pale cigarette from the box, strike fire from a pink butane lighter. She took a sip of the tasteless coffee from the office machine, whose only value was to wash down cigarettes, and with her other hand she slipped the beads in the pocket of her white lab coat along their string. Not that Peg's cigarettes really tempted her. Marissa smoked—used to—real tobacco: Marlboro Reds, or Luckies when they could be found, the short Camel straights, something that would turn even her fingers brown, let alone her lungs. She hadn't quit for health reasons. It was a mortification, and she felt it that way; the stale weak smoke from Peg's exhale, blowing across her face in the autumn wind, was just a nasty smell, but enough to fire her craving.

Peggy arched a plucked crescent of eyebrow. "How long's it been?"

Marissa worried a bead on her hidden rosary. "Six days," she said.

"Five hours," said Peg. "Forty-three seconds."

Both women laughed briefly. Peggy tipped her ash onto the pavement—the same hexagon-scored concrete she'd seen spooled out by U.N. nation-building efforts all over the Third World. The wind skirled the cylinder of ash toward the narrow end of the trapezoidal courtyard, where a row of waiting clients smoked in the windbreak of the retaining wall and drank from containers hidden in paper sacks. It was just early autumn, but the breezes had a bite.

"Seriously now," Peg said. "You're halfway home. Or better. First day's the worst, just pure hell. Then the first week's bad. Then after that—" She took a drag and blew it out over the head of her cigarette, held vertically before her face, "—it never gets any better!"

Marissa looked at her, then away, toward the narrow end of the courtyard. In the space between them and their clientele, pigeons hunted crumbs through a windblown litter of snack wraps.

"What?" said Peggy, stepping on her butt with the fat soft toe of her fleecy boot. "You think I don't know how to quit? I do it all the time!"

Marissa smiled thinly at the old gag, watching a pigeon peck its way closer to her own sneakered feet. She'd counted her way to the rosary's cross. Claude had bought it from somebody on the rez, he'd told her, but it was finer than the usual tourist trinket, the beads satiny and sleek, the crucifix made of two different woods: light cross and a black Christ.

"We used to club those things by the thousands," Peggy said, looking down at the same pigeon. "Back when they were thicker than snow." She made a fake retching sound. "Lord, I wouldn't eat one now if you paid me."

We who? Marissa wondered briefly. Peg's name and her pleasures were strictly Irish, her hair dirty blond and her eyes an impish green. Marissa had once blundered on her personnel file, where the statement that Peg was one-quarter Oglala Sioux had struck her at first as some kind of mistake. Later she took a closer look at Peg's cheekbones and the way she walked, and decided after all there might be something in it. Something that could make Peg's regular slurs on their clients a sort of speech within the tribe.

"Those were passenger pigeons," Marissa said, considering that whites had probably hammered more of them to death than the Indians ever did. "Not the same thing, I don't think. Who knows, they might have been tasty."

Peggy snorted, stood up and kicked at the pigeon, which responded with a form of technical compliance, fluttering about a yard away from Peggy's boot. Then the wind hooked down in a spiraling whoosh and lifted the trash and the pigeons all at once. Marissa followed the path of their flight to the thin end of the courtyard. The south wall of the building had two entries, one for Indian Health Services and the other for the counseling service that employed her and Peg. These were two ostensibly separate entities, but as Peg liked to quip, they did a lot of screwing around in the back alley. Looking at the huddle of clients waiting by the wall, Marissa felt a pang that was more than just wanting a smoke. She hadn't realized Inez was there until the girl flipped back the fake-fur-lined hood of her stained parka. Inez was beautiful, so much so that she'd been a poster girl for the college she dropped in and out of. A métisse, more obviously Lakota than Peg, with long sleek hair and a sweet band of freckles over the bridge of her nose. Her belly was just slightly rounded with what Marissa suspected to be an early pregnancy.

Inez didn't seem to notice her sitting at the table with Peg. She blew a smoke ring, smiled and sipped from a paper sack the man beside her offered. The sacks held cans of malt liquor, most likely, or the more recent ready-made canned cocktails, designed for children and street alcoholics. Most of their clients came in for court-ordered drug or alcohol counseling, and most of their payments were winkled somehow out of IHS. They did a little family counseling, and now and then there was a client like Inez who proffered an image of something that faintly resembled hope.

Peg stood with her knuckles resting on the flaking white paint of the mesh tabletop, looking toward the other end of the courtyard. "My people," she said, with her usual fine blend of sorrow and contempt. "Well, you wanna go in?"

Marissa didn't answer. She hadn't really registered Peg's

question, which seemed pale and distant because her mind had returned to last night's Exercise and its queer incomprehensible result. Inside the white patch pocket she balled the rosary, feeling the bony details of the crucifix rasping against her palm. The world in which she practiced the Exercises seemed to have nothing to do with this one; they were two utterly separate sequences of events, though she didn't know if they were mutually exclusive. It pained her to be thinking that, and it wasn't her own style of thinking either; the level of abstraction was Claude's. What, after all, was the point? Once she had wanted to do good, and now she did this, which was a living, though a meager one.

"Girlfriend?" Peg was frowning at her now. "You all right in there? You look a long way gone."

"Oh nothing," Marissa stood up and shook herself. "I had a funny dream last night is all." But of course she knew it had not been a dream.

33

"The eye of our intention," Claude was saying, with the rasp and flare of a match as he scraped it on the striker. He leaned forward across his folded knees to light the candle between them on the wooden floor. Marissa looked down on the top of his bony, close-cropped head, sprouting a silvery down like dandelion seed. He wore his favorite sweater, a black crewneck riddled with tiny moth holes. This view of him gave Marissa a peculiar watery feeling, like looking at a puppy before its eyes had opened.

She too was kneeling, sitting on her heels. It was a remarkably painful position if held for long. Claude had inured himself to it during a sojourn in Tibet. He tilted his baldish skull, whose shadow shifted on the wall behind him. In the dim his eyes seemed to acquire an ascetic slant.

". . . makes the difference," he breathed slowly, "between an Exercise and ordinary trance."

The eye of our intention. Claude had told her not to think of him as pastor or confessor, nor to call him Father, although he was a priest. He was her guide, through the Exercises. Like—

But he did have an intuition for when her intention faltered. For her confusion, when she was confused. He looked at her now across the flickering candle flame, as if withholding a hint of a smile. As if somehow he knew the odd interruption of her Exercise two nights before: the image of a meteor hurtling down into the dark. The eye of her intention had wandered then—Marissa knew it, would not willingly admit it.

"Set and setting," Claude announced.

Marissa rolled a little on her already-aching knees. "What are you talking about?"

His smile became visible now. "You know, we used to cooperate with other religions sometimes." By *we* he meant the Jesuits. "Not here so much, but sometimes in the East. Considerably. Maybe too much. As if any and all religious practices were really all about the same thing—the Divine— but in a different aspect."

"And so?" She returned his smile with her mouth, encouraging, her eyes turned down.

"Set and setting is a phrase from LSD culture," Claude explained. "There're a hundred ways to enter a trance. What happens inside it depends on your expectations and your guidance. The cultural surroundings, so to speak."

Marissa raised her eyes from the candle to his face. "But you still believe?" she asked him.

"Lord, I believe!" Claude said, raising his open hands. "Help thou mine unbelief!"

They laughed. The room, which was drafty, grew a little warmer.

Claude said, "Shall we begin?"

The candle was a fat white cube, unscented, its four walls faced with thin slices of agate. The reddish-brown whorls of the cross-cut stone warmed with the interior light. Shadows of their two kneeling figures loomed in the corners of the ceiling. A voice resonated, Claude's, not-Claude's. . . .

. . . to bring to memory all the sins of life, looking from year to year, or from period to period . . .

She was careful not to look at him.

... first, to look at the place, and the house where I have lived; second, the relations I have had with others; third, the occupation in which I have lived

It was equally possible that Claude sat mute with his lidded eyes and his lips slightly parted, and the voice she heard was an inner one, a fusion of her study and her familiarity with his tone.

Fourth, to see all my bodily corruption and foulness;

Fifth, to look at myself as a sore and ulcer, from which have sprung so many sins and so many iniquities and so very vile poison.

She heard these phrases clearly, as her eyes began to turn backwards in her head, and yet she was having trouble with the composition, which in this Exercise, as in the previous one, seemed difficult because abstract.

to see with the sight of the imagination, and consider that my soul is imprisoned in this corruptible body, and all the compound in this valley, as exiled among brute beasts:

Her eyes, turned backward in her head, saw no such thing. Yet she was somehow aware that the candle was a barrier between them, like a trench full of burning brimstone—why must it be so? The spark she saw tumbling into darkness now had a shape, a bright rectangle like the form of a small mirror, flickering and turning as it fell. The mirror image was a face, a long Modigliani oval, with something streaming away from its edges like hair or snakes or blood. Animal persons rushed at her from the walls of the cave: bison, bear, a mastodon.

an exclamation of wonder with deep feeling, going through all creatures, how they have left me in life and preserved me in it; the Angels, how, though they are the sword of the Divine Justice, they have endured me, and guarded me, and prayed for me; the Saints, how they have been engaged in interceding and praying for me; and the heavens, sun, moon, stars, and elements, fruits, birds, fishes and animals☐and the earth, how it has not opened to swallow me up, creating new Hells for me, to suffer in them forever!

Now she struggled up through syrupy layers of this dark somnolence; her eyes burst open as she broke the surface. She hoped she had not groaned or cried aloud. The candle flame was ordinary, small. Across it, Claude seemed to look at her quizzically. She knew that much more time must have passed in this room than in the cavernous space where she had been.

Blood rushed painfully through her cramped legs as she cautiously unfolded her knees. An aurora of gold speckles swirled across her vision for a few seconds before it cleared. Claude's regard was knowing now; he *knew* she had seen something unusual with her inward eye, while she knew that she could recover and understand it when she would, and that she would not tell him now.

Claude came up from the floor like a carpenter's rule extending, long arms, lean legs in his black jeans.

"All right?" he said.

"Yes." Marissa's smile felt warped on her face. "All right."

Claude looked as if he would offer a hand to help her rise, but didn't. She got her feet under her and rose on her own. It was difficult to understand the awkwardness of their leave-takings, which were frequent after all. She had seen Claude spontaneously embrace obese and foulmouthed drunken women from the rez. The space between their bodies seemed a chasm now. He reached across it, briefly clasped her hand, then let it go.

34

From that night and the next she could recall no dream but on the third morning she woke with a comprehension of what she had seen in the dark furrow where her Exercise had strayed. "But you *know*," Claude seemed to be saying to her in the space of her mind, and she did know now, exactly. It hurt. but she was more glad of the pain than not. She was proud to have figured it out on her own. She had something to bring to him now, like a treasure, her confession.

It was early, but Claude was an early riser, and Marissa saw no reason to wait. Though they had not planned any meeting this morning, she might if she went quickly catch him for a bit before either of their workdays were due to begin. She dressed quickly, dragged a brush through her dark hair. No makeup, she decided with a tick of hesitation, for she didn't normally wear it to work.

Her ancient little Toyota pickup rolled over the side streets of Kadoka till its windshield framed the church. Over the white lintel was affixed an electrified image of the Sacred Heart, exploding the burning cross from its upper ventricles, its Valentine contour wrapped in yellow-glowing thorns and weeping a tear of marquee-light blood. Marissa loathed this artifact and wished that Claude would have it removed. His predecessor as parish priest had raised the funds to install it.

Connected to the church by a passage of coal-blackened brick, the small seminary where Claude resided was three-quarters empty, most of its windows dirty and dark. Vocations had dwindled on the rez, where a few handfuls of young men once had seen the Church as a portal to a better life. Of course, especially since the scandals, vocations were a problem nationwide. . . . An ambulance was parked alongside the seminary, its back doors open, siren quiet, red lights revolving slowly. On the far side of the white marble steps Sister Anne-Marie Feeney stood solid as a fireplug, her shapeless shoes set apart on the pavement, cool wind twitching the black cloth of her habit.

Marissa's mind could not yet construct the thing she wished to be other than it was, but as she got out of the truck she was already thinking, *if I got up on the other side of the bed, put my right shoe on before my left, if a butterfly flapped its wings in China, if then if—* A pair of shoulders hunched in a white scrub top appeared in the doorway, backing awkwardly toward the first step, while leaning forward into a load.

Sister Anne-Marie registered her presence and waved her imperiously back with her roughened red hand. Marissa continued to advance, as the nun pointed more insistently at something behind her. Her lips moved, but Marissa heard nothing. She looked over her shoulder and saw that she had left her driver's door hanging open across the bike lane, which the town had recently established by dint of drizzling a line of white paint across the pot-holed pavement. Sister Anne Marie, who transported herself on a rust-red Schwinn three-speed, was militant on the subject of the bike lane.

Marissa turned back and slapped her door shut—irritated, though knowing she was in the wrong. She advanced again toward the seminary door, where the two paramedics had now emerged with their stretcher and the long figure laid out motionless upon it, covered from head to toe with a white sheet. With no particular urgency they rolled the stretcher in. No eye contact with Marissa or the nun. Sister Anne-Marie had caught Marissa's elbow in her blunt grip—had she looked like she would throw herself onto the, onto the——-? But now the attendants had closed both doors and were climbing into the front of their vehicle.

She dipped into her pocket and touched the rosary he had given her. The other sequence of events was vividly present so clearly present to her still: she arrived to find Claude sweeping the seminary steps, one of many banal tasks he claimed for himself around the grounds of the church. He looked up, mildly surprised, but already more pleased to see her than not, his smile still not quite perceptible as Marissa glanced at her watch and stopped herself from quickening her step. She did not have to be at work for forty minutes, so there was time to go around the corner and have a cup of dishwater coffee at the donut shop—time enough, and so much to tell, and finally someone she could safely tell it to.

The sun broke over the peaked roof of the church and flooded the sidewalk where they stood with light.

She had apparently missed a few things Sister Anne-Marie had been saying, ". . . a mickey valve, a mighty valve—oh I can't remember exactly what, but Father said it wasn't serious, the doctors were watching it, supposed to be."

She looked at the ugly electric sign. Claude's heart had a hole in it then, if it had not just blown up. Marissa brought her eyes down to the nun's face, which was the same color and texture as the blood-red brick of which the older parts of the town were constructed. Take away the wimple and she might have been looking at the face of a career alcoholic, one of the sterno-strainers. But it was only high blood pressure in Sister Anne-Marie's case, she knew.

"I didn't know," she heard herself say.

"Father didn't tell many people."

And now Marissa searched the nun's face for something along the lines of suspicious knowledge (an insight she had carefully denied herself)—an unspoken What makes you think *you* had a right to know, you little minx? Instead she found only a gentleness she could not bear.

"Child," said Sister Anne Marie. Marissa broke away from her and walked stiff-legged to her truck.

Early to work, she leafed through her dossiers, barely seeing them with her parched eyes. It was supposed to be a paperwork morning; she had no appointments till late afternoon. Just Jimmy Scales, and he was not likely to show. Marissa knew he had skipped his court-ordered piss test and that she would most likely be spending a piece of her afternoon writing him up for it. The molded plastic chair across from her desk, where Scales sat sullen and uncommunicative for forty-five minutes every two weeks. It would be a paperwork day, then, not just a paperwork morning—well, she could catch up on some of those files. A break midmorning, telling her beads in her pocket while she watched Peggy smoke her weak, toxic cigarettes. Yogurt or a stale packaged salad for lunch. She could populate her whole future with such banalities, as if instead of being doled out one at a time the events had all fallen out of their box.

She yanked the sheet with Scales's basic stats from its grubby folder and dropped the rest back into the metal file drawer. Peggy ran into her in the entryway, coming in as Marissa went out.

"Where you off to?" Peggy asked.

"After Jimmy Scales."

"What? Would that be a rational act? He didn't even miss his appointment yet."

"No," Marissa said. "But don't I know he's going to—am I Nostradamus or what. "

"Girl, you look like you seen a ghost," Peggy was wagging her head slowly. "No, you look like you *are* a freaking ghost."

At a gas station on the north bank of the White River she stopped and bought a pack of Marlboro Reds and tossed it on the dashboard. She'd done that before when she quit smoking—once, for a whole sixteen months, an unopened pack on the corner of her desk proved she was stronger than her addiction, and that her clients might be stronger than theirs. A parable in pantomime. Sometimes she had given the pack to a client, in the end.

At the border of the reservation she pulled over to enter Jimmy Scales's supposed address into the small GPS unit improvisationally mounted on the cracking dashboard of her truck. It came up somewhere west of Sharp's Corner. Marissa wasn't familiar with the area. She knew her way to the IHS hospital on East Highway 18, and to Oglala Lakota College, where she had briefly worked in the health center.

She missed the turn she should have taken at Scenic and drove blind across a narrow waist of Badlands National Park. On the far side she kept following 44 as it twisted south into the rez, and presently found herself passing through Wanblee. The wreckage of a couple of houses torn up by a tornado lay scattered over three acres of ground south of the roadway. A little farther was a white frame church, with a quaint wooden belfry, photogenic. She pushed down the thought of Claude. There'd be a funeral. When would it be? Her future. . . . A handful of boys in droopy shorts and shirts were popping skateboards off the concrete stoop of the church. One of the more daring rode crouching down the welded-pipe stair rail and survived the landing. Swooping in a wide turn over the asphalt parking lot, he glanced incuriously at her truck as it rattled by.

Her dry eyes burned. West of Potato Creek she began to overtake a pedestrian. Slender, with glossy black hair so long it swung around her hips. A half-open backpack swung from her shoulder by one strap. She turned, lifting her chin, and signaled not by raising her thumb but pointing her hand peremptorily to the ground, as if to command the truck to stop.

Inez. Marissa's heart lifted slightly. She leaned across to pop the passenger door. Inez slipped off the backpack as she climbed in, then shrugged out of the denim jacket she was wearing.

"Wow Miz Hardigan, whatcha doin' all the way out here? Can you gimme a ride down to school?" Inez wore an orange tank top and the round of her belly pushed a gap between its hem and the waistband of her jeans. In her slightly distended navel glittered a small bright stud. She had not stopped talking: "I'd of been late to comp class if you didn't stop—" she pointed at the corner of a rhetoric textbook sticking out of her backpack "—I dunno, it's kinda boring anyway, I thought I might switch to the nursing program anyway, Miz Hardigan you musta done nursing, right? Hey, can I take a cig? Hey, cool truck, I always liked 'em, my uncle used to have one once, back when they were sorta new."

Marissa nodded at the pack on the dashboard. It was not like Inez to chatter this way. Marissa knew her as calm and slightly mysterious. She had already peeled the cellophane from the pack and lit a cigarette with a lighter she'd squeezed out of her jeans pocket, then let it burn down unnoticed between her fingers, as she picked obsessively at some invisible something between the hairs of her left forearm.

Oh Christ, Marissa thought. Do you know what that's doing to your baby? Do you know what . . . she didn't say anything. She couldn't have, as there was no chink in Inez's prattle for her to have slipped in a word before they reached the entrance of the college. Marissa dug in the pocket behind her seat and fished out a scare-you-off-meth brochure. . . . Unfolded, it displayed the stages of a twenty-year-old woman aging forty years in two. Inez shoved it into her backpack without really seeming to see it at all, but she gave Marissa a hurt look from her wiggly eyes as she hopped out of the truck and slammed the door.

In a devil's elbow beyond the college, Marissa narrowly missed a collision with a horse-trailer, though the road was otherwise empty and their speeds were low. She pulled onto the shoulder and sat there, shaking with the fading tension, watching the trailer recede in her side-view mirror. A painted rodeo scene flaked from its back panel: cowboys and Indians, horses and bulls. Marissa saw that Inez had dropped her lighter on the passenger seat when she got out. The translucent plastic showed a quarter-full of fluid. And the cigarette box lay on the dash, cracked open. Another few months into a meth habit and Inez would have automatically stolen it.

Marissa got out of the truck to smoke her first cigarette in over a week. The blast of unaccustomed nicotine dizzied her so much that she had to brace a palm on the warm, ticking hood of her vehicle. In one corner of her mind was the thought that this was not really a pleasant or desirable sensation. In another: *Now I am going to cry.* But she didn't cry.

Sharp's Corner was no more remarkable than Wanblee had been. The GPS led her west onto a gravel road that soon degraded itself into a packed dirt track. Where the track petered out into blank open prairie, the GPS unit went dark. Marissa had a state map in her glove box, but on that the reservation proved to be a nearly blank white space, like the African interior on the maps of Victorian explorers. Her tires were worn, and it would be idiotic to break down out here; if the GPS had failed her cell phone probably wouldn't get a signal either.

Nevertheless she drove on. The prairie was neither as featureless nor flat as it first seemed. There were billows and hollows full of thorny scrub and small twisted trees. In one of these pockets appeared a tin roof streaked brown with rust. Marissa steered toward it, thinking that she might have blundered onto the Jimmy Scales domicile after all.

She set her parking brake and got out. The small house sat half in, half out of a thicket of evergreen brush, at the bottom of a dish in the prairie, scattered with sharp white stones. It did not exactly look abandoned, but the door hung open in a way that dismayed her. She started to call to the house but did not. To the left of it the rusted carcass of an old Mustang stood on blocks and beside it a washing machine so ancient it had a wringer bolted on top. A dented aluminum saucepan lay upside down among the stones.

The sky darkened abruptly, though it could scarcely have been noon. Marissa looked up to see a black squall line hurrying from the west, a dense inky cloud that blotted out the sun. She could no longer remember why she had come here. Out of the thicket to the right of the house came an old man with long white hair, wearing a green quilted vest with the stuffing coming out from its parted seams. He shook a rattle at the end of one bony arm and made a thin keening sound with his voice. Although he did not seem to see her he was coming toward her certainly, purposefully, as if everything in this day, in her whole life, existed to carry her to this moment and him to her. When he had reached her, his free hand took hers.

Marissa said, *Why?*

You have a hollow in your heart, the shaman said. Or maybe he said *hunger.* The rattle shook in his other hand. *Hunger. Hollow.* Now Marissa was weeping, with no sound or sobbing. She only knew because the water from her eyes ran into the neck of her shirt and pooled in the shell of her collar bone.

Go to it now, the shaman said. *Don't hesitate.*

35

If then if. When had she first played this game? Oh, in her early childhood, surely, many times but for trivial cause. The first time she had ever played for money would be sixteen—no, it was seventeen years ago. Her age at the time had been sixteen.

She drove due north as best she could figure, and faster than she probably should. The GPS unit had come back to life but she didn't look at it. Since her meeting with the shaman she had not been able to stop crying, and it was as much as she could do to see the road.

She could play the game with another plot line. If Claude had had a healthier heart valve. If he had been more solicitous of the unhealthy one he did have. Then, then they would have gone around the corner that morning before work and sat, each cradling a cup of burned coffee, while Claude turned on her his comprehending smile and she told him—what and how would she have told him? It did not seem so clear and easy now as it had that morning in the moment before she sprang out of her car, so eager she left her door hanging open across the bike lane, or no, that was because she had been startled by the ambulance. What if the ambulance had not been there. If Sister Anne-Marie had not been there rooted wart-like to the concrete and robed in black as if she were the angel of his death. . . .

If the butterfly waggled its wings again, then it could be different in another way. Take away the coffee shop and put her on the path to a conventional confessional, the carved wooden phone booth in a corner of the church, and behind the screen was only Claude's shadow. He wouldn't be Claude at all, only Father. And she, Marissa . . . well you might as well take away the master's and the college degree and the faded ambition to somehow better people's lives, take away the Exercises too while you're at it and leave her an ordinary nondescript little nurse turned social worker, alone in her early thirties except for her work and of course the Church, bearing into the confessional her burden of guilt for an action cast off when she was in her teens. The guilt itself a Catholic thing, so carefully inculcated in her, like some pale and mildly toxic flower cultivated from the stubborn soil of the plains. So easily the words would have bloomed through her lips and blown through the screen to his forgiving ear.

I abandoned her. I abjured her. And worst of all I forgot her. For years I forgot that she ever existed. TillUntill I saw that spark going down in the dark.

Marissa had stopped crying now. She dragged a sleeve across her face, piloting the little truck through a cloverleaf to bomb eastward across I-90. Her mind mercifully quiet for a moment, she listened to the pistons pump in the engine. Every part on this vehicle had been replaced and some more than once, so that now it was invincible, the same as her own dented heart. She was going toward the hunger now, full tilt. Or the hollow. Whereas for half of her life, until today, she'd been trying to go away from whatever it was. Now she meant to do what the shaman had told her, though as yet she didn't quite know how.

The signs for Wall Drug began to whip past her now. Her mind started to work again, *if-then-if.* If Claude had never entered the priesthood—no, not that one. Go further back. If the Jesuits hadn't got sucked into the I Ching when they went to China. Or if the Jesuits in the western territories had adapted to Lakota ways as they had done with the Chinese. Her mind tumbled out of the sequence. Back to where she started.

If she hadn't lied to her parents to go camping—that was wrong. But she had so wanted to go with Georgie to the grasslands south of Pierre. The truck was new then, or new to her—the big gift for her sweet sixteen. It had a cap and they brought a tent with them, but they never put it up. It was late summer and the sky soft and clear to the horizon. Georgie beat down a pallet of the sweet-smelling grass and laid a tarp over it, then an Indian blanket. If they hadn't been fifty miles from a drugstore. If she hadn't fudged on her count of the days. If the sunset light in Georgie's brown eyes hadn't melted her, why then they might have stopped at the other, not-quite things they did when there was no protection.

Had she not been surprised and pierced by her own desire? The same quickening, though more equivocal in the latter case, that she felt when looking down on Claude's bowed head (as she would never, ever do again). How fleeting the pleasure, compared to the long, slow battering of its consequence. To be sure, the Church had always taught so. She had nine months to contemplate it—no, it was less, because for the first month she hadn't known at all and for most of the second she wasn't quite sure.

If I had only done otherwise then. But now she was coasting down the ramp into Pierre. The town had grown since she'd last been there, in a disagreeable way with which she was familiar. It took her twenty minutes to pick her way through newly rundown shopping strips to the parking lot of St. Mary's Hospital. These buildings too had been expanded. There was a new façade, adobe brown, and an abstract cross resembling a glint of starlight splintered by a lens.

She walked down to the Missouri River and stood on the edge of Griffin Park, smoking another Marlboro and staring across the water at the yellowing leaves on the trees of Framboise Island. There was a little boat basin not far off, and when the wind rose she could hear hardware ringing against metal masts. Most of the streets hereabout had the names of long-gone Indian tribes. Marissa had spent six penitential months of her junior year in high school here in Pierre, with a friend of her mother's who'd agreed to take her in. She kept up her schoolwork with a correspondence course. Her mother's friend was wearily devout and escorted Marissa to mass almost daily. Back home her absence had been represented as a semester abroad, though she doubted many had really been fooled.

Later on when she went away to college it seemed like a peculiarly quaint way to do things at the end of the twentieth century, even in the remote place where it all had occurred. She told no one she met in her new life, though more from embarrassment than shame. The taste of tobacco made her think of Inez—that was how unwanted pregnancies were managed nowadays. Marissa had come here, stood near this same spot, on that afternoon half her lifetime ago. She hadn't smoked, though, because of the baby.

Back at the hospital, she walked into the general reception area and sat in a chair for a few minutes, watching the traffic; there was more of it than she remembered. Presently she got up and walked through the double doors at the back. No one prevented her. The floor plan had changed, or she didn't remember it. There was no reason she should remember it; she hadn't been here long.

Orderlies in blue scrubs passed her, then an intern came by at an urgent trot, the tails of his lab coat flapping. Marissa realized she was still wearing her own white coat from work, and that it served her as a sort of camouflage. Her mind bifurcated—in one part she was painfully conscious that she didn't know what she was doing and that this was not at all the way one set about doing the thing she was trying to do. In the other part she only heard the richly textured sound of the shaman's gourd shaker, which drove her forward as if through a dream.

She got onto an elevator at random and got off when it stopped to admit another passenger. Deliberately, she walked toward the nurses' station. A nurse was coming the other way, in a smock festooned with cartoon animals, carrying a clipboard in one hand. She was a good thirty pounds overweight and had a remarkably pretty face, from which she looked at Marissa with a flicker of suspicion.

"May I help you?"

Marissa settled back on her heels. "I had a baby here."

The nurse cocked her free hand on her hip. "Well. Congratulations."

"Seven. . . ." The rattle in Marissa's head was like surf. "Seventeen years ago."

The nurse was not exactly looking around for rescue, but Marissa recognized something like her own body language when a troublesome client approached the border of self-control. "Miss, I—"

"July sixteenth," Marissa said desperately. "Nineteen ninety-three."

The nurse's plump lips parted, but instead of saying whatever it was she glanced down at the chart in her hand.

"Wait a minute," she said. "I think she's here."

Now Marissa knew that she *had* gone insane. "She can't still be here."

"I mean, she's here again." The nurse turned her head slightly, and fixed Marissa with one puzzled green eye. "You didn't know? She's the girl from the cave."

36

The stone was blue now, the color of turquoise, but soft like clay; she could move through it. She was aware of other women with her, circling through the blue stone wall. She did not know them. They were shades. On one side the cave, the other the world.

The blue clay substance sucked at her calves. Really it was softer, more liquid than clay. She was free of it now, completely free, standing by herself on the ledge. What had become of the blue shade women she didn't know, but they were no longer with her. She knew they were her kin, her guardians, but they had gone away somewhere and she was standing alone on the ledge, looking out over a world she did not know.

Below the ledge was a green meadow, sprinkled with stars of white and yellow flowers. Water lapped at the edge of the grass. The water was wide, a metallic gray color, and it went all the way back to the horizon. Something moved in it, an enormous sleek black rubbery creature, grazing on weeds that floated on the water. The weeds had purple trumpet-shaped flowers and the animal person was eating the flowers too. There were more than one of them she saw now; animal persons whose name she did not know.

Something else should have been down there. A different scene, with different persons present. She could not quite remember what it was. A shadow passed over her, a shadow with wings fleeting over the rock, and she remembered the hawk, watching the hawk. The hawk had been feeding. The shadow was gone.

She turned to look behind her. The wall of stone was no longer blue, but a grayish brown, with a vertical black slit in it where she had come out. Must have come out. She had the vaguest recollection of going in that way. Not from this exterior. On the back of her eyes was an image of the blue women, passing through the wall in a misty dawn light, as if they were wading a stream.

That antlered shape now looked as if it were bursting out of the opening to the cave. She had seen that before, before, and there were other images too on the rock shelter wall, but it hurt her head to try to recall them. There was more to the antlered-shaped form than before. The crudely incised outline was still there, but now it had been enhanced with colors, fat cinnamon brown and a bloody red, and the colors gave it a quick animation, so that it was no longer one thing but two: a stag that was becoming a man, or a man turning into a stag.

And her eyes went dark. She had looked at this image, a part of it, with someone, another person, not an animal. She could not—the bear. In the cave, the bear had been looking at her. As if they shared one eye. . . .

Now the blue women were near her again, circling her with that sort of stuttering step, sort of a dance step they used to wade through and through the molten rock stream. Then black darkness, nothing she could see, but a sawing gasping sound all around her. A growl. Two syllables spoken into her blind ear. Oo. Ee. Oo. Ee. A voice was calling, but she would not come. She would stay here.

Her vision cleared. She rocked on her heels, then steadied herself. The moment's dizziness had now passed. She turned away from the cave's opening to follow the shadow of the hawk around the ledges.

37

Hunger was a star in her belly, radiating fronds of light. She had been heavy, squeezing into the cave, heavy, cold and somnolent. The mouth of the cave was rimed with a dagger-like frost. Afterward a long time was blank, till the star was born in her slack gut, its fronds reaching through her like tentacles of a jellyfish. It was this hunger star that had awakened her.

In the darkness she clutched at her face, but something was wrong; it was not her face, something covered it. A long proboscis, a mask, a muzzle. Covered with fur and full of white teeth. The darkness was full of a gravelly snarling. She clawed at the mask and rolled her head from side to side.

The walls of the passage squeezed tight on her flanks. Strange, for she must be leaner after the long sleep. But it was so. Light blazed ahead. She was coming free, out of the rock and onto the ledge.

In the high distance, in the darkness she was now leaving behind, a voice.

Jesus! She's torn off the ventilator!

And another calmer tone

Wait, it's all right. It's all right. She's breathing on her own.

But she was going away from those words, which were only syllables; they soothed and meant nothing.

On the ledge she straightened to stand a little unsteadily on her hind legs, and wrinkled her nostrils to read the spring air. Her cinnamon pelt hung on her, loose as a robe. Below, a tangle of white and yellow blossoms in the meadow. Every year it seemed to her it had been so. Black beings were splashing in the water at the meadow's edge. She had eaten one once. A smaller one. Slick skin and rubbery fat encased the meat—an agreeable blend of textures on her white teeth, and the blood running salty over her chops. With curved black claws she grazed her muzzle. It was clearly hers; she fit into it, smooth and tight.

But these black beings were too big, and she was too weak and too giddy for hunting now. She must feed the hunger star something easier. Beneath the snarl of flowers there were roots to dig. She dropped to all fours and loped toward them.

38

The ledge wrapped around the cliff wall to the north. There was a narrow place and she closed her eyes and pressed her face against the rock as she inched across it. The sun-warmed stone grateful against her smooth cheek. When the ledge had widened she opened her eyes. On the boulder opposite she expected to see something: the stain of the small death that had fed the hawk. It was not there.

On the horizon there had been a r—. A r—. The word would not come. Even the idea would not come. Would not quite come. It had been a surface on which people traveled in—. The word would not come. Hard shiny things that beetled along.

No, everything had changed since last she passed this way. Now the dried-mud hills were green, and some were wooded, and in the low places there was water everywhere, so that some of the hilltops looked like islands. With the glistening of the water she was assailed by sudden thirst. She began to head down the slope of the ledge into the valley.

Here and there were scatterings of stones . . . not along the ledges she descended, but farther away, on the hillsides and the hummocks that rose out of the water. The stones were flat, for the most part. Something about them seemed unaccidental. But she could not think clearly about that.

The water on valley floor was still, or moved with a syrupy slowness. Its color was a brownish green. Behind her thirst was a dim understanding that still water was not safe to drink. She could hear running water too, somewhere under the ledge where she now stood. The still water at the foot of the cliff was rippling where it was fed by the spring.

She lay on her belly on the ledge and reached over with both arms, hanging her head. The cold shocked her wrists and hands before she saw the upside-down crevice in the rock from which the clear, bright water sprang. She cupped water to her face, spilling most of it, and drank, then lay and rested. It seemed that all the flesh of her body was opening and expanding to receive this water, like a sacred thing. Now her thoughts became more clear.

She wet her hands again, and as she sat back on her heels she rubbed cold water into the hollow between the tendons of her neck. Now when she looked at the stones piled on the green hillside across the water it seemed obvious they had been gathered by hands.

It was not far down now to the water's edge, and it was a narrow channel, moving slowly. How deep? Almost to the tops of her thighs when she waded in, opaque emerald water swirling in question marks at her movement. She crossed quickly and came out on the other side and looked back. The spring water fell onto a flat rock, then purled over it into the green water of the spring and rippled out. There was another ripple there too, not the expanding half circle from the falling water, but a zigzag with some other cause. An enormous snake, three times the length of her own body, was swimming up against the faint green current. She had been in the water with it moments ago. But the snake did not seem interested in her. It swam steadily upstream; she watched it away.

From the flat rock where the water fell there were stones that crossed the stream, set close enough together that she could have walked over on them without even wetting her feet. Set. For some reason she looked up toward the top of the cliff, high above where the cave mouth would be, around the bends of the ledges. There, rocks had been piled to represent a Person, legs set apart like an archway, arms stretched wide and flat like the wings of a p——. . . the word would not come. Again the peculiar doubling in the space between her eyes, as if there was some other awareness there, which could not find its words.

So there were People here. Had been. And in that other time there had been other people, whom she knew. Who. . . . Where were they now? The sun had dried her legs. She walked along the stream's edge, sometimes passing a scattering of stones. Surely there was something deliberate in their gathering. Maybe they had not yet been finally arranged or maybe they had fallen down from that arrangement.

It was bewildering, though, the windings of this stream among so many hummocks that looked so much alike. Did it matter if she could find her way back? She tried to note the scatters of the stones as she passed them, but these looked too much like one another.

At the bend of the stream was an archway of piled stones. No arms, no head, only the arch, about her waist height, so she had to go down on one knee to look through it. She looked back through the archway the way she had come. Within it was framed a single standing stone, a long way off, perhaps farther downstream from where she had crossed, for she didn't remember passing it when she came this way.

Moss grew on the near side of the stones of the arch. She touched it thoughtfully with a fingertip. It was green, velvety, a little damp. At the sound of a bird's cry she turned her head, a little startled. She couldn't find the bird.

She stood up and walked around the arch and looked in the direction she had been going. Yes, another standing stone was framed, equally far away. The second stone was nowhere near the stream bank, but far distant in a dry cleft between the hummocks and the wooded hills. She rose and began to follow the line that had so been drawn.

39

Ahead of her something flickered and moved in the tangled grass. A bird, but not the one she had heard before. She remembered the shadow of a hawk passing over her on the ledges, and the thought that she had followed in the same direction. But that was not this hawk. One of its wings was folded up properly but the other was fanned out in an odd angle over the grass, and it dragged as the hawk hopped forward.

So it could not fly. Something pulled at her other awareness. She had seen meadowlarks behaving this way, feigning hurt and flightlessness, hopping and fluttering over the hay field to draw a person away from the nest. But hawks did not nest on the ground.

She followed it. The hawk hastened as best it could, scrambling forward with it talons, beating the one good wing against the grass. The wing would lift off the ground a little, not very far. She stopped pursuing to let the hawk rest. When she moved again, the hawk hurried forward. She allowed a constant distance to remain between them.

The color of the light was reddening, deepening. The sun had begun to sink toward the hills and higher ranges to the west. There was something ominous in that, the coming dark. She wanted to feed, and to find fire. There was hunger but it seemed to be outside of her, ahead of her. She moved toward the hunger, where she felt that it was. The new urgency of her progress seemed to alarm the hawk. With a great effort it fluttered and clawed its way to the top of the standing stone they had been heading toward.

She stopped for a moment to let it settle. One flat round yellow eye looked at her always. When she began to move again she paused with every step. This hawk was speckled on the front, its back and wings a deep reddish brown. Not so different from others she had known in that cloudy elsewhere that came before, or maybe a little bigger.

The stone was not so high after all; it came up to her clavicle. She and the hawk were eye to eye. But it was not as it had been with the bear. The two eyes didn't merge to one. The hawk's iris was yellow, glowing like a ring of translucent shell. She looked away, keeping the hawk just barely in the edge of her vision as she came almost near enough to touch, not knowing how she knew it would calm the hawk, but knowing that it would. She could look directly at the talons clasping the stone, the big, bright yellow hooks of them.

When she was near enough to touch she rolled her left forearm up the stone and rubbed against the backs of the hawk's legs. She didn't know where this idea came from either, but after one quick swivel of its head the hawk stepped backward onto her wrist. Heavy. She took a backward step from the stone and carefully bent her elbow to bring the surprising weight of the bird to the central line of her chest. The hawk was settling, flexing its talons. A drop of blood where a claw had pierced her purled along the tendon of her inner arm.

She bent her legs to sight along the top point of the stone. They'd lost the sun already, behind a wooded hill to the west. In the twilight she thought she could just make out another arch, framed in what looked like a pass between two hillocks.

She walked that way, adjusting her balance to the new weight of the hawk rocking on her forearm. Now the hawk must feed, and she must feed. The hunger was outside of her, ahead of her somewhere. She felt that she must move toward it. When she stopped for a moment and flared her nostrils, she caught an odor of blood on the wind. Blood and maybe a thread of smoke too. She balanced the hawk and walked on, farther into the hunger.

40

By the time she reached the next arch of piled stones it was
fully dark. No moon, and the stars that swam overhead were
unfamiliar. She could not find the next standing stone she had
seen framed in the arch. The hawk was quiet; perhaps it was
sleeping where it rocked on her forearm.

The blood smell and the hunger were nearer now. In the
dark, she was not so confident about going toward those sen-
sations. But they defined a direction, and she went that way.

Ahead was a whistling sound like a bird, but not a bird.
Up hill from where she walked in the declivity between two
hummocks. The birds had gone to roost by now. She'd heard
their voices stop, an hour since.

The whistle stopped and now she heard a tapping, chinking, of stone on the stone. That was intentional, that sound.
Also the blood smell was that way. Near. She climbed toward
it. Behind a rock there was a fire glow too.

A Person whistled to her over the rock.

There was meaning in the whistle. What did it mean? It
was a greeting, or an invitation, she knew.

She could not get a very good look at the black silhouette of head before he ducked down again out of sight. Still,
she went there. The chink sound of stone on stone continued.
The grass ended and it was a rocky ascent but her feet automatically found the same footholds that the Person's must
have done.

When she first saw him her breath caught, for he seemed

crowned with horns. The antlered beast-half-human whose image she had seen, exploding from the slitway to the cave. Then the Person shifted his head to look at his work and the illusion vanished; it was only that he had happened to set the antlers of his kill on a stone just above where he was working. He was using a heavy stone pestle to flake a new edge on a knife of pale flint.

There were strips of meat drying on a stone the fire. Her belly rolled. She must feed the hawk first, though.

She made some sort of sound with her voice and the Person put down his tools and looked at her. The Person was young, she felt, not so much older than herself. His nose was flat and his face was round, or almost heart-shaped, framed in thick dark bristles of hair. There were crests of hair on his arms and legs and his sex was hidden in a swatch of it, she supposed. He was well clothed in his own hair, for summer weather anyway. Only the face and the belly and chest showed leathery bare skin. Although expression was hard to read in the strange face, he did not seem surprised to see her. It was as though she was expected. He must be a dreamer like herself, one who walked in dream.

She looked at the unbutchered leg of the stag and the Person, understanding, took up the flint he had been chipping and cut two or three bloody strips of meat. The hawk arched its head back to receive them. Her own hunger had moved inside her now. The Person was now offering her something else—a band of leather from his kill, with the hair still in it. She didn't understand and then she did, shifting the hawk from one arm to another as he wrapped the raw leather, hair side in, around her forearm where the talons had raked. The raw side of the skin molded to the wounds on her forearm like a balm. The hawk settled on the gauntlet.

The Person took a strip of meat from the hot stone above the fire, and fed it to her as she'd fed the hawk. This meat was not dried yet but mostly cooked and it was good, and juicy. The Person kept feeding her strips of it and smiling, until she shook her head, though still feeling the shape of a smile on her own face. Then his smile drained and he crouched down, behind the sheltering rocks, and presently picked up a stone-tipped lance.

She herself had at first heard nothing, but then she felt it. Whatever it was. The presence. The other awareness that tugged at her mind from time to time. Cautiously she peered up over the rim of the fire stone. What she saw was herself, girl with a hawk, edged red with firelight, half hidden behind a sheltering stone. She saw this with the eye she shared with the bear standing just at the tree line as it rose to enormous height on its hind legs as if to greet her. Eye to eye across that distance. Or just one eye.

The Person was beside her now. He was empty-handed, no longer holding the lance. He breathed a whistle into her ear, and though she still didn't understand what it meant, she knew he understood what was happening, and probably better than she did.

The bear dropped four paws onto the ground and lumbered off into the trees. Did it look once more over its high shoulder with the reddish yellow eye?

The Person had curled on a pelt to sleep. She sat beside him, back to the warm stone, hand on her knee to brace the arm that held the sleeping hawk, feeling her gaze and the bear's still entwined as she lowered herself deeper into dreaming.

41

They called her Julie. Whoever *they* were. Julie Westover was the name heading the chart that hung from the foot of the hospital bed. The room was full of clicks and beeps, blanketed by a leisurely sighing sound. The ventilator, sucking and sighing. In a high corner near the door a bracket held a television chattering aimlessly; local news.

Marissa went to the window. Fortunate for Julie that there was one, if she had been able to see it. The window overlooked a tattered greensward of the park, and beyond, the slow brown progress of the river. In the park, a man pushed a small child in a swing.

Southern exposure. The room was suffused with amber light. Marissa worked her way through a grove of hospital machinery to the bedside. The girl was wrapped in cable and tubes, like tentacles of an octopus. On a monitor, hiccups of a traveling, beeping green dot marked out her heartbeat. Steady enough. The ventilator masked her face, flex tube curling out of it like an elephant's proboscis. Her hair was dark, with little round patches shaved out of it here and there to bring electrodes to the skin of her skull.

Something from the TV snagged Marissa's attention. She glanced up. The anchorwoman had a handsome, horsey face, framed by two wings of orange-blond hair that curved from a center parting to not quite meet again at the point of her chin. The hair had a metallic sheen that pixelated on the screen, jumbling with her shimmering green suit jacket.

Reception poor. The glossy lips worked against a faint screen of static—*and for cave girl Julie Westover it's the thirteenth day in a coma. Doctors cannot expl*— Marissa somehow had found the remote and switched the television off.

Julie. The *cave girl*. What name had Marissa imagined for her? None. There was none. The counselors at the adoption service had advised her not to name the baby, not if she really meant to give her up. For similar reasons she had never really looked at this child before today.

She can't see you.

Julie's eyes had opened. No recognition in them, certainly. That is, she didn't recognize another human presence, or any other object in this room. Her eyes were cinnamon brown, like Marissa's own. After a moment, they slipped shut.

Marissa turned again toward the window. The angle of the sun had changed, and a rage of autumn light rushed over her like a wave. She closed her eyes and leaned into it. Through the plate glass, the light warmed the surface of her skin. For a moment she thought she was going to faint. She popped her eyes open, regaining the reality of the room.

Routine noise through the open door. Someone was pushing an empty gurney down the hallway. It passed. In the room across the corridor a voice repeated in a dead monotone, *callmyson, callmyson, callmyson, callmyson*. There was a quality Marissa recognized from time she'd served in other hospitals: void syllables of dementia.

Someone was sitting in one of the mint-green molded plastic chairs by the door. Squatting, rather; he'd caught his boot heels on the edge of the seat, long legs folded up like a mantis's. White wires to an iPod ran off his dark shaggy mass of hair. There was some sort of textbook balanced on his knees, the cover scrawled over and the corners frayed to feathers of gray cardboard. Marissa couldn't tell if he was reading the book or not. His head was tilted over it slightly, but he wore wraparound sunglasses with bulbous yellow lenses, like the eyes of a fly. The sun, still pouring in from the glass, reflected from those lenses so harshly she couldn't tell if he was looking at the book or at Julie or at her; he might have been staring at her the whole time.

She can't see you—had this person said that? Could he have been in the room all along? Certainly she had not heard anyone come in. When she looked at the battered textbook it occurred to her that Julie's world must be full of such objects. But the impenetrable eyes unnerved her. She felt defensive, almost frightened, and thus angry. Pulling the front of her lab coat straight, she rapped out sharply, "Who are *you*?"

42

Jamal could hear Karyn, still screaming and sobbing somewhere back behind him, but it was hysteria, no more than
that. Screams had a completely different timbre when someone was doing the screamer material harm—he remembered
that sound from another life. And no one was molesting
Karyn right now because Marko and Sonny were both after him, or in fact Jamal was leading them away from Karyn
and Julie, the way a bird, pretending to be wounded, decoys
predators from the nest.

In the half-light of the moon he was quicker than they
were on the ledges, which he had explored a number of
times before this afternoon. Beyond the boulder where he
and Julie had watched the hawk feeding, there was a spot
where he could drop down from one ledge to another below. He pressed silently against the stone, into a crevice that
hid him from the moon. Marko, probably Marko, passed
over him. The white beam of the big mag light played over
random patches of the stone. Jamal had his ear flat against
the rock face and for a moment he thought the mountain
had a heartbeat, then understood it must be his own heart
he was hearing.

Now he could hear Marko coming back from the point
where the higher ledge petered out into thin air. Where was
Sonny? Karyn wasn't screaming anymore, so maybe Sonny
had gone back to calm her. But the silence unnerved Jamal.
Marko would be going back in the direction where Julie was,

where Julie had gone into the cave, and Jamal thought maybe he should have tried to follow her in there. He thought he could just squeeze in, and he was sure enough that Marko couldn't, but—

He caught up a piece of shale and flung it against the boulder opposite the ledge where he was crouching, and heard it shatter against the harder stone. That stopped Marko. The mag light beam played over the boulder, lighting up the stain where the hawk's kill had bled, but maybe Jamal only imagined he saw that, and out of the corner of his eye. He was already scuttling down the ledge to the desert floor.

The moon seemed to brighten as it climbed, and Jamal wondered just how visible he was, a ragged black shadow hovering over pale sand. Too visible. Marko shouted, and picked him out with the mag light beam. Almost at once one of the Harleys growled to life and Jamal saw the headlight surging toward him across the sand-pack. Sonny, then, had gone back to the bikes. If Karyn was making noise now he couldn't hear it over the engine. And he was already running, dodging in and out of two cones of light, then just one, for Marko must be trying to find his way down the ledges to come after him too.

No cover here on the open sand. Before, he used to go out with his brothers and some slingshots to hurl rocks at tanks and jeeps, and then they'd scatter through the boulders of another desert, with the large clumsy vehicles lurching after them. Another world. In this one he had two hundred yards to go before he'd reach the first high hummocks of painted mud, and the motorcycle was gaining on him fast. By dumb luck he tripped into some sort of ditch, dry streambed maybe. It was shallow but he'd lost the headlight beam and right away he began crawling, worming rather, over gravel and sharp shale. No point worrying about snakes. His left palm landed on a flat cactus, filling itself up with spines, and he crawled over it, still keeping low.

Sonny's bike shot over the ditch and went on without

stopping. But the other engine had started now. Marko was a little brighter than Sonny and when he hit the ditch he stopped. The motor eased to idle. Jamal waited for the mag light beam. If he picked up his head he could see he didn't have far to go to the first channel winding into the hummocks, but it was better to lie dead still. Marko was a long way off and the light beam was diffuse by the time it reached the heels of Jamal's boots, which must have only looked like more cactus or debris. After a moment the beam shifted away, and Jamal got up and dashed the remaining distance to the first clay hill and began to climb it, scrambling on his hands and knees, working his way across the steep slope at a diagonal until he dropped into a pocket, almost like a foxhole.

Marko had mounted the bike again and was systematically working his way along the dry gulch with the headlight. Farther out on the desert plain, Sonny's headlight swooped around and began to return. Marko stopped at the foot of the hill and played his flashlight up the slope. Fortunately he was no tracker. By then Sonny had pulled up beside him. The engines died.

Jamal was so close he could hear them muttering, though he couldn't make out what they said. Then Sonny raised his voice.

"Jamal? You out there? Jamal, come on back, man. We're not gonna hurtcha!"

Good-cop-bad-cop, Jamal thought, picking cactus spines out of his palm by feel. It hurt when he mouthed the words; he'd popped his lip against something, crawling low.

Marko was muttering again, then Sonny, louder: "Jamal? Man, we can cool this out. Come on out, man. We need to take care of the girls."

Marko's lines, in Sonny's voice. Jamal kept quiet and low. Then Marko's voice boomed.

"Jamal? Jamal!" Then in a slightly lower tone, "Well fuck it. If he wants to die out here by himself we'll let him."

For twenty more minutes he watched headlights looping

and searching in figure-eight patterns over the sand. Then they joined and went back in the direction they'd come.

By dawn he'd worked his way northwest about half the distance to where he thought the road cut through—maybe, it was only a guess. He didn't want to go back to the campsite. Marko and Sonny would have disabled his bike or got Karyn to ride it out of there. Or if they were waiting for him, maybe, there'd be no escape.

When the light was full he climbed a north slope and studied the distance for the sheen of asphalt. He had to wait for a car to pass before he could spot the road. He memorized the contours of two crazy sand-drip peaks that had framed the car and then he climbed down and started for that spot, only it was near impossible to go straight in the right direction, unless he wanted to climb every hill in the way. They were crumbly and it was illegal to walk on them too—not that he cared in this situation but—

Walking the old dry channels between the hills made it easy to lose his sense of direction. A compass would be a nice thing to have, and water. Especially water. In a time before history these hills must have been islands in a land of lakes. He put a pebble in his mouth, to build saliva.

The sun was tilting, reddening at his back, before he climbed over the lip of the road and crouched, exhausted, on the balls of his feet and the knuckles of one hand. He had no warning of the first car coming. It arrived around the bend at high speed and in eerie silence: one of the new hybrids that got by without combustion most of the time. When Jamal jumped up swinging his arms the car swerved sharply, first toward the mountain wall, then over-correcting to the edge of the precipice he had just climbed, where it just managed not to hurtle over. Then it was gone around the bend.

Jamal retained a flash of lipstick framing a cell phone. That was it. He looked down at himself: clothes torn and bloody at the knees and elbows, his left hand swollen from cactus venom—there was a good chance nobody would stop for somebody who looked like that, especially now it was beginning to get dark.

He began to walk downhill along the serpentine rubber tracks the car had laid while losing and regaining control. How far it was to the nearest town or village or crossroad or wayside gas pump or ranger station he had no idea at all. Sunset was a red filament burning like forged metal at the horizon's edge. Julie had been in the cave for almost twenty-four hours, he thought. Maybe there was water in there. Maybe she had survived the fall.

The patrol car came around the bend, revolving blue dome lights flashing but with no siren. The young Smoky hopped out with a hand on his pistol grip. Mirror sunglasses stopped Jamal from being able to tell just how he was being scanned but he had the sense of being compared to a description.

"All right, you. Hands on the roof there. *Come* on. Give it some weight." The patrolman hooked one of Jamal's ankles out so that he practically fell against the car, at the same time he frisked him, quickly finding the swing-blade clipped in his pocket.

"The fuck is this, son?" The patrolman flicked the knife open in one hand, studying the serration and the tanto point, while pressing Jamal's head down with the other, gripping him by the nape of his neck.

I was camping he wanted to say, but when he opened his mouth he was too parched to make a sound.

"Okay, I'm not gonna cuff you. Get in the back." Head pressed down by the big bony hand, Jamal obediently climbed into the back seat. The patrolman slapped the door shut and got behind the wheel, twisting to look at Jamal through the wire mesh between them.

"Let's lose the shades there, boy."

Jamal took off the yellow sunglasses. To his surprise the patrolman pushed his own glasses to the top of his head. Their eyes met through the diamonds of the wire. Probably there were not too many years between them.

"Got a call about some wild man running around out here. On a bet I'd say that's gotta be you. You got anything to say for yourself?

Julie. The word wouldn't come out.

"You don't start talking some English pretty soon I gotta think you're one of them Ay-rab *terrorists.*" The unmasked eyes squinted. "Or you might be a Messcan, I don't know. Hey. *Habla español?*"

Jamal tried opening his mouth again. The pebble clicked against the back of his bottom teeth.

"Be that way, then." The patrolmen lowered his shades and put his hands on the wheel. "Maybe you'll have something to say at the station." He popped a U-turn, burning more rubber, and roared back the way that he had come.

Jamal rolled his head against the seatback. He still had the feeling of being watched. Yes, the rearview mirror framed two mirrored teardrops. He coughed the pebble into the palm of his hand.

"Fuck me I'm an idiot," the patrolman said. The brakes slammed on and the car shuddered to a stop. He reached to the floor and came up with a blue-topped bottle of water. "Here," he said, sliding back a gate in the mesh between them. "Cut the dust."

Jamal turned the cap from the clear bottle and held a sip of water in his mouth before he let it trickle down his throat. Much as he would have liked to slam the whole pint at once, he knew it wouldn't be a good idea. He thought he could feel the parched cells in his tongue and the walls of his mouth expanding. He took a slightly larger swallow.

"Dude." The patrolman had pushed up his glasses again. "About how long were you out there anyway?"

Jamal shrugged. "A day . . . but Julie."

"What Julie." The patrolman's eyes narrowed.

"Julie," Jamal said. "She's still in the cave."

43

Julie's mom walked into the police station with a half-smoked Virginia Slim in one hand and a quart of Diet Coke in the other. She wore a smock printed with tiny multicolored teddy bears, long enough to reach halfway down her bowed legs, and over the smock a blue vest with a Walmart name tag pinned to it. She didn't look right or left when she came into the dim room, but headed straight for Jamal as if her flight path had been programmed to something in his blood.

Jamal was under no restraint, but his only move was to take off his sunglasses and hold them folded in his lap. His neck flexed like green wood but he didn't let his head turn with the blow, which dragged nail scratches across the line of his jaw. Julie's mom backhanded him by reversing the same motion, swinging her hips into it like an expert golfer. Her knuckles rebounded from Jamal's cheekbone; again, his head hadn't flinched from the blow, and he was looking straight at her with his naked gray eyes. Julie's mom paused for a moment then, and stood planted, looking into her palm as if to find a fortune.

"Lady!" the desk sergeant said from his high chair behind the grubby counter. "You can't smoke in here."

Without glancing up at him, Julie's mom tossed her cigarette out the open door. She'd discarded the Coke bottle with the first blow; it drooled a semicircle of brown syrup across the linoleum floor. The overhead lights were out except for one flickering fluorescent tube so there was only a wedge of noonish light thrusting in through the doorway, not quite reaching Jamal's own mother, who sat in the shadows of a far corner, expressionless under her black headscarf, except for the flash of her dark eyes.

Julie's mom raised her blunt head toward Jamal again, and cocked back her right arm.

"Ms. Westover," Jamal said. "You can beat me till you break your hand. I wouldn't blame you."

44

In the late afternoon light of the desert there was a sort of haphazard conference between highway patrol, Murdo police and a search and rescue team that had choppered a dog in from Sioux Falls. Murdo was such a small town that even a random highway patrolman could pull rank on the chief of police, who was comforting himself by bullying Jamal.

"Little shit-bird," he said, heavy jowls shivering. "Don't tell me you were out here all by yourself with your girlfriend."

Jamal said nothing. He was figuring time, as the shadows lengthened. Forty-four hours, or forty-six, since Julie went into the cave. He inspected his palm, which was pockmarked and still swollen from the venom of the cactus spines. The police chief raised his ringed fist.

"I wouldn't bother," said the patrolman who'd found Jamal on the highway. "If anybody could smack it out of him we'd already know."

The police lowered his hand. "Why didn't you bike out to get help then?" he said. "Why walk it?"

Jamal shrugged. "Flat tires." The highway patrolman was looking down at the scooter where it lay dumped on its side in the sand. Marko and Sonny had been subtle, for them. Instead of slashing the tires they'd let the air out and even replaced the valve stem caps when they were done.

"Both of them," the police chief said. "Yeah, we saw that already." He gestured broadly. There were long loops of tire tracks all on either side of the dry streambed Jamal had used to crawl to shelter. Marko and Sonny had taken their tent but left a scattering of beer cans and one of the collapsible coolers. The search and rescue dog, who wore a red vest decorated with a five-point star, was sniffing around Jamal's dome tent, which had stayed in place, weighted down by its rocks.

"Come on," the police chief said. "There was a party here. It's obvious. You didn't just come out for date night."

"People come out here all the time." Jamal pointed up to the ledges. "Look at the graffiti."

"Is that right?" The police chief's eyes wouldn't follow Jamal's gesture. Jamal found himself looking at the big oval Shriner ring on one of the chief's thick fingers. He was squinting a little from his right eye, because his cheekbone had swollen some from Julie's mother's backhand.

"Hey kid." The highway patrolman was beckoning, shaking two cigarettes out of a pack of Camel filters. Feeling he'd been given permission, Jamal walked away from the chief. He accepted a cigarette, though he didn't normally smoke. The patrolman snapped a Zippo for him. Jamal relaxed a little. The patrolman had made an effort to be nice to him since Julie's mother popped him in the station. Jamal was not actually under arrest, and the patrolman had even found a chance to slip him back his knife.

The unaccustomed tobacco buzz was making him a little dizzy. He looked around. The police chief had shaded his eyes with one hand to stare up at the ledges where the spray-painted tagging surrounded the cave mouth. At this distance the old animal designs were not apparent. The purple and red KAOS tag stood out brilliantly in the day's-end light. Invisible beneath it, the bear totem Jamal had once figured out with his fingers like a blind man groping to read Braille.

Twenty yards behind him Jamal could see the silhouette of Carrie Westover behind the tinted windows of a double-cab white pickup the Murdo police chief had driven to the scene. They hadn't let Jamal's mother come. However, on the horizon behind the truck, he picked out a matchstick figure he felt sure was one of his older brothers, which comforted him, though he knew his brother would come no closer, and could not affect anything that happened here.

The search and rescue guys were shaggy, mustachioed, dressed in plaid shirts and jeans. Their dog was now whiffing a pair of faded bikini underpants. They'd asked Ms. Westover for some of Julie's unwashed garments, but Jamal didn't know why she couldn't have found a pair of dirty socks.

One of the search and rescue guys was sniggering over the panties, snuffling louder than the dog. He had only just opened his mouth to speak when the patrolman socked him on the upper arm.

"Knock it off," the patrolman said. The search and rescue guy gave him a sharp glance, but he didn't say anything more.

The patrolman threw down his cigarette butt and ground it into the sand with his boot toe. "These guys. . . ." he said. "Think they're Delta Force, I don't know."

Smoking had made Jamal's cottonmouth worse. He'd been dry in the mouth since his day in the desert and no amount of water made any difference. He read the patrolman's watch upside down. Forty-five hours. Forty-seven.

"I don't see what the dog's got to do with it," he said. "I know where she went. I already told them."

"Sure," the patrolman said. "But it looks like the dog agrees with you, at least."

The dog had led the others up the ledges; by the time Jamal and the patrolman caught up the dog was straining into the slit opening of the cave. He looked back over the desert plain. Carrie Westover had left the truck and stood in front of its cattle-catcher, arms folded across her burly chest, planted on the sand like a gravestone. Probably she was looking up at the party on the ledge, but the afternoon light was slanting so harshly that Jamal could not make out her face. When he checked again where he thought he'd seen his brother he could see nothing but the red blaze of the sun.

The dog wanted to go in the cave. To Jamal it looked

something like an Airedale, though not a hundred percent. He'd tried to pet the dog when it first arrived but the search and rescue guys had waved him off. A dog on duty, working, working, it showed no interest in Jamal either. One of the search and rescue guys was studying the old petroglyphs on the wall above or under the tags. The other one held the straining dog by its collar and a fold of loose skin. He grunted and skipped back abruptly, pulling the dog with him, dodging a thin stream of bats that came from the top of the slit like smoke.

"They come out the same time every day," Jamal said. "Almost. Every day it's about a minute different. Always around the time the sun goes down." He wondered why he and Julie hadn't seen them. They'd been somewhere else on the cliff side, he guessed, admiring the fine wafer of the moon.

The police chief and the patrolman had turned from the cave mouth, to watch the bats scattering like flakes of ash across the dimming sky. The search and rescue guys were both looking intently at Jamal. "You know a lot about this place, don't you," one of them said. "Have you ever been in there?"

"No," said Jamal. "But I'm ready to go."

45

Folding his elbows and shoulders together, Jamal burrowed into the cave mouth like a mole. Stone edges scraped the back of his forearms and chafed against the top of his scalp. There was a moment when he really felt like screaming. Then the passage opened, a little. He could move his arms out from his body now. He could stand straighter, and had room to turn around.

But for the moment he kept facing forward, into the cave. He touched the flashlight they'd given him, tucked in the front of his waistband, but he didn't take it out to turn it on.

There was a much larger space in the darkness before him. Air currents, a change of temperature. No, he didn't know how he was aware of this expansion, but he was.

Somehow he didn't want to shine a light into it. He thought of calling. Julie. Julie. He didn't call.

"Hey kid?" It was the police chief, worried. "You in there?"

One of the search and rescue guys snorted and said, "Where else would he be?" The voices echoed, warped as they rounded a bend of the passage, where a weak stain of day's-end light spilled across the wall. The cord attached to Jamal's back belt loop tugged. He reached behind himself and yanked back.

"I'm all right," he said. "Just wait a minute."

There'd been a few minutes of argument over whether or not Jamal should go into the cave. The police chief, suddenly solicitous, had objected that he was a minor, a civilian, untrained. But there was no one else who could fit. And there was nothing else to do. Jamal had known that he would go, from the moment the idea occurred to him.

He turned and began to reel the cord toward him, pulling in heavier lines, some tackle and a sort of harness that could be used to help get Julie out if she needed it. One of the search and rescue guys had said what everyone had to be thinking. If she were in shape to get out on her own, she would have already done it.

A walkie-talkie crackled from a clip on his belt. The search and rescue guys had given him that too, though they doubted it would work very deep in the cave.

"Kid, you hear me? Testing, over."

Jamal lifted the gadget and squeezed the talk button. "All right so far. I'm going on in." He thumbed down the volume dial, reducing the static to a whisper on his belt, and turned into the deep darkness before him. He could feel in his spine how the space expanded, bloomed out before him, like the passage where he stood was a stem and the cavern beyond it its tremendous black flower.

The idea of turning on the flashlight was somehow like the idea of calling Julie's name . . . his voice would only echo back, he thought, sealing him into solitude. And the light's beam would only bounce back on him, he felt. But now he had to use it, because—

He panned the beam across the floor until, about fourteen inches in front of his feet, the floor disappeared into inky blackness; the vast, expanding space that he had sensed. Within it the beam simply disappeared; it was like shining a flashlight into the night sky. He tugged on the climbing line to be sure it was made fast outside, and began to inch his way to the lip.

When he turned the beam downward his heart kicked in his chest. Julie was there, about fifteen feet down, and the light seemed to catch her glassy eyes, open, unseeing, so he thought she must be dead.

Hastily he set up the climbing tackle on the rim and rappelled the short way down. Julie was motionless, her eyes closed now (maybe the other thing was some illusion?) Could she actually be sleeping? Her legs curled under her, but not in a way that they had to be broken. The smooth round of her cheek was warm to the touch, though the touch didn't rouse her. He felt an exhalation stirring the hairs on the back of his wrist. *Julie wake up.* He didn't say it. Now he could see that her halo of hair was widened by something spilled over the rock, a paint stain? No, he could smell the blood. Dried blood clotting the back of her hair when he lifted her head, feeling all around her skull for a fracture, but there wasn't one, not anyway that he could feel. A hairline crack he wouldn't have detected.

Julie slumped into him. Warm all over—that was good— and he could feel the rhythm of her breath against his own ribcage. Maybe he shouldn't have moved her though, maybe—but there was no way he was leaving her here.

He fed her limp arms into the harness. The climbing tackle worked as intended; in a moment he had hoisted her up. Only there was no place down below to fasten his line. He climbed it cautiously, with Julie still dangling over the drop, balancing her weight with his. In a moment he had drawn her away from the lip into the passage and he thought, as he crouched there gasping, that the worst of it was probably over.

The walkie-talkie whined on his hip but Jamal thought he was too close to the aperture to need it. He called out toward the entrance. "I've got her. I'm bringing her out."

The worst part was working her through the passage. No way they would ever fit through together. Jamal would have to drag her, and that wouldn't be good, or feed her into the tight part from behind. Try that. He soon realized she shouldn't go head first as he'd first thought, not when she was unconscious and unable to help. Julie wasn't especially heavy, but there was nothing so awkwardly massive as human dead weight. He threaded her feet into the tightest part of the passage. It reminded him of breech births he'd seen one summer when he'd worked for a vet, but at least this way he could cradle her head, which was cut but probably not broken.

"Easy," he called, because they had got her feet, then her knees by the crooks of them, and they risked pulling her head free of his hands. He turned sideways in the passage, where he also had to crouch, sucking in his gut to make room for Julie's torso to pass along the furrow in his body, passing almost through his body. He was supporting her head with only one hand now because he couldn't turn far enough to use both, and now her head with his hand under was out in the open air—*Have you got her head?* he called, and already he felt other hands basketing under his, and a warm lick of a dog's tongue on his knuckles, so the dog must have clocked out for the day.

Jamal retracted his arm into the cave.

"Buddy," the patrolman was saying, "You got her, man! You got her, come on out."

"I," Jamal said. "Gotta get." What? The flashlight, but it was tucked in his waistband now. The ropes and tackle. Not that either really.

"We'll get that all later," a search and rescue guy said. "Ja- Jamal? Come on out now."

There was no reason it should remind him of Sonny and Marko calling for him, night before last, promising they weren't going to—Jamal was already back in the wider part of the passage. He had already spun himself down on the rope, like a spider, to the place where Julie had lain.

The space was not the same infinitude into which he'd shone the light from above. He knew it, though the flashlight was turned off. He was in the spot where Julie had been, a passage that was deep and long but not so wide. He could brush either side with his fingertips if he reached his arms as far as they would go.

And there was a presence here. Julie and not Julie too. It was more than just that she had recently been here in her body. Something was still here, another. Something lay within the wall Jamal was facing, but with his light extinguished he could not say what. And there was something further down the passage, in the direction of the intermittent currents of cool air caressing his face.

Strange that he was not afraid. He was not simply curious either, but somehow compelled.

The walkie talkie crackled on his hip. Jamal switched it off, and on second thought discarded it. He still had the flashlight, though unlit, as he began slowly and carefully to make his blind way into the greater darkness of the cave.

46

Now the stone was red, warm and elastic; it reshaped her head as her head squeezed through it. That small warm leathery hand was still holding hers in a firm and reassuring grip, and at the same time a hand supported her skull at the base, guiding it through the tight red clasp of the passage. Then with a wet rush she fell into the startling cold of the open air, which was full of a terrible brightness, so that she cried out from the shock.

A liquid whistle answered her cry, and she was gathered into a heartbeat that was hidden in warm fur. She knew it, this heart-drum; she had been listening to it all her life long, she knew. The soothing whistling sound continued, and her mouth stopped crying. Her mouth whimpered now and was at the same time searching, behind her weak insistent hands as they probed through the fur. Her mouth found a rubbery nubbin that released warm milk into her body, and the whistle settled into a sigh. The heart-drum inside her body locked onto the beat of the drum she felt through the warm, milk-giving fur.

She had not yet opened her eyes, but burrowed now, in a warm soft feeding blindness. A part of her that was still Julie thought now with a jolt of surprise, *I am my own mother.*

47

She rode a skin slung on the mother's back, her head beside the mother's head, her eyes beside the mother's eyes. Her vision was the mother's vision. Still they shared one heart.

Her hands inside the mother's hands gathered greens and dug for roots. A green stick was pointed, hardened in the fire to do the digging. There were plants for healing, others for food. There were roots for healing—a brown one forked like the arms and legs of a Person, and roots for eating—a round one with the crisp white taste inside.

Inside the mother's hands her hands scraped skins with a stone scraper. Her teeth chewed rawhide strings to a serviceable softness. With a stone knife a Person flaked for her she cut up meat for eating. Inside the mother's heart she knew the names of animal persons who gave such nourishment to the People. The names were shaped in that half-melodious twittering clipped off by quick clicks of the tongue. There was a *hawk*. There had been a *bear*. But they were not called so in this tongue and she was too deeply buried in the mother to reach the mother tongue.

There was *fire. Water. Fire-drill.* Names of the animal persons. Her hands inside the mother's hands rolled the fire drill until her leathery palms were nearly burning and she crouched and made her lips a flower to huff a spark into the tinder. *Fire. Meat.* A *torch*, which she could hold up to the edge of the vertical slit from which her Person had somehow been extracted. But the darkness of the *cave* was such that it devoured all the light.

Inside the cave there were other times. A time of many lives gone when the People had walked out of the far north through deep crevasses in the vast ice mountain, hunting an animal person with long matted hair and tusks and an angry bellow when stung with a spear and a long snout that moved like a serpent, and it could grasp and hurl a branch or a Person, and many many lives gone before that when fire shot down from the sky like an angry icicle and the People learned how it slept in wood and learned their ways to wake it. Time is not straight like a spear, but round like the moon, and inside the *cave* time went around and around in a dark spiral that included times of many many lives to come—she knew but she did not know how.

The injured hawk waited, perched on a stone cropping outside the overhang of the cave. It ruffled its feathers and shrugged its wings, except that the hurt wing would not come to the position of the other. Slowly that wing relaxed and fanned out and down over the surface of the rock where the hawk perched, covering the gray-white streaks of its droppings. The yellow eye closed and the hawk's head tucked down behind the one raised shoulder. Its consciousness stopped.

48

Inside the skin bag, with rawhide strings made supple by the working of her teeth, the mother carried the fire drill everywhere the People traveled. Inside the mother's heart and hands she was herself *fire-bringer*. She spun the stick between her hardening palms and puffed a spark from the bloom of her lips into the tinder. Fire grew, meat cooked, the People fed.

Sated she sat by the waterside, in the reddening light of the close of day. The valley, which in many lives to come would be a crumbling, dusty dry place, was full of water now, in this crater of the great moon-shape of time. Channels of turquoise-colored water snaked among the green hilltops, reflecting the fading blue of the sky. A Person walked along the bank, head cocked to watch for a shadow of fish beneath the opaque surface of the water, balancing a light spear in one hand.

To her left a Person was scraping a shaft, to her right a Person was chipping a large flint spearhead, and behind her near the slit of the cave mouth a Person was gathering different colors into little points of horn. She was chewing rawhide strings to soften them, taking sticks of hide from a stiff pile to her left and laying down the chewed strings in a soft pile to her right. The faint flavor of the hide as it relaxed brought back the sensation of the meat she had recently eaten and the texture brought back the feeling of the strip of hide that the Person had wrapped around her forearm, its flesh bonding with the scratches left by the claws of the hawk. The soothing motion of her jaws relaxed her in the direction of dream ...

... again the stone turned soft like clay; she could move through it. She was aware of other women with her, circling through the red stone wall. She did not know them. They were shades. On one side the cave, the other the world.

Her eyes rolled open. It was dimmer now, and some of the People had gone away from the water's edge. A ghost of moon hung in the opposite side of the sky from the setting sun. She watched the sign of an animal person making its serpentine wave beneath the surface of the water going south, and when the water had stilled again, another animal person arrived, mossy carapace lifting out of the reflection of the moon, but larger, so much larger, and the head emerging with its dark eye in many wrinkled folds, looking at her but without appetite or intention. The eye was simply there, floating calmly in the ancient body of the *turtle*, and she saw how the curve of the vast shell met its reflection in the water to complete its orb, and there was a meaning in that which eluded her, slipping out of the reach of her mind like a fish shivering away from a thrust of the spear. Something else was happening now: a hawk, circling tight and swooping to claw a bright fish from the darkening water, just at the edge of the turtle's shell. Rising into the air with a shriek, the hawk turned the fish in his talons to match the fish's tail to his, dropped it, stooped to catch it again almost before it had broken the water, then carried it to the peak of a boulder to be torn, eviscerated, consumed.

Blood from this small kill staining the stone. All clear in her mind's eye, clear and real as if she'd seen it with the eyes of her body. But the secret was elsewhere, in the moment *hawk* twinned with itself, touching its reflected talons, the way the two halves of the turtle's shell composed a squashed sphere like the gibbous moon.

Inside the rock shelter, the mother slept by the cooling embers, breathing with the faintest whistling sound. She saw how she was apart from the mother now, though the small strong hand that had helped her into this world remained the same, resting on its swollen knuckles, palm up by the fire-pit. The other hawk, the one she fed, slept on the rock cropping outside the cave. This hawk, the one she had brought among the People, could not yet fly, though day by day its injured wing folded and unfolded itself more smoothly.

49

She was coming again to the People, bringing the wounded hawk on her arm, following the stones they piled, coming to them again for the first time. So she was strange among them now, strange as when she first pulled free of the stone, because of this familiar on her forearm, his talons curled around the strip of raw hide bonded to her skin, so that hard as the hawk gripped he dented her flesh but did not break it. The hard grip of hawk's talons held her in this world.

She fed the hawk with strips of meat, before the meat was tongued by fire. Around them People gathered, watching, whistling and twittering to each other over this strange thing that had arrived among them. Hawk cocked its head as it took the meat, the flat yellow circle of its eye shining on her. Hawk left her forearm and fluttered awkwardly a short distance to a boulder where it perched, fanning out its wings. Now the wing that had been hurt held the same shape as the other. Hawk turned its head to the side, yellow eye shining, the curved beak open. The hooked beak probed the feathers of its wings.

She waited till the wings had folded, till the mica-flat eyes appeared to close. Standing below the boulder she raised her forearm and nudged the back of the hawk's legs, till the hawk with a feathery sound in its throat stepped back and settled, closing its claws tight on the strip of hide. A murmur went round among the People who were still there watching; by this time some had gone away.

Then when Hawk rose from her arm she fell as if the beating wings had stunned her. The wings had grown enormously larger, with the force to move more air, a rush of wind that flattened her into the grass and held her there, continuing to press her down with a revolution of wings that strobed over the sun. Perhaps she heard a whistling among People who might be coming to her aid, but her eyes had rolled back into her head; she could not see them. She floated in a rain of the horn-point colors: umber, ochre, now a near scarlet red, and there were the three spirals swirling around each other— a triple helix, the dots drawn toward each other but never quite touching, as though a magnetic energy that held them together held them a certain distance apart.

She rose up in the loose skin of the bear, shambling over the rock ledges in the fluid sparkle of spring sunlight. The bear's own warm intentions warmed her, but the vortex was still drawing her down, so that the bear turned from the light and folded itself into the slit of the cave mouth, descending to the place where horn-point colors melded it into a bulge of cave wall stone—one eye looking backward, raised toward the faraway light.

With a pop like a cork shooting out of a bottle she was released into midair, her sight seated now behind hawk's eye, widening a circle in its deep blue gyre. Hawk's eye scanned the ledges for prey, but for the moment there was none. The animal persons etched on the face of the rock shelter wall had been obscured by other colors rolled over them—dark but with an unfamiliar gleam—and on the ledges were warm-blooded creatures, surely, but too large to be taken. They must be People of an unfamiliar kind, clothed in skins of the most unnatural colors, with strange colors shining from their lips and claws, and hair as fine and soft as milkweed. Harmless, surely, but too large to be taken. Hawk's eyes passed over them and on.

50

Ascending more gradually now, the ledge wrapped around the cliff wall to the north. At a narrow place where Karyn hesitated, Julie reached back to urge her along, and then they had come out, giggling, into the warmth of the sunlight. Julie let go Karyn's wrist and turned toward the lowering sun, raising one hand to shade her eyes, wishing now she'd brought a pair of sunglasses. On this side of the cliff the striped stone hills were densely grouped together, shallow, dry canyons snaking between them. The first phase of the sunset picked the landscape out in bands of turquoise and rose.

"Wow," said Julie, "We could be on the moon."

"Yeah, you think?" Karyn had slumped back against the rock. Wider in the hips than Julie, she wasn't quite so nimble on the ledges. Also it seemed she'd already had a pop of something, who knew what, just enough to make her jolly, and a little unstrung in her limbs.

Karyn cocked her head to the sky. "What's that?"

The whole desert valley resonated with an airy silence. Then squeaking, like a hamster in distress, and it grew louder, but there couldn't be a hamster in midair. From below the lip of the ledge where they stood, the beating wings of a hawk came into view, flogging the air as it flew to perch on a crag some twenty yards away.

Julie pulled out her phone to take a picture.

"Don't," Karyn said. "Oh gross. . . . How can you *watch* it."

The hawk tightened its talons and the squeaking

abruptly stopped. Julie didn't know if she wanted to watch and she wanted to ask what the hawk had caught, and there was no way that Karyn would know. It couldn't be a hamster of course, and it was bigger than a mouse, and furry. A prairie dog. Did they have those here? She watched the hard bright eye of the hawk as the curved beak dipped, cut and penetrated, then emerged with a shuddering strip of bleeding meat. There was something dreadful about it and yet—

Karyn was crowding Julie from behind, using Julie as a shield as she peered over her shoulder, her breasts lowering, heavy and warm, into Julie's shoulder blades. "It's disgusting," she said. "Oooo, I can't watch this, it's too awful."

Karyn covered her eyes with her hands, then peeked out through her laced fingers. A delicious shudder blunted itself on Julie's back every time she peered out through the finger-lattice. Karyn was just the same in horror movies, Julie realized, punctuating her furtive glances with luscious little shrieks, and getting herself a lot more worried and bothered than she would have if she'd just opened her eyes as wide as Julie's and watched the splatter scenes straight through.

Dumb. Still, Julie felt an affection for the frightened girly-girl routine, though it had been quite a while since she'd tried it herself, and she had never performed it half as well as her friend. She swung her shoulder under Karyn's and wrapped one arm around her waist. Karyn clutched at her, still watching the hawk. Julie remembered how Karyn would act this way when she talked about the tape Sonny and Marko supposedly had heard, the one where you could hear bears eating the stupid guy and his girlfriend.

She thought how Karyn didn't understand the difference, which Julie herself could less understand than feel. Karyn had always been the leader, since the friendship first struck up in middle school, first to sneak out at night and first to sneak into R-rated movies, first to go steady, to sneak parents' liquor and find ways to get pills and pot. She was the first to grow a woman's body and to have sex and to have steady sex with

Sonny. *Advanced* sex, Karyn claimed sometimes. But that was just about the only area where Karyn was ahead of Julie now, and in other ways, less tangible or clear, Julie saw that she was going to pass Karyn soon, maybe had already started to.

And now she seemed to be looking at the two of them as if from somewhere on the moon. Julie saw that Karyn's horizons would be shrinking after high school. She'd log a couple of years at community college, then most likely would marry Sonny, assuming Sonny got himself unstuck from Marko (since Karyn had enough sense to know that Marko would be worse and worse news as all of them got older), and the two of them would spend their lives in some small town like the one they were raised in, creating other people like themselves.

As for Julie, she had no idea what her own life would become, and that made her feel dizzy, as if she were falling or as if she might fall, so she tightened her arm around Karyn's waist. When Karyn squeezed her back, that dislocation turned into a sort of sad warmth, like Julie was already missing Karyn, though Karyn was still right there with her.

The hawk had finished its meal and flown, and Julie and Karyn turned from the death stain on the boulder, set their backs to the wall and looked out toward the horizon. Karyn's squeeze turned into a nudge.

"Girlfriend," she said. "Where you sleeping tonight?"

"With you?" Julie forced a laugh.

"Come on," Karyn said. "We'd have stayed at my house if it was gonna be that. You know me'n Sonny—"

"I know," Julie said quickly, deft as she usually was in forestalling Karyn telling her more on that subject than she wanted to hear. "Only with the tents we got it looks like you and Sonny and *Marko*."

"Get out!" Karyn pulled away, but she was laughing. "We're not freaks like *that*—Marko's staying out in the open—says he likes it under the stars. Sonny says so, anyway. So we get some quality alone time out here . . . and you—"

Karyn patted Julie's cheek. "You must of thought about this before now."

"Of course," Julie said, though she hadn't exactly thought it through.

"Do you like him?" Karyn gave her an elbow nudge. "You like him?"

"What do you think?" Julie said.

"Get serious!" Karyn said, then she herself did. "I dunno. . . . He's weird. *They're* weird. They're foreigners. My Dad says he can't figure why anybody would eat the food they fix. Much less pay for it. Dad says they could be Ayrab terrorists the whole pack of them."

"Come on."

Karyn looked down thoughtfully. Jamal had climbed to the top of a boulder on the flat sand near the tents. He sat cross-legged, looking out toward the sunset. The yellow bubble sunglasses made his pose more insect-like than it otherwise might have seemed. He was completely contained in himself, Julie thought, like that silver-gray orb of his tent.

"Okay," Karyn said. "I'll tell you one thing I like about him is I think he's strong. He's not very big but I think . . . he's strong. You know? And I know he likes *you*." Karyn switched her hips, winking her navel stud above her skintight jeans.

Julie thought of Jamal, when the dog had rushed them. He'd put himself between the dog and her right away, but not suddenly. It was like he had always been planted there, like a tree. One hand behind him, palm down to the ground, told her she should be that same kind of still. After a while the dog stopped snarling. Its back relaxed and it walked up to Jamal and sniffed his knees and the fingers of his gently outstretched hand and then it went away. Jamal had made nothing of it all, after the dog had gone. He didn't say anything about what had happened, and he didn't walk any closer to Julie than he had been before, although she wouldn't have minded if he did.

Asked you first, Karyn said. "Okay I like him," Julie

blurted. "Okay I *like* like him." At that she knew she would share Jamal's tent and also that he wouldn't touch her any more than she wanted him to or not at all if she didn't want it. She was opening her mouth again to ask if Karyn had brought along any extra protection, because Karyn sometimes showed off Sonny's favorite types of condom in her purse, but Karyn was staring at the boulder again.

"Oh disgusto," Karyn said. "Julie, look, Julie, it's *drinking the blood.*"

Julie looked. A butterfly had lit on the stain of the hawk's kill. As it imbibed the blood its wings stirred the air, an iridescent, heavenly blue. Julie shivered as the butterfly took flight.

"I trust him," she said, and knew it was true.

Out of the darkness where she lay she could still see the butterfly as if at the end of a telescope tube, its wingtips delicately revolving. And yes it could have happened like that. Could have been as innocent and simple as that. But then she would not be in the cave, and it mattered more than anything else that she be in the cave.

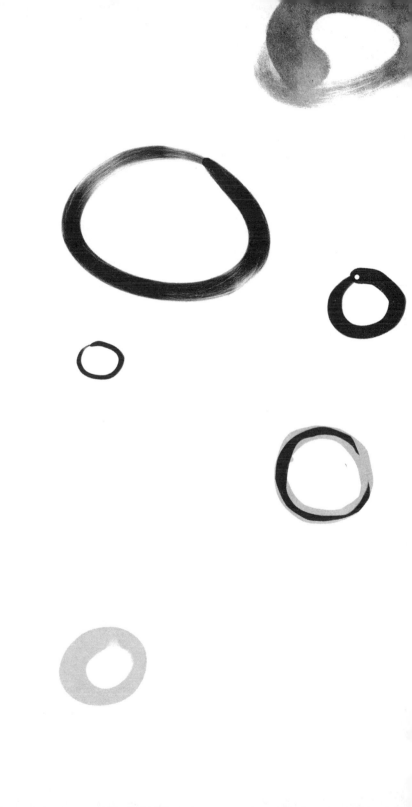

51

Jamal piloted Marissa down Highway 15 into the streets of the little town. Faster perhaps if they'd come on I-90. But the two-lane road was calmer. In wind-dried fields along the road were billboards advertising a Wild West Town and presently they passed the attraction itself, or its weathered board gateway, surmounted with quasi-comical mileage arrows and a bleached cow's skull with horns. Beside the gate, heeled over on a missing wheel, was a remnant of a stage coach.

"It's fake," Jamal said as they passed. It was the only remark he had made since leaving the hospital, other than things like *turn here.*

"They're on the west side," Jamal said now. "Turn right up there on Lincoln."

Marissa made the turn. It seemed a little ludicrous to talk about the "West Side" of a town no better than ten blocks square.

"Left here," Jamal said. "All right. There's the house." He didn't point, only half turned the yellow bulbs of his glasses to indicate which house he meant. Marissa braked. Beside the little white brick ranch was a flimsy carport with an arched plastic top, empty. When she looked at it she seemed to see it crushed beneath a weight of winter snow.

"Does she have a car?" Marissa said? "I don't think anybody's home."

"She's got a car." Jamal turned a thin smile on her as he popped open the passenger door. "You'll hear it coming. She works at Walmart, down on the bypass." He glanced at the clock on the truck's dashboard. "Should be out of work already."

"Don't you want a ride somewhere?" Marissa said. "Or—" She was wishing he wouldn't leave her here alone. But Jamal was already out of the cab, walking around the hood to the driver's side. Marissa rolled down her window.

"I dunno how pissed she is at me still," Jamal said. "Probably better if I'm gone when she gets here." He was offering her a takeout menu he'd pulled from his windbreaker pocket. Marissa looked at it uncomprehendingly. Some kind of Middle Eastern place.

"It's my mother's restaurant," Jamal said. "Stop by when you're done. You just go down Lincoln and over to—"

"There's no way I'm not finding it in a town this size," Marissa said, forcing a short laugh. Jamal laughed also, and waved a hand as he turned from the truck. In a moment he was around the corner, out of sight.

West side. She looked at the little brick house again. A gutter was loose at the corner by the carport. It made a metal scraping sound whenever it caught the wind.

She put the truck in gear, drove half a block to the dead end circle and shut it off. Through the rearview mirror she could see the approach. There was a newspaper on the dash, but she couldn't concentrate. Her stomach unknotted, knotted again. If she smoked it would pass the time but she hadn't smoked since that day with Inez.

She got out of the truck and walked to the edge of the asphalt, shading her eyes against the lowering sun. Here civilization ended, at least for now. She thought of the phony ghost town in the opposite direction. Beyond this border there was scrub and dry prairie, a few tumbleweeds. When she looked to her right she could see the sun gleaming red on the rusted railroad track that ran away to the northwest.

Engine noise made her turn. An old blue Toyota with a hole in the muffler turned into the gravel drive of the white house. Under the carport the engine coughed dead.

The woman who got out was burly, like a knotted tree trunk, overweight but not morbidly so. A plastic grocery sack was looped around one wrist. She wore a Walmart smock and a black eyeshade whose band confined a wavy tumble of graying blond hair, long enough to spill over her shoulders.

Marissa got her legs to start walking toward the house. Something was wrong with her proprioception: she could feel her heart rhythm but not her feet striking the ragged pavement. Conscientiously, she breathed.

"Mrs. Westover?"

Key in the side door, the woman turned toward her, eyes slitting over puffy red cheeks. But she didn't look like a drunk, Marissa decided. Just sunburned, or windburned, and why wouldn't she be suspicious of a stranger?

"You from the hospital?"

"Yes," Marissa said. It was simpler, and not exactly untrue.

"Do I have to let you in?"

"No," Marissa said. "You don't have to let me in."

"Huh," Carrie Westover said, hefting the bag as she pushed the side door open. "Well, you better come in, I guess."

They were in the kitchen, a small linoleum square. Carrie Westover unloaded her bag into the fridge. Frozen peas, frozen fries, a pack of hamburger pale with fat. She pulled a bottle of Diet Coke from its plastic ring before storing the remainder of the six, then squinted at Marissa.

"You want one?"

Marissa shook her head.

"I got beer. I think." She leaned her torso into the fridge, searching. She's not a lush anyway, Marissa thought, or she wouldn't think; she'd know. Unless her taste was not for beer. Carrie Westover unfolded herself from the fridge and handed Marissa a can of Coors Light. She took it, feeling condensation dampening her palm. Carrie's hand was small considering her overall bulkiness, like a bird's claw. No rings.

Marissa followed her through the next room, darkly blinded, with leatherette furniture and a hefty TV. The house seemed to have a shotgun plan, like a trailer. Where were the bedrooms? Julie's room? When Carrie opened a door at the back the dust motes in the interior glowed in rays of sunset light. There was a low wooden deck with web chairs and a metal table, supporting a jumbo ashtray.

"Cooler out here," Carrie Westover kicked off her Crocs and put her bare feet on the seat of the chair opposite the one she sat in. "Sorry," she said. "I'm on my dogs all day."

She lit a cigarette, the same pale brand that Peggy smoked, in the rundown courtyard behind their work. In Marissa's mind, the count of the vacation days she'd already consumed in this venture lit up. If she didn't return soon she'd be into sick days also.

From the deck they had a pleasant view of the sunset, across the receding railroad track.

"Are there still trains?" Marissa asked.

"Once in a while." Carrie blew a smoke ring. "Usually when you just went to sleep." She pulled off her eyeshade and tossed it onto the table. "You didn't come out here to ask me that."

"Julie," Marissa said, setting her unopened beer on the table. "So. You live alone with her here?"

"Since thirteen years, yeah." Carrie closed her eyes for a moment. "No, I think it's fourteen."

"No siblings." Marissa practically winced at the word herself. She'd slipped into social worker mode and she didn't know how to get out of it. "Brothers and sisters?"

"No."

"She was doing okay in school?"

"College prep. Okay, not great."

"But it's good to be in college prep."

"Best they got."

"And the um, father?"

"Hey Missy, where's your clipboard?" Carrie dropped her feet to the board floor and leaned sharply forward, all hackled up like a threatened dog. "You people all keep

coming after me like I got the answer—well, I'm looking for the same damn thing myself. I never had any real
trouble with Julie—not like some people do with their
kids—but come to find out she was hiding things from me
and I still don't know just what. I thought she was spending
the night with her girlfriend. I didn't even know they were
running with those two motorcycle punks. If I'd known
I'd of put a stop to it. I didn't know till the call from the
cops and after that your guess's good as mine. I don't have
the first idea what went on out there that night. Docs can't
say why she won't wake up, and then all you people keep
coming around like if you poke me enough I'll come across
and tell you."

"I'm sorry," Marissa said.

"Right," Carrie sat back, exhaled another cloud of
smoke. "You're sorry. You want to show me some ID?"

"I'm—" Marissa said, and stopped. She had to get off the
wrong foot somehow and there was no way to do it but jump.

"I'm the biological mother."

Carrie squinted at her, closing her right eye. "The what?"

"The birth mother. I—Julie's adopted, I knew that from
the start. I had her and I gave her up."

"You had her and you gave her up." Carrie broke her
half-smoked cigarette stabbing it into the overflowing ashtray.
"Why you skinny little snot-nose bitch—who sent for you?
You have no right to be here."

"I have a *wrong!*" Marissa shouted. She didn't know how
she'd chosen the word but she said it again, more quietly, as
she closed her eyes. I have a wrong. A wrong of my own making. She felt herself falling into it, as into a deep well. An inner
space, dark and limitless, with no point of orientation and no
light. There was no way to get a foot under her or to begin
to find her way out.

Behind her black lids she saw the shaman coming toward
her out of the thicket, over the scattering of sharp stones,
keening and shaking his rattle and looking at her with his

159

sad otherworldly comprehension. It won't help if you cry, she thought. She didn't cry.

Carrie Westover didn't look angry anymore, just tired. No doubt she had every right to be exhausted. Her feet, which she'd put back on the chair seat, were small, small-boned like her hands, and didn't really go with the gnarled body, which looked as if armored by battering.

Marissa picked up one of Carrie's feet and began to massage the knot under the instep with her thumb. When she realized what she was doing she thought the other woman would surely pull away, maybe even strike her, but Carrie only sank down in her chair and sighed.

52

He dozed in the green twilight of the hospital room, listening to the click and burble of machines, the steady whisper of Julie's breathing. A feathery shadow in the white bed, her face turned toward the dark window. She was still, waiting. Now and then the nurses exchanged a few words as they passed in the corridor. From outside he could hear the throttle sound of a big motorcycle engine, idling into the lot. Two engines. First one cut and then the other. Jamal opened his eyes and put on his bubble sunglasses, adding a yellow tint to the green, a different ghostliness to everything, as if he was submerged in an aquarium.

"The drool in the lotus," Marko said.

He was standing over Julie's quiet bed. Beside him, Sonny hulked uneasily.

Jamal remembered Julie, aware in her yoga pose, hands in a mudra over her head—how in this flower of her youth she had at the same time seemed ancient. It surprised him that Marko retained some picture in his mind of this. No doubt it was not the same picture. But Marko was not as stupid as he sometimes seemed.

"It's a problem for you if she doesn't wake up," Marko was saying. "A problem for us if she does."

"I think it's also a problem for you if she doesn't," Jamal said. He was standing now, light on the balls of his feet.

"Yo," Marko said, more sharply. "We never did anything to her. She just decided to run, that's all."

"I wonder," Jamal said. "Does Karyn tell it all like that?"

White teeth in the shadow of Marko's smile. "You know, that might not have been Karyn's first movie. And Karyn's out of the picture now."

"She went to her sister's," Sonny said hastily. "In Rapid City. She's gonna finish school over there."

Jamal, of course, already knew that; impossible not to in a town so small. He wondered if Sonny missed her, how much.

"That's what the girls do when they're pregnant," he said.

"No," Marko said. "Karyn had an upsetting experience. Which was nobody's fault. It just happened."

He reached as if he would touch the fan of Julie's hair on the pillow. Jamal moved slightly. Marko withdrew his hand.

"This one's not talking," he said. "I guess that leaves you."

"You're not going to take me down here," Jamal said. "There's too many other people around."

"No," said Marko. "We're going to let Ultimo take care of you."

Jamal reached toward this idea with his mind and couldn't feel anything about it whatsoever. No surprise, no fear.

"Do that."

"All right, then," Marko said, as if the matter had been amicably settled. He flipped his hand idly, moving toward the door. "We'll see you around, little bro. Unless for some reason we don't."

"I'll keep it in mind," Jamal said. He tried again, without success, to measure the seriousness of the threat. He couldn't even seem to remember exactly what Ultimo looked like. Ultimo's silhouette in his mind was like a wormhole into some other universe.

"Jamal?" Marko had turned in the doorway. "What's in that cave?"

"It's just a big black hole in the ground," Jamal said.

"No, man," Sonny said, with a queer urgency. "The Smokey said you wouldn't come out—like for an hour. They were calling and calling. They thought you were gone."

"Bears," Jamal said.

"Bullshit," Marko said.

"I don't mean just bears," Jamal said. "There were all kinds of animals. And people who were partway animal." He thought for a second. "I don't mean like you."

53

At first there was only the sound in the darkness, damp thump like a heartbeat and a high dry rattle on top of it. The dark enveloped her with the viscosity of tar. She struggled with it, for sight, breath, movement. The heartbeat sound jarred the core of her body and she clawed at the tar with a windmill movement of her hands, stirring it out and around herself in a sort of chocolate whirlpool. Her vision cleared and she saw him sitting cross-legged on a round smooth stone and slapping with one hand at the belly of the gourd, which he shook by its crookneck with the other hand. Here was the rattling sound that sat on the top of her head and resonated with the damp thumping pulse that drove into the hollow at the base of her skull until the matter of her brain began to shatter into pebbles like the ones that made that rattle in the gourd. She was spinning in the opposite direction from the tarry vortex that revolved around her. White hair on the back of the shaman's hands, not separate hairs but a pelt, and the shaman's hide vest had a pelt on it too; it hung open to reveal white body hair on the chest or breast through which two black and rubbery nipples protruded. Always the splintering sound of the gourd shaker. The eyes of the shaman were red-rimmed and recessed under heavy brow bones, like the eyes of some ancient androgynous ape, and somehow under their regard her own eyes rolled backward.

The tar of the vortex around her began to separate into colored threads like the rainbow colors of gasoline spilled

in water. The threads broke into particles, and now she was
spinning in a shower of light looking down on the body
of the woman Marissa who lay unconscious with her hair
bleeding out on a white pillow and her hands folded over
her chest like a corpse. The points of color were painfully
bright, and through a gap in the helical curtains of light she
looked down on the person of Marissa with pity and fear for
her confusion and loss.

the eye of my intention
to move the feelings more with the will

with a crash Marissa fell back into her body and jerked
upright from her pillow, her mouth open wide in the form
of a scream, though only a desperate panting came out. The
dry rattle from the gourd had stopped. The heart of that hard-
beating *thump* was her own.

54

Jamal's mother's restaurant was installed in a former Wendy's, Marissa thought, or some other hamburger chain anyway. A portable marquee at the driveway entrance announced The Magic Carpet, and under it in moveable block letters a list of specials ; she didn't recognize any of the words. The lot was better than half full, many cars with out-of-state plates.

Inside the smell was rich and delicious. Marissa had been eating very little since she came to this place, mostly yogurts she kept in a Styrofoam cooler in her motel room on the bypass. She sat down at a corner table, or rather a former fast food booth. The menu dizzied her, however, words running away in a blur. A freckled girl about Julie's age stood over her, slender hip cocked, clicking her pad with her pencil.

"I don't know what to get," Marissa said helplessly.

"That happens." The girl shot her a quick smile full of braces, and turned toward the back. Behind the fast food service counter a bead curtain had been dropped, screening the kitchen. All the good smells came from there. The curtain parted, and Jamal peered out; Marissa didn't recognize him at first because of the white apron and because he wasn't wearing his sunglasses.

"*Harira*," Jamal said, with a nod. Apparently it was a decision on Marissa's behalf, because the waitress made a note and took the menu. Presently she brought Marissa a glass of hot sweet tea. A few minutes later, Jamal came and set a white bowl in front of her, redolent with cinnamon and other less familiar spices. He had taken off his apron. He sat down in the booth across from her.

Marissa tasted. "My God this is good!" she said. "What is it?"

"People eat it after sundown during Ramadan," Jamal told her. "When they don't eat during daylight."

"Oh," said Marissa. "Is it Ramadan?"

"No," said Jamal. "It's good soup any day."

Marissa ate steadily and drank her tea. Little had been done to the décor of the place, except that the fluorescent lights were turned off, and a small oil lamp had been set on each formica table. The difference in atmosphere was considerable. By the time she had finished her soup the restaurant had mostly emptied out. Jamal called: "Misty!" and the girl brought her a plate of honey-soaked baklava.

"Why are you here?" she asked Jamal.

Jamal shrugged, with his long thin smile. "Because my mother has no daughters. My brothers, they do other work."

It wasn't the question she had meant to ask, but she didn't elaborate. She could see a hooded shadow moving behind the beaded curtain, amid a clatter of pots and pans and the rush of a dishwashing stream.

"How's it going," Jamal said.

"With Julie's—with Mrs. Westover?" Marissa said. "Carrie. I don't know. We talk . . . but why should she trust me? And—she doesn't really know anything. Not about what's happening now. The doctors don't know—"

"Nobody knows." Jamal said. And for a moment they were silent, looking into the flickering light of the lamps. Marissa was reminded—

"What goes in this Ramadan soup?"

"A lot of things. It's supposed to be lamb. But here we use buffalo." The long crooked smile. "It's easier to get."

She wanted to ask Jamal what he had seen in the cave. There were rumors. He had stayed down there a long time after Julie came out and there must have been some reason for it.

A small woman came out through the bead curtain, and circled the counter to sit in a corner booth. It was she who wore the dark hood, and her ankle-length skirt made her seem to glide without stepping. In the lamplight her eyes were dark and lustrous. She did not appear to be looking at them, but inward.

"You can sit with my mother sometimes, if you want," Jamal said. "She drinks tea in the afternoon when it's quiet, and sometimes after closing."

Marissa glanced at her again, not wanting to stare. "Another time."

"She will receive you."

"Thank her for me," Marissa said, struck by this odd formality, and the strangeness of not being directly introduced.

The parking lot was dark and mostly empty, and the light of the waxing moon spilled in through the plate glass window. Misty was blowing out lamps at the empty tables. One by one those yellow points of warmth disappeared from the surrounding silver glow. Through the glass a shadow fell across their table, and Marissa felt Jamal go on alert. She sensed that they were being watched, like prey. She didn't want to look but she did: a huge man, straight as a spear shaft, stood with his face almost touching the glass. His face was weathered like wind-worn stone, with his hair pulled back in a snake-like braid. His hands looked hard and heavy as stone. On his forearm Marissa recognized a tattoo that some of her clients had, the ones that had been to prison. He was not looking at her after all, but fixing Jamal with a deep, neutral gaze. Jamal, even without his sunglasses, didn't let his own eyes turn away.

When the man had turned to walk slowly away, Marissa felt her breath whooshing out of her. "Who the hell was that?" she asked.

"Oh, the baddest man in town," Jamal said. "Ultimo."

What's he got to do with you? she wanted to ask. With us? She couldn't find a way to say it.

"They say he's an Indian, or some kind of half-breed,"

Jamal said. "He's got a place somewhere in the desert, out past the El Fake-o Wild West Town. He does, you know, illegal stuff. Drugs. Porn. Dog-fights."

The lamp in the other corner had gone out; Jamal's mother was no longer there. Jamal leaned forward, scanning the lot and the street beyond.

"He's gone," he said. "Come on. I'll walk you out."

They stopped by the bed of her truck and stood with the moonlight pouring over them. The town closed down early, no one else was about.

"Jamal," Marissa said. "Where's Julie?" And don't say in the hospital she thought and don't say . . . don't. She had no fracture, no brain bleed, no injury to explain why she wouldn't wake up. Marissa thought of the dream she'd had before Claude died and of that space she'd seemed to fall into, during her first meeting with Carrie, the dark hollow full of wrong.

Jamal was mumbling, "I don't know. . . ." But then he looked up and said, "Behind the moon."

55

"Do you want to go up?" Jamal said.

Marissa craned her neck. They stood below the rock shelter, on the desert floor, with the shadow of the cliff just beginning to reach toward them. She looked at the zigzag pattern of ledges leading up to the cave mouth: an irregular slit in the stone, pinched to a point at bottom and top. The sight of it made her breath come short.

"If you get close you can see the old pictures," Jamal said. "They're like scratched in the stone, underneath all the tags."

Marissa took a step forward and stopped. What had Jamal seen in the cave? She wanted to know what was in there, certainly, but she didn't want to go in. The idea of climbing the ledges dizzied her. Her one step toward the cliff face felt like it had been repulsed, by some kind of magnetic energy.

"Not—" she said. "Not now."

Jamal looked at her; he didn't turn his head but she was aware of his eyes moving inside the bubble sunglasses.

"You okay?"

Marissa backed up and steadied herself with a hand on the warm hood of her truck. Jamal moved around her and brought out a bottle of water and a straw hat from behind the passenger seat. Marissa was looking at the shadow of the cliff on the desert floor and thinking it looked like a pool of dark water, or oil, or a bottomless drop into nowhere.

"Drink some water." Jamal set the hat on her head.

Marissa filled her mouth from the bottle and, with a

slight effort, swallowed. Without looking she felt Jamal's concerned regard.

"I'm all right," she said, returning the bottle to him. She fanned herself with the hat, put it down on the ticking hood, and smoothed back her hair with both hands, looking up at the puffy graffiti letters, KAOS, that edged the mouth of the cave.

"What is that supposed to mean?" It was such a stupid question she was that much more surprised by his answer.

"Sensitive dependence on initial conditions," Jamal said.

Marissa turned her face toward him. "Come on. A gang of JD taggers can't be thinking that."

"Probably not." The crooked half smile as he looked away. "But I am. And so are you."

Marissa felt a strain in her face from her widened eyes. "How do you even know something like that?" The schools around here couldn't be that good.

Jamal shrugged. "My brother does physics. He gave me a book."

"You know, it gets me sometimes." The memory of Claude pulled at her dizzily, repelling her at the same time it drew her in, like the cliff shadow. She would have told him this part if she'd had time to understand and frame it. "It's like I never made the choice because I didn't see there was a choice to be made. Like I just saw one thing to do and so I did the one thing and that was it. And any little thing I did could have made it different."

Jamal was listening. The sun was beginning to go down behind the cliff, which made the shadow of the cliff reach farther toward them. She noticed how the upper pinch of the cave opening pointed into the molten core of the setting sun.

"I was in love with a priest," she said. "Fuck me! A celibate Catholic priest—of course I didn't know, I didn't let myself know what I was feeling. . . ." She didn't know why she should be telling this to a boy half her age, a child really, she might say.

"What happened?" Jamal said.

"He died." Marissa laughed bitterly. She didn't cry. "He just—woke up dead one morning, some heart thing nobody knew about. Almost nobody. . . . And it gets me sometimes, how it could have been different. How everything could have all been different. If I didn't step on a crack."

Jamal nodded. "It was like that out here that night."

Marissa looked at him. "What?"

"When I was with Julie, up there." Jamal raised his chin to the ledges. "It was like something big was going to happen, good or bad, you couldn't tell, and the least little thing you did would change it. Or like a bazillion things had already happened and all of them were true—And Julie . . . Julie could feel it too. I know she did."

Jamal took off his sunglasses and looked Marissa in the eye. They were close to the same height—had she noticed that before? Jamal's eyes, unlike his mother's, were a translucent gray.

"But if you'd done something different back when?" he said. "We wouldn't even be here. I wouldn't be me and you wouldn't be you and there wouldn't be a person named Julie."

"You know this," Marissa said.

"How close is your soul to my soul!" Jamal told her. "For whatever thing you are thinking, I know."

"Jesus." Marissa stared. "What *is* that?"

"Rumi. A poem by Rumi. He was a Sufi mystic."

No, she thought, whatever he was, Jamal was no child. What he must have seen and done to get from wherever there was to here. . . . She shook her head sadly. "My life feels so small."

"I don't know about that," Jamal said. "The big part's inside of you."

Marissa wrapped her arms around him and kissed him on the mouth. She hadn't known she was going to do it but she wasn't shocked at what she had done. Jamal relaxed at her touch, shifting their weight against the fender of the truck, and his lips parted slightly, but he didn't kiss her back. She pushed away and rested her two hands on his shoulders. And he probably doesn't even know it himself, she was thinking.

"My God," she said. "You're in love with Julie." A comforting warmth spread through her.

56

Aimless and restless, Marissa drove west of town on Highway 14, then turned north on 63, a narrower road that eventually ran into the Cheyenne River Reservation. The land was flat and almost featureless; here and there on either side of the road were a few depressions that held shallow ponds. She passed a pole gateway to a ranch but there were no buildings in sight down the long gravel drive beyond the cattle gap. A mile or so farther on she began to catch a harsh ammoniac smell. Rolling up the truck windows did little to blunt it; she wrapped a cotton scarf around her face.

A quarter mile ahead she saw a Humvee heeled up on the shoulder, indistinct in the gathering dusk. Above on a low rise was a small ranch house, which she felt sure was the source of the smell: meth lab. She thought of doubling back but that maneuver might attract too much attention if anyone had noticed her from the house or the roadside vehicle. The prospect of pursuit made her stomach flop. Nearing the Humvee, which looked like an army surplus vehicle rather than the commercial version of the car, she pressed the gas and picked up speed. She was aware of a vague silhouette in the driver's seat, though she had taken care not to really look in that direction.

Bald peaks blocked the horizon, and the road slipped into a cut between the hills, then emerged and curved around the soft corner of a large plowed field, its plowed earth empty, dust stirring under the wind. The road ran almost due west through another cut in the mountain stone, then opened as it veered to the north. There was a bridge over a branch of the Missouri River, and she stopped short of the crossing. She left the truck without bothering to lock it—there were no vehicles in sight, nor any sign of human activity around three-sixty degrees of the horizon. On the far side of the bridge was a deep expanse of forest.

Wind whipped her hair across her mouth when she stepped onto the bridge. With one hand she caught it back and used the other to wrap her light jacket more tightly around herself.

Halfway across she stopped and faced the wind. It seemed to her now that she must have come here supposing she might discover some sign or portent . . . another inscrutable ancient mystic walking toward her out of the wilderness of the rez. Now, though, it seemed wrong to enter; the place was not empty, but empty for her. She was alone here and feeling very small. *Small* was the word she had used with Jamal. What in the world had possessed her to kiss him like that? The action had overpowered her somehow; she'd done it with no apparent trace of thought. At least he hadn't seemed to resent it, or embrace it as some sort of cougar come-on. Why should she think that Jamal understood what she was trying to do better than she did?

In a blue haze near the horizon a cluster of dark specks was circling above the brushy treetops. Squinting didn't bring them into better focus, but still she could surmise they must be vultures. The light was fading. Time to go.

Back in the truck, she inspected the GPS to learn that there was no reasonable way back other than the way she had come. Well. In this part of the world the news did not surprise her. And the sun had set; she would pass the lab under cover of darkness, and after all she was only going by on the road.

A half mile out, she saw the house lights up on the rise, then another light—an orange flare—arching up from the roadbed. In the silence it made her think of a shooting star.

When the two lights met, the house caught fire all at once, star-shaped explosions blowing out the windows and front door. The sound struck a second later, along with a sort of shock wave; by then Marissa had shut off her headlights and pulled to the side of the road. Call someone. No. The house burned furiously, with continuing explosions. A couple of smaller episodes of fire separated from the shell of the building and ran away into the dark. That howling sound could not be human; it must only be the wind screaming through the flaming timbers.

What was she waiting for?—the wide-set taillights of the Humvee came on. The vehicle lurched up into the road bed and the red lights *thank God thank God* began to recede. Marissa waited for them to disappear, mentally composing answers to questions from an imaginary cop. Why did you stop here? *I wanted to wait for the fire to die down, I was afraid an explosion might hit my car.* Did you see anyone around the building? *No No it was too dark I was too far away.* What were you doing out here anyway? *No no no good answer to that one.*

She started her engine and urged the truck forward, eyes rigidly straight ahead as she passed the burning house. Nothing on the road or anywhere, just the white dashes of the centerline furling up under her wheels. She'd gone fifteen miles before she heard sirens, and if her stomach clenched it was for no reason—not cops but a fire truck ripping past her at full speed.

57

Marissa coasted her truck past The Magic Carpet. It was somewhere close to midnight—she had stayed with Carrie Westover that late. A single lamp glimmered through a bead curtain. Marissa bumped her brake pedal, a gesture at respecting the stop sign, but made a right turn without breaking the momentum of the truck.

Two blocks south, where some fast food restaurants and the town's one bowling alley and bar were still open, there was a steady stream of traffic: teenage cruisers, shouting and laughing and blasting car stereos. Their strength was swelled, on weekend nights, by kids from other towns and ranches scattered over the plain. Residents along the cruise loop didn't like it, but the police wouldn't shut it down till 2 a.m. Obnoxious as the cruising might be, it was a sign of some kind of life, and a lot of other towns on the plain had been pithed out completely by methedrine, mortality, and emigration to the cities and the coasts.

How little acceleration could she use and still keep her truck rolling? On the flat pavement a kind of perpetual motion seemed possible. Marissa made two more right turns, barely tapping the gas pedal. Across her hood, beyond the candlelit window of The Magic Carpet, she faced again the streaming cruise traffic, the sound of it going around like a loop. A gaggle of girls in a pickup bed collapsed in laughter. One of them had pulled her blouse open as if to flash the onlookers—with a bikini top, Marissa would bet, not her bare breasts, not in this backwater—but who knew?

Her truck nosed through another right turn. Marissa was cruising her own solitary circle, silent except for the night breeze ruffling through the open windows of the cab. Why was she doing it? There was no intersection with the other cruising loop, full of noise and light, where Julie must have passed some time—Marissa knew she had, in fact, from Carrie Westover.

She turned again, repeating the circuit, thinking of the hooded figure sitting calmly behind her candle in The Magic Carpet. *She will receive you.* Queer the way Jamal had put it. But no more queer than the way Marissa kept circling the place.

On her third pass she shut off her headlights so they wouldn't glare in the restaurant windows and parked the truck. She didn't think she'd shut the door hard but it banged in her ears like an explosion. She couldn't think of what to say. If the restaurant door was not open she would get back in the truck and drive away.

But the glass door yielded smoothly inward when she pressed the metal bar. She walked directly to the booth in back, her sneakers squeaking slightly on the linoleum floor. Behind the flame of the oil lamp, Jamal's mother sat in enviable stillness. She didn't make any visible sign, but Marissa felt welcome to sit down, and she did.

In the mix of warm lamp's glow and the bluer ambient light from the street, the woman's eyes seemed large and dark and liquid. They were beautiful eyes; Marissa had noticed them before, striking even beneath the dark hood, across the meager width of the shadowed room. Marissa studied the lamp on the table between them, an orb of glass with inserted wick, such as she had seen in many restaurants before. For some reason she'd expected a slipper-shaped thing out of the Arabian Nights—a lamp that might confine a genie.

Presently the woman got up and carried her tea glass

through the beaded curtain into the kitchen and after a short while returned with two fresh glasses of tea, one for Marissa.

Marissa sipped. It was minty and sweet. She had no clear notion what she was doing here. The visits to Carrie Westover made some kind of ordinary sense, she supposed. By comparison to this. In her early twenties Marissa had trained as a masseuse and she had won Carrie partway over by working on her feet: flexing the bunions and working the kinks out of the arches and the cramped calf muscle and stressed-out hamstrings. In return, Carrie showed her scrapbooks and home video and told her stories about Julie. The documents petered out when the girl was still quite small, around the same time Carrie's husband left, Marissa gathered.

After the videos ran out they had just watched TV, an alien experience for Marissa, who for the last decade or so had preferred to read something, or try to meditate. Carrie sat on a recliner, legs up, flexing her toes inside her socks. Marissa homed in on her aura of comfort; she thought the massage work she'd done had helped. On the screen was local news; a reporter standing before the shell of a burned house festooned with police tape. Behind him, medical personnel carried away charred objects on stretchers. The image was day-lit, the hillside bleak.

Earnestly the reporter recited his script. *No survivors. . . . House believed to have been abandoned. . . . Nearest neighbors more than five miles away. . . . Emergency responders arrived at the scene too late. . . . Degree of destruction makes the cause of the fire uncertain and identification of the bodies difficult. . . .*

"Serves'm right," Carrie muttered, crossing her ankles and glaring at the set. "Sketcher scumbags."

The shot returned to the studio. "Thank you, Tom." The same newswoman with that glossy reddish blond helmet of hair; she touched her tongue to her lips and leaned toward the camera. "No suspects and no clear evidence of arson so far," she announced, and Marissa shifted in her seat, thinking, *but*— The newswoman turned her head slightly, as if to address a partner just out of the frame. "But of course these places blow up by themselves, don't they? Meth labs are a dangerous game." Again she faced the camera. "I'm Janice Rivington for Kay Ee El Oh." A shuffle of papers. "Today marks the twenty-first day of apparent coma for cave girl Julie Westover. Medical—"

"Oh shut up, Janice." Carrie squeezed the remote and the screen went dark.

Monkey mind, Melissa thought. But tonight it circled more than it scrabbled, like the cruisers orbiting the square. With an effort she brought it back to the The Magic Carpet, soft flicker of the lamp on the table, the warm cup cradled in her palm. Still, she couldn't hold the moment, remembering now that her last sick day had been consumed twenty hours back, which meant that her previous life had expired. She, or the life she had lived before, had just that simply ceased to exist. Oh something could probably be worked out and repaired with Peg and the bosses, despite the vague and lackluster quality of the excuses she had filed by voice and email, but the idea of fitting herself back into that life was like trying to wear a pair of your old bronzed baby shoes. She had left that place, and now she was here. Where was she?

Regaining the present with a minty sip of tea, she noticed that despite her uncertainty she didn't feel uncomfortable, but instead unusually relaxed. She was aware that a wordless something was taking place between her and the other woman. As if the smooth fluid regard of the other was melting something inside of her.

Jamal's mother placed her hand over the back of Marissa's hand. Marissa was flooded with the thought of the kiss she'd pressed on Jamal out in the desert. Here was another touch that somehow, against expectation, seemed to be turning out all right. The other woman's palm was warm and dry. Against her knuckles Marissa could feel the calluses of all her kitchen work. Also Jamal had told her that his mother had made carpets as a child. She had been compelled to do it. The magic of The Magic Carpet was that there were no carpets involved at all—a sort of inside family joke.

You want to be where she is, the other woman said. Marissa didn't know what language she had spoken, or if she had spoken out loud at all. She didn't even know what was the native tongue of Jamal's family or what country they had originally come from. But she did know that the other woman was quite right in what she had expressed.

She remembered the rosary, still in her pocket, but didn't reach to touch it. Since Claude's death, or a few days before, Marissa's faith had been playing tricks on her. It did not mean she was losing her faith, not necessarily. Claude himself had suffered doubt; it was something they had talked about, a little. They had not talked about the probability that Claude had also deceived himself, maybe more than a little, about the nature of his interest in her.

She still practiced the Exercises sometimes, sometimes at night when she couldn't sleep, though no longer with the strict purposefulness that Saint Ignatius of Loyola had intended. Now it was just a way to wind herself down, to still the self-conscious chatter that usually bounced off the walls of her brain, sometimes to open a passage to the wide cavern inside her psyche that Jamal had called the big part of her life.

The eye of my intention. . . . To move the feelings more with the will. As the words articulated in her head she flashed on that dream not long ago, the one that had felt more like a vision, had left her lost in that cavernous inner space. But here, she felt the other woman guiding her, as Claude had done, her hand like a hand on a tiller. As she went down, she was stabbed by the unexpected recognition that in the other life where she kept the baby and somehow raised her to adulthood she still arrived in a moment like this one, where the person called Julie tore herself free and vanished into a life of her own, leaving Marissa alone among strangers . . . though a wise and sympathetic stranger in this case.

. . . an exclamation of wonder with deep feeling, going through all creatures, how they have left me in life and preserved me in it. . . .

Instead of a spark going down into darkness she was winged perception rising in clear sky.

58

The fear of it! To be hurled, naked, into high thin air, like a stone out of a sling. But after the first breathless moments she knew she could rest at the top of the arc. She would not fall.

Hawk's eye was a flat gold disc, with a black shining circle at the center. Hawk was nothing now but eye and air. The eye transparent. . . .

Caught in its clear center was that ancient animal person, who moved, despite his staggering size, with weightless grace through a green glade. Snaking through the branches, long as a python, his trunk gathered leaves and tucked them into the shovel-lipped mouth between white ivory tusks.

She felt the solitude of Mammut in her own bones. Like herself, he was not proper to this place and time. He had returned to the People from three-lives-gone, out of the spirit stories. But in his flesh, with all its rich weight. Old and alone as he was now, with his eye like a marble, dark pearl losing itself in watery folds of skin.

Her twinned selves floating between the worlds, touching at the coccyx and the back of the skull. She was seeing with the same eye that saw her. With shouts the hunters rolled away a boulder from points themselves three-lives gone. Black points, flaked from a glassy stone; People said the stone was found near a fire mountain away in the west. Whistling, they bound points to new shafts with fresh wet sinew.

Mammut was not mired in bog this time. He moved freely, lightly too, considering his legs were big as tree trunks.

He seemed slow, or he was in no hurry. He was eating as he moved, stripping the trees of leaves and green branches.

Hawk might have reached him in an hour's flight. But hills and valleys and streams to be forded lay between Mammut and the People. Long spears tipped and ready now, they began to move, loping north along the riverbed, and crossing where they knew it to be shallow. No more whistling among them. In silence they kept the long loping stride, which could be sustained for a long time. She was with the eye of the hawk always, and she was in the curved space between the backs of the two worlds, and also with her own spear, among the People.

Marissa fell awake; it was a giddy vertiginous fall, down the spiral of a terrifying scream till she came to herself sweating and shaking in one of those molded plastic hospital chairs. Had she screamed aloud? Perhaps, but there was no one in the room to hear it, only motionless, unresponsive Julie, feathers ruffed out on the pillow—she lunged forward, sure she had seen the harsh eyes and cutting beak of a raptor framed on the coarse hospital linen . . . but when she reached the bedside there was only Julie's dark hair spilling over the pillow, as always.

She was alone with Julie in the greenish dim of the room, blinds drawn against the daylight, tick and burble of machines. An aquarium. She laid her fingertips against Julie's cheek and felt the child's warm breath come and go across her knuckles. All right then, she was here, in this world only. With a terrible headache branching toward either side of her forehead . . . from something like tree roots prying into her brain. She looked around the room for painkillers but whatever Julie got was by IV, so she covered her eyes with her hands for a moment. The pain subsided in her head but there was an odd sensation in her palm, like the haft of a tool or a weapon.

59

Bear. She had been Bear at her first awakening, and she was Bear again, along with Hawk, running, flying beside herself as she ran with the hunters and floated in dream. Bear dug in the earth, pressing the square muzzle deep in the fragrant hole, breathing in news of the underground. Bear clawed out roots and ate them, while Mammut broke branches with his trunk and stripped them of the leaves. They had, it seemed, no interest in each other: Bear doglike, small beside the greatness of Mammut, the two of them indifferent, eating the different things they chose.

The stream of running hunters divided around the glade, as yet unseen. Bear knew their presence by their scent, and grew wary, but did not stand or run. In Hawk's eyes she saw the pattern of their movement. Leaders, who had passed the glade, finding a patch of sodden ground, growing cress and yellow flowers, soft enough, though not quite swamp.

Hunters ran into the glade. Mammut saw, but did not care. His little eye turned past them without interest, these small things. He seemed to have no knowledge of the People.

Bear had been hunted. Eaten sometimes. The heart and gall bladder, rich store of fat and flesh. After the feasting, the hide scraped and cured to make a warm robe. Bear stood up now, astonished at the hunters. Vast she would be, if not for Mammut. Bear dropping to all fours again, lumbering to disappear into the brush; Bear looking out from the stone of the cave wall curious to see frayed twigs spreading color from the horn points onto the stone: two crossed lines with a circle at the top of one made the hawk a simple flying eye while below the hunters boiled out from the bones of an animal person already killed and consumed, glossy obsidian spear points dulled with blood. She heard the clatter of the shaman's rattle, much, much louder than before. And a growling, snarling sound was very near, as if inside her, like the splitting of roots dividing her brain—in darkness she raised her hands to her head and found it heavy, broad-boned, pelted. She struggled to lift it off, tear it *off*; it would not come off but light did come—the swirl of brilliant colored points, its movement driven by the rattle, the interlocking coded helix with the eyes of animal persons swimming amidst its folds. Now she saw an image reflected as in water, if water could stand upright on a wall: a woman whose bare breasts heaved as she fought with both hands the bear's head, *her head*

Then just Marissa, standing before a mirror in Julie's room, wearing only a pajama bottom and tearing at her own hair for no evident reason *you want to be where she is, to*—the rattle sound was above and all around her and then it stopped and she was outdoors under a dome of troubled gray sky in the midst of that same scatter of loose stones, though she saw no sign of the shaman or even the clot of brush he had emerged from.

"It's Hell."

Marissa turned to find Carrie, standing with the tenacity of a cypress, hands on her hips, back slightly arched, blue Crocs rooted into the asphalt as they looked. By reflex Marissa folded her arms across her breasts and discovered that, thankfully, she must have thrown on a shirt before coming outside.

It was *hail*—that must be what Carrie had said, and certainly that was what this stuff was. Hailstones, not those jagged rocks from the different place, the other time. Marble-size white pellets of ice beginning to melt as the sky above them dissolved into indifferent, vacant blue.

60

The gourd rattle fizzed like a rattlesnake's tail, like a rasp of
rough breathing, and the hunters spilled out of the cage of
bones across the cave wall, breathing fast, though not yet
winded. It had not exactly been pursuit, for Mammut had no
mind to run. The first spear jabs were only pricks, not even.
Stone points could scarcely pierce the pelt of matted hair,
long and tangled, brushing the ground. And People had lost
memory of this hunting, three-lives-gone. Bear they knew.
Bison they'd begun to know. Mammut was a story told by
grandmothers, who themselves had never seen Mammut with
their own eyes.

The hunters circled, whistling, dancing. Some made
a drumbeat, clapping hollow sticks with stones. Mammut's
huge ears fanned forward, back. The little eye revolved in the
great head. In the eye of Hawk, through branches Mammut
had stripped of their leaves, she saw this august animal person
as if caught up in a swarm of gnats.

A hunter darted forward and thrust into a hairy flank,
hard enough to sting. Mammut bellowed, and broke the spear
shaft with a shudder. With the snaking gray trunk he caught
a hunter by the heel and threw him altogether out of the
glade. The hunter landed, rolling like a leather ball, in the
patch of soft ground, and came up from the cress and yellow
flowers, wet and muddy but unhurt. He caught up another
spear that someone passed him and thrust it now between the

tusks, toward the impenetrable skull plate between the eyes, no threat, but a goading challenge.

Mammut trumpeted and made a rush at him. Others pricked at his hindquarters, and Mammut turned, sweeping his trunk along the ground, spilling several of them over. He trampled one; the others rolled away.

Now the hunters widened their circle. In turn they rushed Mammut from one direction only, jumping to prick the base of his tail, until he turned and charged them, trumpeting, the horn of his trunk drowning out all their whistles. The first hunter to be thrown danced and capered before him, drawing a charge that broke Mammut clear of the trees, out into the open where Hawk's yellow eye saw it all plainly now. That first hunter rushed and pricked at the trunk itself with a spear point, so that Mammut's weak little hairless tail stood up like a stick and the tusks lowered and Mammut made a thundering charge, the hunters throwing themselves clear as Mammut's great weight hurtled ahead till he went down in the boggy ground to his front knees.

Hunters circled, uncertain what to do. The bolder of them pricked at the tough hide and tangled hair. It was good, it was what they had intended, but they could not remember anywhere among them what came next. They circled, jabbing uselessly. Mammut bellowed. He would soon free himself from the bog. His hind legs were working on solid ground, struggling to pull the forelegs free.

A hand spread color, ochre and umber, onto the shadowy wall of the cave. In the red torchlight the image flickered. The body of slain Mammut opened and hunters came out of it like a swarm of bees. The color spread across the wall and the hunters swarmed around Mammut sunken to his knees, flourishing the twig-like spears and thrusting them. Her hands wrapped around a spear shaft, driving a razor-sharp lava-stone point into the place back of the hampered foreleg, the point slipping sideways to pass a massive rib, passing that last resistance to sink home. All in a rush and a great trumpet, the air went out of Mammut then. Heart's blood came bursting out of the wound and soaked their joined hands on the spear shaft.

In the air was Hawk's harsh cry. Hawk folded his wings in the air and was falling. Ground rushing up, with the great kill at its center. Hawk stooped upon it, blinded by the falling wind.

61

Hawk was still falling, but now falling up. Maybe Hawk had become a fish. His wings long fins that stroked the water, fanning him toward the surface. Above was a yellow-green watery light.

Beyond the surface was a cool dim space, like an underwater cave. There were people there waiting, as if in a trance. A woman in a sort of blue jerkin, thick-bodied as a troll. A spidery boy with translucent amber shells that covered his eyes. A slender woman, taller than the first, with loose black hair and a dark, hollow gaze.

The cave covered them like the dome of a tent. They were all looking down, as if waiting for something, or hoping for it. They were looking toward her, but they didn't see her. She couldn't break the surface of the water to enter the space where they were. Her hands spread flat on a firm surface, solid though invisible. It wasn't stone, like the times before. Maybe instead some sort of rock crystal.

In the desert there had been a tent, a silver-gray dome, light as a bubble, and she had looked at it and sensed its reflection, symmetrical beneath the sand, where someone had forgotten to peg it. Two worlds invisible each to the other, invisible but present.

If she pulled back her hand a ghostly image of it remained, like a damp handprint on a pane of glass, fading as it dried. The handprints in the cave were framed in black, and they fit her own hands to perfection. If she kept pressing she could come through, as she had come through the stone before; the stone had softened, like wet clay. She could come out of one cave into the other. That was what the people in the space above her wanted her to do.

That woman, the one of the three she didn't know, turned toward her. She didn't move. It was an inward turning. She had been looking down at Julie the whole time, but now she saw her and knew where she was.

She was back to back with herself and facing both the realms at the same time, curving outward into both realms. Below, the First People circled Mammut and cried the joy of the great kill. Above, the other cave, which was a world she also lived in.

But where was she? Behind the moon.

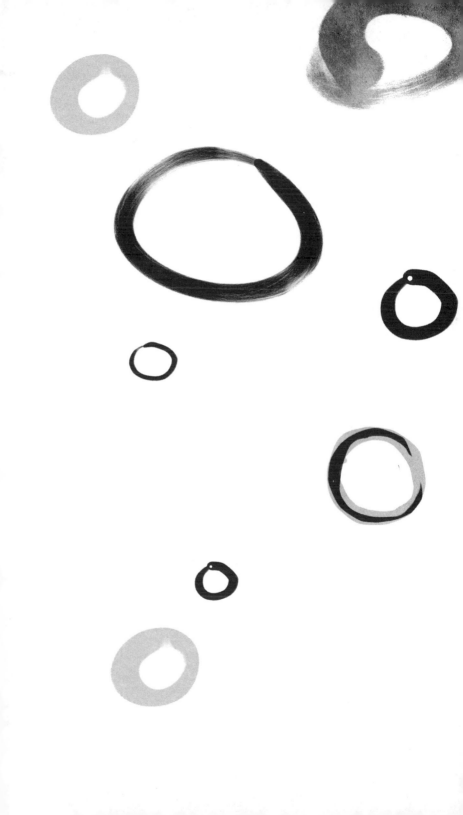

62

"For school," Carrie Westover said. "I think it was a project for school." She leaned in the doorway of Julie's childhood room, wrapped in a pale green quilted robe, her hair still damp from the shower. Through a thin wall, the water heater whined. Marissa sat on the edge of the bed, holding up a fat blue book, a study of prehistoric Clovis people. On the cover, a mastodon labored over a red earth plain. Buried under the dirt, flush with the cover's lower edge, was a picture of a flaked stone spear point.

"Well, g'night," Carrie said. Marissa heard her Crocs shuffling into the next room, the whine of bed springs as she settled her weight and kicked off the shoes. The water heater's shrilling stopped abruptly.

Marissa wanted the room to tell her something. She had stayed there now for several nights. Carrie had invited her, and Marissa was running low on money, though she hadn't yet run completely out. The first night the loose gutter squealed with the wind, and the next day Marissa went to the hardware store for some roofing nails and tacked it down. She found other small jobs around Carrie's house and did them, discovering she'd learned more than she thought from week-ends volunteering to help Claude with various repairs in the church and crumbling seminary.

Carrie had accepted her, as she seemed to accept everything eventually, like stone receiving water that slowly wears it down. The massages also helped. Marissa had brought

Carrie back from the edge of plantar fasciitis, she was reasonably sure. Carrie said it was much easier now, to walk through her shift. They were hiring at Walmart, Carrie said, but that was Marissa's idea of hell. She'd sooner waitress at the Magic Carpet, not that there was a place for her there. Grind cloves and chop up garlic in the kitchen. The town was far too small to support a masseuse, and anyway people in a place like this would probably think that "massage" was code for "prostitution." But she was sure she could find nursing work somewhere reasonably nearby, when it got to the point she absolutely had to.

The Clovis book was densely academic; Marissa couldn't get through a page of it without going to sleep. She'd read the same paragraph over and over, mind wandering away from the text. Strange choice for a high school girl. The book didn't look much used, and maybe Julie had just been captivated by the cover and bought it by mistake. On the bookshelf opposite the bed, fringed with an array of tiny plastic dinosaurs, were more accessible books about Indians and early man. Marissa crossed the room and took down a copy of *Black Elk Speaks*, opened it, closed it, put it back in its place.

In a desk drawer, Marissa had found a modest collection of arrowheads, but Carrie didn't know if Julie had found them one by one or bought the lot. She didn't seem to have known they were there. What did Carrie know about Julie? She did well in school, with little prompting, but not so well that anyone would denounce her as a *brain*. She was pretty enough, but not enough to make a mother worry. Carrie had raised her as a single mother, from the time Julie was two. The marriage had dissolved so soon after the adoption that Julie would have no memory of the man who had briefly posed as her father, who'd stopped sending child support when she was ten and whose whereabouts, since then, had been unknown.

Marissa might have done the same, she thought. If a butterfly waggled its wings in Cambodia, say, instead of in China. The idea didn't stab her, as it had at first. When she had wept among the scattered stones of Pine Ridge, somewhere even GPS couldn't find her. No it was a duller pain. She thought of Carrie's mute ability to spread shocks all over the surface of her being; that way they didn't knock her down.

There was an infinity of possible lives, and after all she only had this one, but what if all the lives were somehow happening anyway, all at once? There was the Julie who lay unresponsive in this coma that wasn't really a coma, like Sleeping Beauty waiting for a kiss, and the other Julie Marissa seemed to have seen floating up toward her like a revenant from underwater, her eyes open with some kind of recognition, her mouth about to open with a greeting, her hands flattening, palms out, on the invisible barrier between them.

She thought for a moment of trying an Exercise, sitting cross-legged on the floor, but instead she worked her shoes off with her toes and stretched out on the narrow bed, still with her clothes on. Julie's pillowcase was printed with little emerald paisley shapes. Marissa reached up and across herself to turn out the lamp. On the ceiling above the fluorescent green stars lit up. They seemed to have been arranged in constellations, only not the real ones in the real sky. There was a pattern that suggested a fish and another that suggested a bird. Julie must have done it herself. Carrie wasn't the sort to imagine it, and wouldn't have time to carry it out.

But then the stars were white, not green, and there was a whole great dome of them, the Milky Way spread out across the velvet darkness. Firelight on the plain below, and near-naked people dancing with a curious sort of stutter step around a skeleton, or rather a carcass; blood was still red on the vast ribcage, which was big enough for her to stand inside. She was watching them and also dancing among them, and with that queer lucidity also aware that this dream might have been inflated out of the books in Julie's room so maybe that was why Julie was dreaming it. That wouldn't explain why she herself was. A hollow sound built from a long way off, like wind in a cannon barrel that would reach to the moon and the mastodon assembled its bones and tusks and rose, turning to face her, one single white-blazing eye burning toward her in the middle of its forehead. The hollow sound became a roar and the floor was shaking under the bedposts and Marissa shot upright as the headlight strummed across Julie's window and the train went tearing by.

It seemed to be a very long train, and it left a big hole in the air behind it. By time the sound of it had receded, Marissa had managed to stop shaking. *Usually when you just went to sleep*, Carrie had told her—that was when the train came by. It was the first one that Marissa had heard. Carrie was inured to it; Marissa could hear the rasp of her sleeping breath, not quite a snore, through the wall behind Julie's bed.

Carrying her shoes in one hand, she slipped out the kitchen door. When she stepped from under the carport she was bathed in starlight. No moon. She walked to the edge of dead-end pavement and looked west. The iron rails caught a glimmer of starlight, as if the passing wheels had burnished them. There was no light pollution in this place; when she craned her neck she could see all the stars.

When she turned back toward the dark house she thought for some reason of that pack of cigarettes she'd bought, the day Claude died, and wondered if they might still be in her glove box, though she was pretty sure she'd thrown them out. Anyway they'd be stale by now. She didn't know why she would want one. Then she saw that her truck was completely gone.

63

In the rear of The Magic Carpet, Jamal stood at the utility sink, draining chickpeas. The water was still hot, and slightly steaming. He shook the colander, poured the peas into a big flat baking dish. The restaurant had been closed for an hour, and his mother had gone to bed, and this was the last chore of the night. He measured in tahini, lemon juice and a little minced garlic, picked up a potato masher and began to crush it all together.

When he looked up he could see his own reflection in the black pane of the kitchen window, and when he looked a second time he became aware of another pair of eyes, inside the mirror image of his own, looking in on him from the outside. He didn't change the pace of his movements. He covered the dish with plastic wrap and put it in the refrigerator, then got out a clump of parsley and dropped it on a cutting board. But really the parsley would be better if he chopped it the next day. He put it back in the refrigerator and flicked off the light, resisting the impulse to look at the window again, though he knew that if he did, now he would be able to see whoever was outside.

Instead he went out the back door of the restaurant and turned the corner of the building. Ultimo had moved away from the kitchen window and stood at the far end of the parking lot, looking at Jamal as if he had known exactly where Jamal would appear. There was no menace in the look, or even any curiosity. It was just looking. Jamal remained, his right hand resting lightly on the edge of the building's painted cinderblock corner. After a little while Ultimo got into his vehicle and began to drive away.

Jamal threw a leg over the saddle of his scooter and followed. Or not exactly; he didn't keep Ultimo in sight, because he didn't want Ultimo to notice him. But at the edge of town he picked up the taillights where he'd expected them to be. There was no doubt; Ultimo's taillights were set much farther apart than any other car in the area.

He kept well back. On a rise of the highway above the phony ghost town he saw Ultimo's tail lights turning in beside the tilted stagecoach. Jamal stopped on the shoulder, waited five minutes. A highway patrol car went by, headed toward town; it slowed as it passed him, but didn't stop.

When he left the road he shut off the headlight of his bike. No moon, but there were stars aplenty to illuminate the rocks and scrub. Wide-set tire tracks wound between the boulders and mesquite, climbing the slope of a low ridge. Just short of the crest he killed his motor and rolled the bike into the shadow of a rock.

He heard barking, a rattle of chain, then the thunk of a heavy car door slamming shut. When the barking subsided he could hear coyotes singing in the far distance. Now and then a car hissed down the highway behind him, obscured for a moment by the ramshackle rooflines of the Wild West Town, then reappearing.

Jamal walked to the top of the ridge and saw a double-wide trailer, Ultimo's it must be, caged by a wide square of chain-link fence. Inside the trailer was just a flicker of turquoise light from a TV. Jamal moved toward it, setting his sneakers down quietly on the rutted track. The wind was in his face, so the dogs didn't pick him up till he was quite near. When the dogs began barking and hurling themselves against the fence, he stopped and crouched on his heels, watching from the shadow of the ridge above and behind him.

No sign of anything inside the trailer except flashes of

light from the TV. Ultimo could be anywhere, in the trailer or in the cage. He drove a Humvee—not the commercial kind sold to civilians, but the original military vehicle. No one knew how he had come by it. The body was dented and punctured here and there with what might have been shrapnel, and the passenger window was gone, replaced with plastic duct-taped to the frame. Ultimo had parked the vehicle inside the wire, just on the other side of a double set of gates, locked shut with a heavy chain.

Jamal stood up and walked toward the fence. The dogs went even crazier as he moved toward them. The fence was serious business: eight feet high, posts set in concrete, a coil of razor ribbon strung along the top; it probably cost more than the whole trailer. There was another, smaller gate, opposite the door of the trailer, this one secured with a padlock through the hasp of its catch. Jamal stood in front of this gate, looking toward the closed door beyond it.

The dogs were fighters, bred and trained for the pit. There were five of them, raging and throwing themselves into the chain link, bashing their muzzles into the gate posts. The biggest had Catahula Leopard stripes, and even he wasn't tremendously big—not as high as Jamal's hip. Jamal thought he liked that one the best. Smooth muscle working under the stripe pattern in the starlight, the hot yellow eyes, the single-ness of intention as he kept trying to rush the gate, as if he didn't believe in any barrier between himself and the blood inside Jamal's body.

But finally the big Catahula gave up. He stood a few feet back from the gate, vibrating still with a low growl, hackles pricked up between his hunched shoulders. The other dogs had given up before him. A couple of them went off and curled up under the hammered fender of the Humvee.

Jamal watched the aluminum door of the trailer. There was a window in it, but it was dark and the balance of light was in favor of the person inside. Now that the dogs were quiet Jamal could hear the voices from the television. Fox News.

He somehow doubted that Ultimo was actually watching that. Ultimo could be standing inside with his nose touching a window and Jamal still wouldn't be able to see him through the starlight reflecting off the pane.

The big Catahula stopped growling and settled down at the trailer's door sill. He was still watching Jamal intently, the yellow eyes glowing like agate. Jamal listened to the trailer, hard, but there was nothing he could hear but the chatter of the television. The dogs didn't bark when he turned away and started walking back up the ridge, but in the distant desert the high, eerie wail of the coyotes started up again.

64

A car was idling on the shoulder of the highway when Jamal got back to his bike. A maroon Trans Am—he didn't recognize it. It took off toward town the moment he lit it up with his single headlight, its rear wheels spitting gravel back against the dry-rotted boards of the fake stagecoach.

Jamal rode slowly back to town. The stars were so bright he would have liked to shut off his headlight again, but he didn't want to risk a ticket on the highway.

Two blocks from the Magic Carpet he saw Marissa's truck pulled to the curb, motor running though the lights were out. He put a foot on the asphalt and throttled down. It was odd for Marissa to be out so late, and anyway he wasn't sure that he wanted to talk to her now. The excursion to Ultimo's had meant something but he didn't quite know what and he didn't have a way to tell about it either. Maybe he could make something up. He was thinking that when he realized that the silhouette behind the wheel of the truck, backlit by a streetlight, had ears. Marissa's hair was long enough that her ears didn't show.

The lights of the truck came blazing on; it lunged at him with a rubber squeal. Jamal froze for a second, almost too long, then twisted the throttle and popped the bike onto the sidewalk. The truck swerved after him, viciously, but caromed off the posts of the parking meters between the street and the brick storefronts, spun out into the street and died.

Jamal could see Marko's knotted face as he struggled to open the dented driver's door. White teeth. The door wouldn't open. Marko threw himself out the passenger door and stalked away without looking back.

"The train woke me up," Marissa said. "They stole my truck."

Jamal, still astraddle the bike, was looking at his hands and his feet, as if surprised they were still whole. The motor sputtered and died under him. He knocked down the kick-stand and got off, steadying himself with one hand on the parking meter.

"I can see that," he said.

"See what?"

"Marko stole your truck."

Marissa dropped an arm over his shoulders and Jamal wrapped his around her waist. They balanced for a moment that way, leaning into each other, hip to hip.

"He tried to kill you."

Jamal, without saying anything, shrugged off her arm. Marissa shivered, from shock or the cold. The night was chilly, and she'd left Carrie's house without a jacket. She walked to the truck and pulled at the driver's door. It wouldn't open.

"Let me do that." A strange voice, with a shade of the ac-cent Jamal didn't have. Marissa stepped back. Two men were standing by the truck-bed, looking at her alertly. One pulled a short crowbar from under his loose shirt-tail and began to work it around the dented edges of the door.

"Try it," he said.

Marissa clasped the handle and the door opened easily. The other stranger went down one knee, peered under the dash below the steering column, and pulled out a set of alliga-tor clips connected by a wire.

"You got the key?" he said. "See if it'll start."

Obediently Marissa climbed in and cranked the engine. She let it idle for a moment and then shut it off.

"Beauty," one of the strangers said, patting the truck's fender as though it were the flank of a sound horse.

"Not so bad," said the other, with the same trace of accent. "Bring it in tomorrow, if you want. We'll knock the dents out for you."

"Bring it where?" Marissa got out of the cab and stood facing the two men. They looked alike, one just a little taller and beakier than the other. They both had their hair cropped extremely short, although their beards were left untrimmed.

"Shifty's, out on the highway," Jamal said. "They work on cars and bikes over there. Not body work usually, but they'll do this for you."

"They will?" Marissa said.

"My brothers," Jamal said, a little awkwardly now. "Omar," he said, lifting his chin toward the taller one, who still held the little pry bar lightly in one hand. "Ramin. This is . . . my friend, Marissa."

"Of course," Omar said. He and Ramin both inclined their heads to her. The movement was slight, but the formality was such that they might both have bowed to their knees.

"Thank you," Marissa said. "Thanks for your help." She must have known before, without really thinking about it, that all the strangers here must know who she was and why she was there. They'd know as much of the story as she did.

"Where'd you get the Trans Am?" Jamal said.

Marissa looked around. Events of the night began swirling in her head, so that she had to prop herself sideways on the truck seat. There was no Trans Am in view.

"Shop," Ramin said.

"Shifty won't like that," said Jamal.

"It's a test drive, brother," Omar said. "That's not the problem."

Marissa looked at the three of them together. They did in fact all resemble each other, except for differences of style. Jamal dressed and groomed as an American teenager, more or less. Omar and Ramin somehow managed to wear their loose shirts and painters' pants in a way that made them look like kaftans.

"The problem is Marko," Omar said. "And that . . . degenerate Indian."

"Look," said Jamal, "I'm glad you're here."

Ramin said something in a language Marissa didn't understand. Liquid, guttural. She couldn't even pick out a word but it sounded to her like a proverb or something from scripture.

"I know you do," Jamal said. "But just . . . let it alone."

"He tried to kill you," Omar said. "Brother, it's gone too far."

"He's trying to scare me," Jamal said.

"What?! Get out!" Marissa said, suddenly angry. "He'd have crushed you like a bug if not for those meter posts."

"Oh," Jamal said. "So three people saw it."

Omar and Ramin and Marissa all looked at each other and then at Jamal, who had clasped his fingers to the bridge of his nose, as if to pinch back a headache.

"Marko'll kick back and think about that," he said. "If we don't do anything, he won't either. It only makes it worse if he does, and Marko's not stupid all the time."

Omar laughed, low in his throat like a growl. "I understand you, brother," he said. "Let Marko lose the sleep."

"What about Ultimo," Ramin said.

Jamal dropped his hand from his face. "I don't know what Ultimo wants," he said, and stopped a moment, thinking. "I don't think it's the same thing as Marko."

65

"You're kidding," Marissa said, when Jamal motioned her onto the back of his scooter's saddle. A tear in the black vinyl had recently been closed with duct tape. Below the amber sunglasses was Jamal's half quizzical smile.

"In my country they use them as taxis," he said.

"But not in this country. They don't. They don't use things like this as taxis."

Jamal's smile briefly became the grin of an older, more confident man, a challenge. He patted the duct tape on the seat with his long fragile-looking fingers. "I bet you don't weigh any more than Julie," he said. "Get on already."

My country, Marissa thought, with the wind in her face, whipping back her hair like a flag. What country was that? It was the first time Jamal had said anything of that sort. Deft the way he'd got her into the saddle. When he grew up a little more he'd be a caution, that was clear. No helmets. She was in Julie's place, cementing herself to Jamal's bony back on the turns. Yet he seemed to drive safely enough. What did Marissa have to keep herself whole for? In fact she was enjoying the ride: speed and wind and her tearing eyes and the solid feel of her chin hooked over Jamal's shoulder. She could have said something into his ear but she didn't. She hadn't ridden pillion on a motorbike since before . . . oh, never mind.

They passed Shifty's without slowing, though it had been their destination. It might have been Omar or Ramin who glanced up at them from one of the gas pumps but he went by in such a blur, Marissa couldn't be sure. The station was west of town on Highway 16, and just short of the interstate cloverleaf, Jamal throttled back and eased the bike off the shoulder. Marissa could have said into his ear *what are you doing*, but she didn't.

They were headed toward the mountain range of junk cars that stood behind Shifty's, blocking a good chunk of the horizon. As the shadows of mounded wrecks loomed over them, Marissa felt a gain of foreboding. She could hear a car crusher pounding metal, out of sight but not far off. Then Jamal threaded their way unerringly to a tin-roofed lean-to, beneath which her little truck awaited her, pristine.

In the space of three days, most of which Marissa had spent in the Saint Mary's hospital room, Omar and Ramin had not only undone the most recent damage but erased every scratch and dent she had ever put into the thing since she'd received it at the age of sixteen. The truck was repainted its original deep blue, and now had a red racing stripe running all the way around it: a line like a razor cut before it starts bleeding.

"Why would they do this?" Marissa said. "You know I can't—I don't—"

"Because you're my friend," Jamal said. He found the key under the floor mat and held it out to her.

She didn't reach for it right away. What does *friend* mean in your language? What do I owe? It came to her then that her old life had completely dissolved and that she might give or receive anything in this new one. She didn't know what the limits were or even if there were any.

"I thought you said your brother did physics," she said.

"That's Ramin," Jamal said, waggling the key toward her nose. "He's over at Brookings half the year but he earns the money for it at Shifty's. Take the key."

Marissa took the key.

"Catch a lift with you?"

Marissa nodded, and Jamal opened the tailgate and

propped up a plank. With an easy balance he rode the scooter up into the bed and secured it with bungee cords he seemed to have ready in the pockets of his cargo pants. Marissa meanwhile had started the engine and noticed that it was running much more smoothly than before.

"What did they—" she started, as Jamal climbed in beside her. She was going to say again that she couldn't possibly. . . .

"Also we like this kind of truck," Jamal said, reaching through the open window to pat the outside door panel. "Don't see so many of them around here, but before . . . they're tough. They're good cross-country. You could mount a belt machine gun in the bed and fire it over the top of the cab."

"I never tried that," Marissa said. Jamal utterly failed to register her tone.

"Do you want me to take you back to the restaurant?" she asked.

Jamal shrugged. "We could drive around."

"Drive around?"

"Test drive, you know. See how that tune-up flies."

Marissa drove clear of the junked-car mountains, then turned behind them into the open desert. She had an inkling that it would be better not to take the truck out in direct view of Shifty's office area. In the distance, opposite the highway, a range of mountains closed the horizon. It occurred to her that in the thoroughness of their repair, Omar and Ramin had erased the evidence of what Marko had tried three nights before.

"Let's go that way," Jamal said. "See how she four-wheels."

Marissa let out the clutch and the truck rolled out smoothly over packed sand.

"Why won't you tell me what happened out there?" she said. Jamal didn't answer. He might have been asleep behind the sunglasses, except that she was sure he was scanning the horizon, where the crooked line of faint, misty mountains was hardening into a more concrete blue.

"Jamal?"

He turned to her then, across the cab, pushing the sunglasses up his brow, so they swept back his long frizz like a hair-band.

"I already told you," he said. "It's hard to say exactly what happened. I'm not sure if anything did. And. . . ."

"And?"

"Julie had nothing to do with it."

Marissa could feel her knuckles whitening on the steering wheel. She made an effort not to speed up. There were rocks and spines to be dodged in the desert, along with detritus from other off-road vehicles.

"She falls in a cave and comes out in a coma. And still she has nothing to do with it."

"I mean she didn't bring it on." Jamal was still looking at her with his naked eyes. "She had nothing to do with bringing it down, that's what I mean."

This thing that didn't happen. Maybe didn't happen. I don't know the code here, Marissa was thinking, as she twisted the wheel this way and that to navigate a path between rock hillocks that looked like inverted ice cream cones, traveling some prehistoric streambed was her guess. She'd met the same difficulty with patients and clients, especially the ones who still lived on the rez, and often she had been able to crack it—not always, though. You had to learn to think the way the other person did, and sometimes you just didn't know enough to make that possible. It occurred to her now that if she'd raised Julie herself she would have been trying to decipher her words, her gestures, discover the underlying pattern, understand what she meant by them. With Jamal it was much harder because there were those other layers, and no way to guess how deep or how numerous they were.

"—then why is Marko trying to kill you?"

"He's trying to scare me. Like I said."

Can't you just be scared and he'll leave you alone? Marissa thought.

"You could——" she began, "*We* could——"

Jamal, now looking through the windshield, was shaking his head. "It's two different things, anyway. We go to the law, or the police. Then they start looking at my mother and my brothers, which people already do around here after all the sh——the stuff they see on TV. People around here, they look at Omar's beard and hair and they see. . . . You know. We could get the short end of all that. Most likely we would."

Most likely he's right, Marissa thought. "What's the other thing?"

Jamal's thin smile, a slight shake of his head. "With Omar and Ramin it's the duties of brotherhood. Pure and simple and . . . very strict. Anybody touches a hair on my arm even, they'll disembowel that person and string him up like a sheep." He turned his gray eyes on her across the space between the bucket seats. "That extends to my friends also, of course."

"They did a first-class job on the truck," Marissa said. The engine was purring like a panther. Tires gripping loose sand and gravel like tracks.

"It's enough for them to do, right?" Jamal said. "I mean, we've been in tighter spots before now, my brothers and I."

In your country, Marissa thought. Wherever that is.

"But here there's law," Jamal said, as if he'd heard what she was thinking. "It doesn't mean you have to go to it every time. Sometimes it's enough for it to exist. The best thing is to do nothing and watch. We've seen plenty of people like Marko before and mostly. . . ."

"What?"

"One way or another," Jamal shrugged, "they take care of themselves."

"Would Marko hurt Julie?"

Jamal uttered part of a syllable, then pulled his sunglasses down over his eyes. "Go over that way," he said. "I think. . . ."

Marissa turned the wheel. The line of cliffs was becoming clearer ahead. Something peculiar hulked on the open sand, like a cluster of outsize bones, and for a moment she thought there was a train roaring toward her but then there was nothing like that all. She wondered where they were going, what Jamal thought about where they were going, but she didn't ask.

"Jamal," she said, and he turned his face to her, eyes hidden again behind the yellow sunglasses.

"You don't like to lie to me, do you?"

"No." Jamal faced forward. "I don't."

66

Two oblong rings revolved in her mind, one inside the other. A grindstone. Some edge being ground. She sat up sharply in the dark, a hand at her throat, located herself in Julie's bed, and with an effort stilled her heart.

Outside it was still, calm starlight glinting on the empty train tracks, glowing on the refurbished surfaces of her truck. She opened the door, pushed the clutch with her right foot and slipped the stick into neutral. Half in, half out of the cab, shoulder against the forward frame of the door, she pushed off with her left foot and when the truck began to roll, swung herself all the way inside.

Like sneaking out. Marissa watched Carrie's dark house receding in the rearview mirror, as inertia carried the truck silently through the first intersection. When momentum began to fail she started the engine, and put it in gear. The idle was enough to carry her forward. In her head the concentric rings continued to turn.

The truck drove to The Magic Carpet, like a horse headed for the barn. Or at least it seemed that way to Marissa, although she knew she must have influenced the direction with subtle movements of her hands on the wheel. Fingertips on a Ouija board planchette.

Her vehicle moved with a buttery smoothness. She slid by the windows of the restaurant without stopping. Jamal's mother was there in her usual spot—yes, but so was Jamal. The glasses of tea and the oil lamp between them. She pulled the wheel and the truck slipped almost silently around the corner. Jamal's brothers had gotten the engine running very smooth indeed. The truck was nosing its slow way around the block and Marissa wished she could know the conversation between Jamal and his mother, but she couldn't enter it without altering it and besides, it was probably taking place in that other language she didn't know. Or maybe it had no words in it all.

In her head the rings grated against each other, without pain exactly, but a kind of annoyance. A fit that couldn't quite find itself. Before she passed the restaurant again she hauled on the wheel and sent the truck down one of the streets toward the center of town, where the cruising went on. There was something more hectic about it tonight. The lights were brighter, the music louder, the hollering more desperate and insistent.

She pulled the wheel to the right and began to circle the circle of the cruising from a block's distance outside of it. She could only *see* the rotating parade of pickups and convertibles and jalopies if she turned her head to the left passing through an intersection but she could feel the movement all the time. The cruising circled inside her circle in the opposite direction, repeating that turning of the rings in her brain in a way she began to find frightening. And the music was wrong, wrong! Deep beating of a loose-skinned drum that seemed to erupt from the bottom of her brain stem, and around this column of sound the fizz of the shaker revolved like a mushroom cloud's halo.

When she looked to the left a diamond-bright light almost blinded her. With her eyes closed she coasted through the intersection and let the truck drift to the roadside, cutting the motor when she felt the tires graze the curb. The moment she popped the door open, the music in her head vanished and was replaced by whatever the cruisers were listening to. She could not exactly place it, but it belonged to the present, which reassured her. But her compulsion to continue circling the inner circle had not gone away, and she continued on foot. The throb of subwoofers in the cruisers' trunks molded her movement into an unfamiliar sort of stutter step. This sense of being shaped and controlled dismayed her too, but it felt impossible to shake free of it. When she passed her parked truck for the second time, the roar intensified, and with an effort she broke the ring of her own movement and turned toward the center of the blinding white light.

A TV news crew was responsible for the blaze of illumination. Marissa skulked behind the cameraman, who panned the long snout of his lens back and forth between two beams of probing light. Cruisers had posted big stereo speakers in the beds of trucks or open trunks of cars . There was an improbable unison to the loud, angry music. Marissa understood that they must have all tuned to the same death metal station, something like that. Many of the people standing up screaming in truck beds or convertibles seemed to be mostly naked and had painted themselves in streaks of red and blue. One was crowned with a bison's head, brown wooly head and black horns circling by, a bloody discharge from the eyeholes as they swept past. Marissa kept to the shadows behind the pair of spotlights. Although she thought she was not likely to be noticed, she still felt a shudder as the bison's head rolled by. Thinking had become difficult: a slow viscous process. A surprising number of women were bare-breasted and daubed with the same dense colors, as if preparing for some savage ritual, or to set out for war. Men in brown uniforms (and without any paint) stood around the perimeter, waiting quietly in doorways of offices or shops. Highway patrolmen. They did not intervene. Maybe there was no reason that they should.

Football. People sometimes behaved this way in celebration of football. Didn't they? But it wasn't football season. Was it? Marissa's knowledge of the world she lived in had somehow become unavailable, and for this reason she felt temporarily reassured to recognize the woman who stepped into the halo of light in front of the camera. That KELO TV reporter, who looked less conventionally attractive in real life—her features larger, horsier. Also, she was distinctly too tall. The wide belt of her tight-waisted suit exaggerated her figure in a cartoonish way. The TV box must flatten her somehow, and make her smaller. Janice Something . . . who did the daily countdown for the *cave girl*. Moved by a pulse of indignation, Marissa stepped forward, but kept herself half hidden behind the cameraman's back.

Janice Something smiled inquiringly at the camera, tilting her head to listen to a spidery voice in her invisible earphone. She touched her tongue to her glossy lip, raised the microphone with its KELO logo as if for a toast, and began to speak. Marissa could hear nothing. The scrum behind the reporter and the roar of unintelligible death metal drowned her out, as effectively as a mute button, and Marissa saw only the automatic set of beauty pageant gestures working silently as the reporter shaped and reshaped her mouth around inaudible words, always smiling, never letting her bottom teeth show.

Painted men wearing animal masks were pressing in around the camera crew now. The masks were synthetic, unlike the bison head that had passed before. Boar's head, bull's head, trout-mask replica. A chant had begun. The chant was intelligible. Janice Rivington's composure began to crack; the flow of her facial gestures was disintegrating.

Janice! Janice! Show us your tits!

Her eyes went white, like the eyes of a frightened horse. A heavy hand appeared on the padded shoulder of her suit, jerking her sideways in the frame, and more hands tore at her lapels. Buttons rattled loose from her blouse and there was a flash of peachy skin. The cameraman lurched backward, and his heavy equipment pack almost knocked Marissa off her feet, but someone caught her before she had quite fallen. The intersection had swirled into battle, and she couldn't retreat the way she had come. Brown shirts were lashing the painted men with black truncheons, cursing, dropping to bind their wrists with plastic ties. A crunch as someone swung a bludgeon at the camera lens. The highway patrol was swinging two-foot-long flashlights. Marissa caught a glimpse of the reporter on her knees, being helped up by a couple of patrolmen, tossing her hair back from her wide, shocked face, clasping her torn clothes together with a hand whose knuckles were bloody from a scrape against the asphalt.

The grip on Marissa's upper arm was friendly but firm; it steered her out of the mêlée and up around the perimeter of the square. Jamal, wearing those yellow beetle sunglasses even at night . . . but it was still bright enough, even though the camera lights had gone dark. Bullhorns were crying for the people to disperse, but there was no enforcement since almost all the deputies were still subduing the group who'd attacked the reporter, whose entourage was nowhere to be seen. The cruising circle continued unabated, cars flashing dome lights and headlights and people standing up in them waving neon-colored glow sticks. The parallel circling in Marissa's head had reached the velocity of a spin. She felt her knees buckling but Jamal's other hand spread long thin fingers across her back to hold her up. He guided her into the shelter of a doorway, where she could stand supported by the frame on either side and look back at what kept happening across Jamal's shoulder.

How had he gotten there, anyway? Attracted by the noise, the shouting, steered by his intuition—who knew, but she felt more secure with his slight body between her and the street, though the vortex in her head had not abated, and she sensed there was more to come. It was coming now: a pickup truck, a monstrous black Dodge Ram, bearing down on them. Marissa saw the winking silver horns on the front of the grille. Driver invisible behind a tinted windshield. Sound stopped, somehow—like a signal failure, or water in Marissa's ears. The truck turned and brought its cargo alongside them: a naked girl standing transfigured like a warrior queen or a human sacrifice, body streaked with paint and her face with blood . . . from the buffalo head she dangled by a horn in one hand. In the other she whipped a handful of flexible glow sticks like a cluster of phosphorescent snakes and her head was thrown back so her bare breasts lifted and her throat swelled in a cry of silent ecstasy. She passed so near that her eyes met Marissa's, though seeing what, who could possibly know? The irises were completely erased, leaving luminescent orbs of black.

Automatically, Marissa tracked her as the truck rolled by, her chin turning over Jamal's shoulder, concentric circles still revolving in her brain. At the end of the block an enormous figure loomed up from the Humvee parked there with two wheels popped up on the sidewalk; its huge hands snatched the girl bodily out of truck bed, rotating her overhead like a trophy, her arms flailing, legs kicking. Sound snapped back on and Marissa heard the air torn by her screams and the snarling of outraged men—Ultimo rolled the girl in a striped blanket that covered her and also seemed to serve as a strait-jacket while the men who had been with her in the truck and others converging from the crowd surged up to reclaim her. Ultimo stopped one of them with a fist, which he seemed to simply hold out in front of him so that the painted man ran his face into it and then fell down—Ultimo also appeared to have two dogs lunging up to the limit of the silver chains he held in his other fist, jaws snapping in the faces of the painted men, who fell back. They were not especially big dogs but their conviction was chilling. The one with a sort of brindled jaguar pattern all over its tightly rippling muscle frightened Marissa more than the other. Still, she made an involuntary motion to go toward the girl as Ultimo pushed her down in the back of the Humvee, but Jamal was already pulling her in the opposite direction—*Come on*, he said, *we've got to go*.

67

Out of the horn-point colors a bear had appeared on the wall of the cave. The bear totem etched in the wall behind the mother was washed in cool moonlight and warmed by the glow of the last coals. The bear stood upright, like a Person, spreading like fingers her curving black claws. She had wanted to stand up like a bear on hind legs and wrest that girl back from her captor. But instead in a dream she shuffled round a post on a chain, and batted down the dogs that leaped at her, jaws wide and white teeth gleaming.

The *fire-bringer* must come hurrying to the glade where Mammut had been discovered in Hawk's eye. Mammut was too vast, he could not be brought back in all his body and bone to the place by the cliff, where his spirit self stayed. But the hunters rolled him up from the bog where he had fallen, where the swamp water was thick and black with his blood. They broke spear shafts and sank into the mud slop. A Person went under right up to his chin, so others had to haul him out by his earlobes. At that, much laughter and shrill whistling.

In the glade *fire-bringer* spun sticks in soft wood till the first sparks were born and then blown into curls of dry tinder, into which they added tufts of Mammut's red-brown hair, acridly burning, while others raised drying scaffolds quickly cut from green wood. The women climbed all over the great body of Mammut's flesh, singing their praise song as they skinned and butchered. Some of the men had begun stretching new skins on old drums, with reddish brown hair still attached here and there, and still damp on the skin side; men stretched and tempered the drums but it was the women who would beat them. Already the mother who was *fire-bringer* too was rolling a slow tempo on a new drum, which in its new elastic hairiness resembled one of the mighty legs of Mammut and shook the earth as Mammut had when he walked in the glade. Presently four such drums were rolling, with the high, dry rattle of a shaker behind, around and above them.

The People brought raw skin bags of heart's blood still warm and salty from Mammut's fading heat, the same blood that had dried on their arms and the killing spear. They brought succulent slivers of liver as if they were offerings, and she fed the rawest bits to the hawk that rode the sleeve on her forearm, and accepted the bits cooked pink for herself. Then there was meat, infinity of roast meat—seized with both hands by the hunters or fed to the drummers on skewers of wood, and the People ate till they were beyond bursting and there was nothing to do but rise up and dance while the drums made the thunder of all four legs of Mammut and the skirl of whistling, the many notes braiding and beating together, into something like the sound of Mammut's trumpet.

A hunter came crouching and stomping with a robe and a mask of Mammut's hide and a thick twist of vine as his trunk. He pranced and stooped and turned and bellowed, and the hunters charged him and retreated, and then they all fell in step behind him as he began to circle the carcass and the fire, where Mammut was being cooked from the inside out. His rib cage had become his oven and before the fire the mother-drummers beat the rhythm, and she fell into the stuttering step of the dancing hunters as if somehow she had always known it. The yellow moon shone down on them above the glade, and everything seemed to be following the path of the moon.

Hawk had moved to her shoulder now, watching. The yellow eye looked through her as she looked through the eye.

The dancing hunter's eye. The Mammut guise was the image of the manbeast that dwelt in the cave, dancing to coax Mammut and all his avatars to follow, to arise and emerge from the crack in the stone surface of the world and walk among the People.

As the sound of the drums faded she could see drumbeats instead, geometric pinwheels and feather shapes eating into her ordinary sight

Less and less did she see the other dancers   but the
        drums were stronger, much much longer
            she was dancing into a trench

round the fire and carcass and the circular track beat drum-
            ming by the dancers
        digging itself deeper into the ground.

Bear, standing on her hind paws and looking into the circle
with not astonishment, but wonder—the old understanding
                of Bear.

            The drums stronger
    the masked hunter gone, inside the burning cave of
                Mammut's ribs

new hunter leading the circle dance weaved and thrust with
        points of the antlers sprouting from his head

    whir of the shaker like a rattlesnake's tail

Mammut rising. A line of women carried coals out of the rib oven to add to the glowing bed of coals beneath the drying rack, where strips of flayed meat dripped and sizzled. Hawk was gone from her shoulder and Bear was gone, but in the cave the painter's hands came loose from the stone where they were embedded. The hands spread color over the stone to shape what happened

make what happen happen make what

now her hands had the hairy backs and the thick black pads of Bear though she still had the dexterity of her fingers—she was dancing on one leg, as if she were no longer moving, though somehow she continued to circle around the deepening trench the dancers' feet, her own, had carved.

When she left her body, left the circle, she went into the ribbed chamber of fire and caught up coals in big bright handfuls and threw them up beyond the treetops into the sky where they became the stars. The yellow moon had vanished now, as if eclipsed by the same dark veil that was sliding slowly over the stars. She heard the drums changing, and the voices changed, and her nostrils caught the scent of rain.

68

What hulked in the sand was a hammered, battle-scarred military vehicle, low and broad and heeled down on the driver's side, as if it was bowing, awkwardly, before the cliff where the ancient half-hidden pictographs and the new tagging were.

"Holy—" Jamal said, "I wonder. . . ."

Marissa stuck the brake, harder than she meant. Her truck slewed sideways and stalled out.

She thought she saw movement up on the ledges. KAOS.

Something coming out of the cave. But really it was coming around the edge of the heeled-down Humvee. A . . . a man. It took more than a moment for Marissa to say *man* to herself about what she saw. Heavyset, dark-skinned and bare to the waist. Indeed he was naked save for a breech-clout. The heavy arms and chest covered with ritual markings, scars, a welt of a brand raised from the skin. He was moving toward them at first, then curving away, as if he had not seen them, did not care. A big man, but not as tall as he should have been. He moved like he was cut off at the knees.

Jamal, staring through the windshield, exhaled with a faint whistling sound. He reached across and pulled the key from the ignition and pressed it into Marissa's palm.

"Come on," he said, and got out of the truck, pressing the door not quite closed behind him, not making the least further sound. Marissa got out and pushed the key over her hip bone down into the pocket of her jeans. Jamal was moving, quiet as a spider, toward the Humvee and the grooved track around it. The bare-skinned man was now concealed behind it, she supposed. Unless he had somehow gone away, but that was hardly possible. The notion of his reappearance filled her with a fascinated dread.

"Tires are cut," Jamal said. Marissa saw now that the Humvee's odd kneeling posture was accounted for by flattened front tires. She looked around; there was nothing, nobody. A cloud above the cliff face was rimmed with the fiery light of the declining sun.

"Who'd do that?"

"He did," Jamal said. "I think. . . ."

"But why?"

"It—" Jamal appeared to be thinking hard. That whistling sound still came with his exhalations, or maybe it wasn't coming from him after all.

"It makes it so—"

"What. *What?*"

"No way out. Or one way out, just one."

The dancer rounded the bumper of the Humvee, petrifying Marissa in her tracks. She recognized that stutter-step, from powwows she'd attended in her teens, was that it? And each step rattled like a snake.

Those markings were jail tattoos mostly. A crowned skull. A spade-shaped dagger. A flaming circle with something inscribed. A pistol grip tattooed into the waistband. Some, wrapping the arms, looked tribal. What she'd taken for a loincloth was a pair of denim cut-offs. She didn't know what to make of the brand, which was just a waffle pattern, broad strips of burn crisscrossed on the left pectoral. Her teeth hurt when she looked at it.

Some sort of script growing out of the eyebrows. Naked eyes which seemed to see nothing, or at any rate nothing of Marissa or Jamal. The whistling sound was more like singing and now she really couldn't tell where it came from. Were the blind eyes bleeding? She could not face them, dropping her gaze as the eyes stroked across her. The bare feet were bleeding, from dancing a trench in the sand. Ultimo passed. The stiff graying braid tied up in a leather thong jounced with the rhythm of his step, and the rattlesnake sound came, she thought, from the strings of cowries and dull brass bells that were wrapped around the thick swell of his calves. Or did it?

The ululation, that whistling sound, seemed to come from everywhere. Nowhere. Jamal's breathing, Ultimo's cracked and bloody lips, the slit opening into the cave on the cliff above. A drum sound, too. A loose skin drum beating from inside the hulk of the downed Humvee, as if the Humvee had a heartbeat. A pierced heart. Claude told her once he had suffered from auditory hallucinations, voices calling his name, or pronouncing nonsensical fragments of scripture. It used to frighten him, till he learned the experience was not uncommon. Twenty percent of all humanity experience such phenomena occasionally, to some degree.

You want to be where she is. To move the feelings more with the will.

"Jesus," Jamal breathed. "He must have been out here all day."

For a moment Marissa was grounded by his voice. She had not spoken to Jamal about what happened the night the cruising had gone crazy. Cruising had since been permanently outlawed, with the local police and the highway patrol augmented by a unit of National Guardsmen to enforce the decree. News and gossip were full of chatter about *barbarians, degenerates, primitives.* A few, certainly a minority, muttered about *police states* and *black helicopters.* Marissa wondered about Jamal's view of the matter, but she had said nothing about it to him, and certainly she had said nothing to him about her dream—if it had been a dream, which seemed less and less certain. Especially now.

Ultimo rounded the bumper of the Humvee and the stuttering clash of his leg rattles increased; she heard Jamal's breath suck in as the vatic eyes raked over them, unaware.

Ultimo was now bleeding from the nose, and heavily, like an animal shot in the heart. Blood ran in and out of his mouth with his panting breath and the keening song he seemed be singing, or that the air around him sang.

Marissa's knees buckled as he passed and Jamal caught her around the shoulders, bearing her up. Her head rocked back across his forearm. Behind her closed eyes she saw the shaman advancing with his shaker, stepping out of a cage of bones, telling her with his mind *I am here to deliver you your dreams.*

Her eyes rolled open, or she thought they did. The cloud above the cliff was bulging. It could never pass, could not release the sun. The sun was too big. She saw emerging from the cave slit a mastodon, an enormous bear, bison and elk and a horned, dancing biped. The boom of the drum had grown deafeningly loud. The shaker's whir whipped her brain like a blender.

"Bats!" Jamal, said, hugging her to him, maybe just to look at his watch, on the wrist he had flung over her shoulder to stop her fall. Had she cried out? From the tone of his voice she knew she had frightened him, but he continued to speak calmly enough, the calm just slightly forced.

"They come out every night the same time. The bats. Or not exactly the same time. It changes every night by like a minute. Call the forestry people and they'll tell you. I think they even have it on their website."

Again his voice grounded her. But now Ultimo had rounded the curve and was stuttering his way toward them again. Blood bubbling in and out of mouth and nostrils, like sucking chest wounds Marissa had seen. She called up some nurse-thinking *it's only a nosebleed, not as bad as it looks*

"Breathe slow," Jamal said, with a greater urgency. He had flattened his hand on her sternum. "Breathe into my hand." No, but it was the eyes, not the bleeding. The eyes bored through Marissa and saw into some other world *you want to be where* as Ultimo passed she followed him, shaking off Jamal—she didn't step into the trench Ultimo's bloody feet continued to deepen, but went on the outside edge of it, imitating the stutter step as best she could, her breath coming hard, like a chant. Hanh a *hanh*. Where, when, had she tried this step before? Jamal was with her, not touching her now but somehow supporting her without any touch, maybe managing the step a little better than she did actually, though she wasn't looking at him or anything, blinded by the sun on the western curve of the circle, the sun having ripped its way through the cloud after all, through a tear of glowing hot, metallic edges. The Humvee hulked breathing Hanh a *hanh*, it was going to get up with its tusks and its trunk it was the train bearing down on her bed it was it was this stutter step was like walking on one leg, the leg like the trunk of a tree with sap running up and running down and the drumming and singing all inside her head pressing everything out, her thought and the self that had thoughts all sinking down through the leg and into the ground

and deeper deeper under the ground Hanh a *hanh* Ultimo tripped out of the trench his feet had dug and unrolled onto his back with a whumpf, as the breath came out of him, eyes still open and staring upward.

Marissa rocked like a tree in the wind, and Jamal did touch her now, to steady her, and now she felt the touch. The material world came back into focus. All she heard was the breathing of the three of them and the quick cry of a hawk floating overhead. The bats, if there had been bats, were gone, diffused somewhere into the darkening sky. An eye-shaped tear in the cloud spun down a sunset beam that crossed the cave slit and stretched across the desert floor to pool its light on the place where they stood. Ultimo's eyes stared into the sun, or maybe they didn't, for only the whites of them now showed.

Marissa drew a bandanna from her back pocket, meaning to cover his eyes from the sun.

"No, don't." Jamal caught her wrist. "He won't be able to come back if you do that. Look."

She looked. The ray of light was pulling away, leaving Ultimo's face and drawing away across the sand like a laser knife cutting toward the cliff wall.

Jamal was kneeling beside Ultimo. He had pulled a bottle of fresh water out of his cargo pants and she thought he would clean the man's bloody face. Instead, Jamal passed his palm over Ultimo's features, not quite near enough to touch, then sat back on his heels.

"But the bleeding," Marissa said.

"Not as bad as it looks." Jamal squinted up at her. "He's breathing."

Marissa leaned in to look more carefully. She had the same feeling now as Jamal, not to go so far as to touch the dreamer anywhere, as if a magnetism repelled her. It was true: he breathed without obstruction.

Jamal set the water bottle inside the claw of his heavy right hand, not touching either thumb or forefinger but screwing the bottle into the sand a little so that it would stay upright. He stood up and took a backward step.

"That's it?" Marissa said. "That's all we do?"

"That's it," Jamal confirmed. "We go our way."

He reached for her hand and drew her toward her truck. Marissa pulled away from him once, not to go back but only to look. With the sun behind the cliff the light had failed quickly. Ultimo lay in silhouette, the craggy face as if carved. She thought perhaps he had closed his hand on the water bottle. Under the blue plastic cap, light lingered in the clarity of the water.

69

Thc Humvee, tires mysteriously mended, was locked behind the double gate of Ultimo's storm fence, but the smaller gate, opposite the trailer door, was not locked. Around the metal posts the chain hung unsecured. The padlock itself was missing. A U-shaped hasp closed over a post was enough to contain the dogs. Unless one of them, the Catahula most likely, knocked up the hasp with his muzzle one time and then they all went out to compete and breed with the coyotes in the desert.

The dogs were not so excited as the first time Jamal had come here. They gathered, jostling at the gate and growling, but they didn't bark loud, or throw themselves at the diamond mesh. After a while they quieted, but remained on their side of the gate looking at him intently. Jamal watched the trailer door. Its window was dark, opaque as before. There were flickers of TV light as before, with a different soundtrack, not news this time. Above the trailer and the rocky basin where it stood, a fingernail moon had risen, carrying a star in the orb of darkness held in its inner curve.

Jamal opened the gate and went softly through and, having closed it carefully behind him, stood still as a tree with his sneakers rooted to the cracked concrete path to the trailer's front step. The dogs pressed around him, in silence, and with small aggression, damp noses cold through the thin fabric of his pants legs. Jamal let his hands hang loose and empty, a little forward of his hips, so the dogs could snuffle his open palms.

A couple of times he felt a lick, but from which dog he didn't know because his eyes were fixed on the window, starlight reflected there in the pane. One by one the dogs went away satisfied, each walking a tightening circle before it flumped down with a little grunt in the shadow of the Humvee. Only the big Catahula remained, his growl diminished to a purr. When the growl had gone away altogether, the Catahula relaxed and came nearer, close enough that Jamal could have traced the jaguar stripes on his shoulders, or rubbed the short ears, which were torn from fights.

When the trailer door opened, a noise of gasping and moaning came out, in pain or in pleasure, Jamal wasn't sure. On the door sill Ultimo appeared, wearing mirrored sunglasses and carrying a carved wooden cane. Seeing himself doubled in the sunglasses, Jamal wondered if maybe Ultimo *had* been blinded by the desert sun. Ultiimo clucked his tongue at the Catuhula and the dog turned away and lay down beside the trailer steps, head on his front paws and eyes still burning.

Ultimo stepped down and used the tip of his cane to flick a dry twist of dog dung away from the cement. So he could see fine, Jamal thought. He wore sunglasses at night fairly often himself.

"You've got a way with a dog," Ultimo said.

"I wouldn't put a dog in the pit."

"No. But you'd go in to get one out, I think." Ultimo had already turned away from him, the heavy salt-and-pepper braid switching between his shoulder blades like a panther's tail. Jamal wasn't so sure that he needed the cane, though he did put weight on it to climb the three steps. In the doorway he turned his head back, with the flash of a silver teardrop lens.

"Coming in, right?"

Inside it was close and mostly dark, and smelled, not too unpleasantly, of dog. Musk, rather; it wasn't all dog. The moans were of sex pleasure, possibly feigned, and now Jamal was certain the sound was canned; it came from the room off to the right, where light flickered from a big plasma screen.

"You like to watch?" Ultimo said.

"No," Jamal said. He had a brief image of the girl he'd seen Ultimo drag out of the truck.

"The tape's copying to disc right now," Ultimo said. "So you know, it's gotta be real time. I can shut the noise off, though."

He reached inside the doorway, found a remote and killed the sound. The screen continued to pulse light, perhaps because there'd have been no light without it. As it was, there wasn't much where they stood in a space that was less a hallway than a gap between two rooms. Jamal was in hand's reach of Ultimo, but he couldn't see where his hands were, or his feet, only the mirrored lenses floating, a head higher than himself.

"You want to hear the bear tape, then?"

"No," Jamal said. "I don't want to hear the bear tape."

"All right," Ultimo said, and this time he sounded faintly pleased, as he'd sounded slightly apologetic about the porn. "Let's go in here."

Ultimo opened a door in the back, where the exterior wall of the trailer would normally have been. Jamal was perplexed, but clearly there was another room, this one with firelight in it. He barely glanced through the doorway toward the TV as he passed; the people writhing in silence there might have been anyone.

"Careful," Ultimo said. "There's a couple steps down."

The new space was built as a T-leg of the trailer, a partial dug-out. Stonework came to Ultimo's hip; the walls above were logs so closely notched and laid they didn't require any chinking between. Ultimo moved along them, more creakily than usual. With his back to Jamal, he muttered, "Got stiff, lying out on that hard-pack."

"And digging a trench with your feet, I guess," Jamal said.

Ultimo propped his cane against the wall and pushed up his sunglasses. Jamal braced himself not to quail at the naked eyes. This look was not so penetrating as others he'd received from Ultimo, though it would have been a stretch to call it friendly.

"You built this," Jamal said. Obviously the trailer had been dropped here first.

"Oh yeah." Ultimo said. "I can do this kind of work. Depends what people ask for."

Jamal looked at the fireplace and chimney. The masonry was no mean skill. And the chimney drew well, leaving behind just a faint redolence of cedar. There were lots of animal skins around, deer hides and a buffalo robe and a great grizzly bear with the head and claws intact spread out on the floor in front of the fireplace. The hip-high stone ledge was decorated with small animal skulls, bobcat and fox, interspersed with candlesticks. Ultimo was lighting a few candles with a long fireplace match. A heavy rifle, a shotgun, and a big compound bow hung on the walls. There was some fishing gear too, but no trophies, other than the hides and bearskin.

"Naturally I work with both hands." Ultimo was seated before the fire, holding both his heavy hands up, displaying a maze of callus and cracks. "You can't survive otherwise. I give people whatever they want."

"I understand," Jamal said. He sat down cross-legged at the edge of the hearth. Ultimo had folded the sunglasses and put them on the table, but Jamal still had the impression of facing a mirror. A stone wall, or the raw face of a quarry.

Ultimo raised his right hand. "I could take you fishing or build you a house," he said. "Would you like to go out and kill a big animal?"

"No," Jamal said.

"You don't want porn," Ultimo said. "Dope neither, I don't think. You don't want to hear the bear tape. I only listened to it once myself. I give people what they think they want. But it corrupts you, to look at things like that. Or listen to them. It poisons your mind."

"What are you?"

Ultimo laughed. "What you want me to be." He reached

behind a pelt-draped chair and pulled up a jug of red wine by its ring. "Have a drink?"

Jamal nodded and accepted a clear plastic cupful. They drank without any toast or remark, looking into the shifting blades of firelight.

"I'm a mongrel," Ultimo said. "If you ask the Census. Or if they ask me, I don't know what to say. Part French, part Spanish, maybe a touch of African too, for sure the biggest part's Brulé. *Sichángu* I should have said. Brulé is a Frenchman's word for it." He drank some wine, and looked at Jamal. "Oh yeah, I qualify for the tribe. I could get on the tit at some casino."

"Why don't you," Jamal said.

"No freedom," Ultimo said. "In fact there's nothing there at all. Nothing I want."

Jamal accepted a new splash of wine in his cup. He didn't quite know what he wanted to know, or if he was close to finding it out.

"You're a quiet one," Ultimo said. "That's good." He took out a short black cigar and lit it, offered the tin to Jamal, who declined. "I don't usually do anything to anybody but I let people do . . . whatever. Sometimes it's not good for them, what they do. Sometimes— no different from you."

"What are you talking about?"

"I've been watching you," Ultimo said. "You're not so different."

"Why," Jamal said.

"Well, that mean-natured punk Marko was worried about you," Ultimo shrugged. "Not for any real reason, I don't think. And then— I just got to wondering what *you* were."

"So?"

"You gave me water. It's the right thing to do. Most people don't know that. It's the most right thing there is to do."

"Okay," Jamal said. "But I don't understand what you were doing out there."

"Some people come to me as a healer, still," Ultimo said.

"Not so many, but they do. And some come looking for a spirit guide. I could say to you now, *I'll take you to the bear.* But kid, I think you been closer to the bear than I have. And that girl, she's all the way inside. Know what I mean?"

"Yes," Jamal said. "No. Not completely."

"There's something out there," Ultimo said. "In there, I mean. It's old, and it doesn't belong to anybody in these little towns around here, or out on the reservation either, and it didn't belong to *Sicháng u.* It's older than any of those people are. But somehow—"

"It belongs to everybody."

"So you do know what I mean," Ultimo said. "And the ways to get there, they're the same, for anybody. I mean the differences don't count. And I—well, you were there. You saw it. But I want to know that what I saw was real."

Jamal drank his wine, looking into the coals. The room was tight and the warmth from the fire and the wine was welcome; it had been growing colder at night as time moved into the fall.

"The animals," Ultimo prompted. "The hands on the wall."

"It's there," Jamal told the fireplace.

"Are they painted on the cave wall?"

"Yes," Jamal said. "No. They were but they were more . . . 3-D. Like they were floating." The dark space of the cave surrounded him again; it dizzied him. Maybe it was only the wine.

"Like they were alive," Ultimo said.

They were silent then, and the black orb of the cave dissipated and Jamal was completely present again in the snug space Ultimo had built behind the several façades he presented to the world. Ultimo offered him the jug again and Jamal shook his head, helping himself to stand with one hand on the stone ledge that ran around the room.

"Better not," he said. "I'll dump my bike."

"Watch yourself, then." Ultimo's hand spread briefly across the center of his back, solid and warm. "We don't want that."

Outside the trailer door the Catahula got up to sniff at Jamal's hand and this time Jamal did fondle, briefly, the stubby, ragged ears. Ultimo chuckled deep in his throat. He was carrying the padlock in his left hand, and once Jamal had gone out he snapped it through the links of chain.

"It's open whenever you come back," Ultimo said, and then, "What *do* you want."

Jamal took a backward step and looked up. The moon was higher in the sky and looked smaller, and that star seemed somehow to have spilled from the crescent. He thought he could make out the moon's whole circle anyway though most of it was dark.

"I want Julie to come back from wherever she is."

Ultimo was shaking his head, fingers entwined in the diamond mesh. "I can't do that one for you."

Jamal lowered his head from the moon.

"The other girl, on the square that night. The one that was wearing the bison head. Her I brought back. Okay, snatched her back. She had got herself into some fairly bad shit."

Ultimo now appeared to be smiling; Jamal could see the white tips of his teeth.

"They call it a *recovery* operation. That kind of thing I can do."

"Okay," Jamal said. "Thanks for telling me." He nodded and started up the slope, but before he had gone more than a couple of steps something made him turn back toward the trailer. Maybe one of the dogs had made a sound.

"Your girl, now. . . ." Ultimo was studying Jamal from his doorway. "If I knew how to get where she's at I would be there. But I don't. It's up to her."

70

Marissa ate her supper with Carrie, two microwaved meals at the kitchen table, and she worked on Carrie's calves and feet and lower back for close to an hour once the table was cleared. When Carrie had drifted off into a grateful, reasonably pain-free sleep, Marissa went into Julie's room and began—

Not an Exercise, because there was no such program, no target for imagination's eye. The rosary hung from a hook on the back of Julie's door—for at least a week Marissa had neglected to put it in her pocket when she prepared herself for the day. Julie had a bounteous teenage girl's supply of candles, many of them with a scent so cloying that Marissa had to open the window, never mind the autumnal cold. Well, she put on one of Carrie's gruesome sweaters. She had made herself a ring on the floor, arranging Julie's arrowheads and plastic dinosaurs in some sort of witch's circle, and if Carrie or anyone saw it all they would probably laugh her out of existence. But Carrie was sleeping and no one would come.

To move the feelings more with the will.

At the moment she thought that nothing was going to happen her eyes rolled back in her head like a pair of marbles and she was no longer where she had been; indeed she was nowhere, floating in a void. There was a rushing sound and a bright light, but she couldn't remember the word for tr- tr- and she was only aware of the light by some sensation of its warmth, because her eyes were closed or maybe she had actually gone blind.

"I can't be here without a guide," she thought, panicking, but then she saw a warm teardrop of light coming toward her. The roar and rushing had all gone and she was relieved she could see the light now, and Jamal's mother's hands cupping the oil lamp as she floated toward her. When she let go the lamp it stayed in the air, suspended. Marissa could see only her face, the soft forgiving oval formed by the *hijab*, but she could feel the other woman's hands, strong on her own wrists, pulling her arms out to the cross position, rotating the right hand palm up and the left palm down, and she could feel the other woman's thought—

Turn with me. Now we will Turn together and the step was simple enough, toe behind heel and a twist of the hips and again and again till the dizziness started, as she and her friends had dizzied themselves as children. Would she slip on an arrowhead, kick dinosaurs around the room? That worry passed and she thought of herself posed like a propeller on a beanie, then wanted to laugh but the hilarity was a deeper, richer euphoria because she was flying in fact, or falling, twirling like a maple seed as she spun down, and her feet had melted together like a ballerina's *en pointe* and were drilling into the floor, soft pine, heating it till sparks flew up and spilled into a furze of tinder, and fire moved from the tinder to the wick of an oil lamp shaped from the hollow of a bone.

Now she could see the walls of the cave and the vastness of it, and coming out of shadow was her lost daughter, naked except for a pelt slung over her shoulder and the ochre and umber streaked all over her, one entranced eye ringed in midnight's black and the other with the color of the moon. Then Marissa slipped behind her eyes and saw no more but the wall approaching; she felt the clutch of the hooded hawk's claws on her shoulder through the bear pelt and the weight of the bear paws with her human hands inside. Drumming, chanting, in her ears and in her blood and she knew somewhere little horns of color were making the hunt of Mammut dance on the wall (or had already done so or in future would).

She knew these songs but was not singing, or was singing them with the blood in her heart. Her feet fit exactly into prints in the hardened clay on the floor, so surely she had passed this way before. There were many handprints on the wall approaching her but not hers, not yet, but when she laid her palms against the wall there was the tingling lock of magnetic connection, and her hands even seemed to sink in a little, as though the stone itself was soft like clay. When she looked to the left there was Julie, dressed in the clothing she'd abandoned in Carrie's house, and to her right was the great she-bear of her clan and her totem, standing on her hind legs and projecting a fearsome, toothy smile, and when she looked forward—

There was—

There—

—and the shaman appeared with his foot-long cane blowpipe and began to exhale black paint over the backs of her hands pressed into the wall but he didn't stop at that as he usually did; he kept on blowing the darkness over her forearms and her elbows, her shoulders and her back, obliterating her completely, erasing every scrap of her being into the whole world's blackest night.

71

Marissa woke up all at once with a jolt, as to the crack of a starter's pistol. She was stretched full length on Julie's bunk, but her awareness roved the room. The rosary hung from the hook on the door. Julie's dinosaurs and arrowheads were back on the shelves. Had Marissa put them away, in her sleep? Had Carrie? By the light in the window she knew it was late, and it was quite cold, with the window still open. The house was still, and Carrie was at work.

She got up and pulled on her black jeans. She'd slept, apparently, in the rest of her street clothes. Her feet were cold on the oval hooked rug, which Julie had made for herself in sixth grade, and colder on the bare wood floor around it. She dragged on a pair of socks and went to the kitchen, where Carrie had left coffee still heating for her. It wasn't quite reduced to tar. She stirred in an alarming quantity of sugar, till the mixture reached the consistency of molasses. Nothing she saw in the room made any sense to her.

Then in her sock feet she went outdoors, carrying the sticky mug, and walked to the center of the dead-end circle, shivering in her shirt sleeves. Here she felt calmer. Except for the railroad tracks, there was nothing in the view that her eyes last night could not have seen: the desert scrub unrolling westward in the harsh clarity of the morning light. Her eyes in Julie's head. The eye of the hawk. Marissa shook her head, like it itched inside. The eye you see with is. . . .

She went indoors, made Julie's bed, and sat again at the

kitchen table. There was a Krazy Kat clock above the sink that should have rolled its eyes and switched its tail, but didn't. Marissa took it down and cleaned away years of built-up cooking grease; when she hung it up again, it worked properly.

She needed someone to explain to her what had happened, or to tell her, convincingly, it had all been no more than a set of mad dreams. Jamal's mother—but her presence in the scene last night must have been hallucination, and in spite of the bright flashes of mutual intelligence that once in a while occurred between them, they didn't have enough of a common language. Jamal himself was wise for his years, but. . . . Then again, Carrie was not to be underestimated. There was a bedrock solidity to her. But Marissa didn't want to make Carrie think she was crazy. Crazier.

I am here to deliver you your dreams, the shaman had said. Or was it I am here to deliver you *from* your dreams? But she had no idea how to find her way back to the one place she'd met the shaman in flesh and bone. If that episode had not been a hallucination, too.

In Julie's room she found her cell phone, the battery dead. She plugged in the charger and thought of calling Peggy Keenan. But Peggy already thought she was unhinged for walking away from her job for no reason. . . .

She pulled her truck into the row of empty slots in front of the Wild West town. The only other car parked there must have belonged to the manager, who sat in the weatherboard ticket booth, listening to football on a transistor, but apparently half asleep. He roused when she skirted the buildings, came out of the booth and called after her.

"Hey Missy! It's over here!"

In spite of herself she turned back for a minute. The man wore a loose flannel shirt over an oil-stained orange tank top. He had a diamond stud in one ear and was missing the two front teeth that meth heads frequently lacked.

"Hey, Baby," he said, climbing toward her. "You don't

need to go back there." His tone was conciliatory, as if they were intimate enough to have quarreled. "Baby, it can't be that bad."

Marissa shook herself, turned on her sneaker heel and kept walking, following the wide-set ruts. Beyond the crest of the ridge she was climbing, a couple of vultures were circling high, their ragged wingtips clawing like fingers at the empty sky.

"Hey Missy!" The man's tone had grown more hostile, but he was also farther away. "You can't just walk off and leave your truck like that. That parking's for Wild West."

The dog pack came ravening at the fence as soon as Marissa topped the ridge. She hesitated, studying the mesh and the gates, till she was satisfied there was no way the dogs could break out of it. Then, tentatively, she began to walk down, watching the front door of the trailer. No sign. Ten yards from the gate she stopped. The Humvee was parked inside the wire, which should have made her think the owner must be there too, and yet that didn't really mean anything. He could have gone off on a horse or on foot or simply vanished into thin air.

The dogs kept hurling themselves at the wire, teeth bared, sometimes catching in the mesh diamonds. The wire began to glisten with their slobber. The biggest one, a sort of olive color with a blunt head and tigerish stripes, was the most determined and relentless, climbing the trailer's steps to hurl himself and hit the gate chest-high, bashing his muzzle till it bled, over and over, relentlessly. But the buzzards were not circling this compound after all; they were half a mile out, above the desert.

"Hush up, you." The voice came from the trailer door, which had opened, dislodging a dog from the top step. "Now just you simmer down."

Ultimo stepped out, scattering dogs with a cane in his left hand, and shaking a square tin box in his right. He seemed to be able to swat the dogs without looking at them. His eyes were steadily on Marissa the whole time. The rhythm of the rattling can seemed to take her back toward where she'd been the night before. Not dream. That other reality.

The dogs had stopped barking and charging the gate. Ultimo tucked his cane under one elbow and pried the tin open, scattering dog biscuits right and left. The dogs claimed their biscuits and went to the shadow of the Humvee or the opposite corner of the fence, where they sat down, chewing, eyes still watchful.

Ultimo unfastened the heavy padlock. Steel links rang against the posts as he pulled the chain free.

"This way," he said, still looking into Marissa's eyes. "I wondered when you'd come."

72

Marko had never yet killed a person or a buffalo. It looked like the buffalo would go down first. He got a buck every year in the season, plus a couple more deer jack-lit on the sly, and he'd been out a time or two after bighorn, with no luck. All that was with a 30.06 borrowed from one of Sonny's uncles. Today what he had was a forty-five automatic, old army issue, which he'd bought bootleg from Ultimo.

If an Indian could bring down a buffalo bull with a bow and arrow he figured the forty-five should be plenty. It would knock down a man the size of Ultimo, or anyway that's what Ultimo said. And it put a good-size hole in you, too. Marko felt a rich thrill of satisfied relief whenever he thought of solving his personal problems that way. *Bang!* through Julie, *Bang!* through Jamal. *Bang!* through that meddlesome bitch Marissa, who'd shown up for no reason from who knows where.

Jamal was the one he'd most like to take out. But going after Jamal was like fighting a bug. Plus he could tie you up with his cunning, which often involved only telling true things, like you can't just walk into a hospital room and start blazing, or not if you want to walk away afterward. Julie might be put away by pulling a plug, only Marko didn't know which one to pull and somebody would notice if he pulled them all—same problem with smothering her with a pillow; there always seemed to be somebody around.

Rubbing out Jamal with Marissa's truck had seemed a

stroke of genius until it went wrong. She could have said whatever she wanted afterward—nobody in town had known her long, and a lot of people already thought it was queer how the two of them went around together. But now—Ultimo wouldn't even talk to him about the problem, plus Jamal's brothers had got involved, or knew enough that they might get involved. Marko had only been three years old when his family started trying to get as far away from Serbia as the shape of the planet permitted, but he still remembered plenty about the persistence of family vendettas and he knew when it was time to back off.

This buffalo had a Circle-D brand, but it had been a long way from home when he separated it from the herd with the bike. Now that was a kick—gunning the Harley in amongst all that galloping, bristling weight . . . like the wild Cheyenne on their painted horses. He'd cut out his quarry without too much trouble, zigzagging the bike and roaring the throttle, and he felt proud of that since he'd never done it before. He'd been driving it for about forty minutes, keeping it moving at a brisk trot. Of course he could have cranked up and overtaken it at any point but he was enjoying the chase too much; also the buffalo was headed back in the general direction Marko would need to come with a truck later on, to collect the hide and meat and the head for a trophy.

The animal was already beginning to tire, but for some reason it started scrambling up the low side of one of the painted clay hills. It was slowing, stumbling on the ascent, but the bike's tires got no traction to climb, so Marko wheeled it down to the dry gulch and went up on foot, racking a round into the forty-five's chamber as he climbed. It would be *mano a mano* now, or no—he smiled to himself at the gag—*mano a buffalo*.

When he came out on top of the mesa, the buffalo had come to a stand, at the edge farthest away from Marko, humped shoulders high and his head low. Marko, pistol swinging in his hand, looked past the animal to the landscape beyond; he felt like he'd come near this place before, only not from the same direction. Behind him, when he glanced over his shoulder, a ribbon of highway stitched through hills. That would be farther away than it looked. A speckled hawk flew overhead, cried sharply and stooped away beyond the cliff edge where the buffalo was standing, head raised now to watch Marko's approach.

Marko had read in a magazine about guys down South hunting wild hogs with handguns, which was plenty dangerous, but those guys had dogs. He meant to shoot this buffalo somewhere behind the shoulder—he'd seen pictures of Indians doing that on horseback, and when they were down on the flat pack he could have done the same thing from the bike. He was beginning to wish he had done that when the buffalo dropped his head and charged him.

He couldn't stop himself from letting off a couple of shots right away, and maybe they had just gone wild but there didn't seem to be anything very penetrable in the space between the horns, the heavy head and shoulders bearing down on him. He wanted to sidestep and get that bullet in behind the shoulder as the animal overshot him, but now he remembered how nimbly the bull had been able to turn while he was chasing it on the Harley—Marko was still looking at the frame of the horns, much closer now, and he squeezed off a couple more straight into the forehead, thinking that might at least spook it, but no—

Another sidestep, but the bull was still on track. Marko yanked on the trigger till he heard the forty-five click empty, and he was about to try to dive out of the way—he'd land rolling, he thought, for whatever it was worth. The buffalo disappeared.

Or rather, it was sucked under the earth. And Marko was too, tumbling down a shifting slope, roots and rocks popping him in the elbows and ribs, trying to keep his head curled in until he flopped out on the bottom.

It was the biggest sinkhole Marko had ever seen or heard

of—maybe four stories high on three sides of it, and as he scrambled up to his feet he was, for an instant, stone terrified—he saw no way out, and there wouldn't be anybody looking for him either. But there was sunlight on his back, and when he turned around he saw a much more manageable slope. At the top, he could even see his Harley in the dry gulch, still securely balanced on the kickstand.

The buffalo hadn't broken a leg; it was standing up and didn't seem damaged in any way, and it also didn't seem interested in Marko anymore. The buffalo was facing the far wall of the sinkhole. It lowered its head and began to paw and snort, but instead of charging, it was backing away.

Hair rose up on Marko's neck, like the hackles of a dog. Peering into the shadow he began to see that the wall of the sinkhole wasn't a vertical wall at all, but a rim hanging over a cavern that the collapsing earth had opened. The thing coming out of the cavern was a bear, something like a grizzly but on a different scale, dwarfing even the buffalo. That's what the buffalo was afraid of, but the bear was coming toward Marko instead, as if it knew him, had been looking for him for a long time, and now had found him. The forty-five was still in his hand and there was even a spare clip in his pants pocket, but his mind was too slow and his limbs were too numb. When the bear was near enough it rose on its hind legs and spread its great arms for a crushing embrace.

White teeth.

It can't be that that big, Marko was thinking. Wherever he turned the bear was before him, blocking out the light of the whole world.

73

The bison came into the dry gulch and stood for a long moment staring at Marissa's truck, which she had pulled to a quick stop the moment she saw it. The animal's head lowered; it blew dust from the ground. It was big, and the horns looked bluish in the midday light. A buffalo was not a wholly uncommon sight hereabouts but this one struck Marissa as ancient, as if it had sprung from a well of deep time. Maybe she had never looked at one closely before.

"Blow your horn?" Jamal said softly. But before she could decide whether to do that or not, the buffalo lifted its head with a snort, turned and went trotting away down the gulch.

"Now, where did that come from?" Ultimo smacked the roof of the cab with his broad palm. He had been riding in the truck bed, in the spot that Jamal had said would be good to mount a machinegun, since the three of them left his place. He tapped the roof a second time, then swung himself over the rail and landed heavily in the alkaline dust. At his gesture Marissa cut the motor. Jamal got out the passenger door and shaded his eyes with one hand. In the spot where the buffalo had been, a big silver-trimmed Harley stood on its kickstand.

"Mmm," said Ultimo. "Let's go take a look."

Marissa stepped out and stood with her elbows braced on the top of the door frame, looking across. The Harley seemed to be balanced on the edge of some sort of pit, or rather a pool full of liquid darkness. Vertigo. It sucked at her mind. The kaleidoscope inside her head revolved and everything turned upside down so that the motorcycle stuck mysteriously to a ceiling of earth and the peaks of the painted hills dangled like stalactites. *I wondered when you'd come,* Ultimo said, his voice pleasant enough until he kicked the door shut behind the two of them, trapping her in some sort of black-dark corridor whose shape made no sense in terms of the outside of the trailer.

The inside and the outside didn't fit. But she had no time to consider that peculiarity because his hands were already choking her and pushing her up the wall. She fought, tried to, but he was hideously strong, thick, impenetrable as stone. Outside the dogs were barking and snarling and hurling themselves against the door. He had lifted her feet off the floor so that she had no purchase to push back, even when she tried to push off the wall, and the wall was wrong too—a trashy trailer partition should have collapsed under such a battering. As her consciousness faded she seemed to hear a sort of voice-over *you set yourself up for this* a sort of shrewish woman's voice *anyone would have seen it coming* like the bitch reporter Janice Something. . . . He wasn't going to strangle her quite to death, she realized. There was a different plan than that. As her head dissolved in a dark swirl of golden motes he released her throat and let her slump down for a moment, her heels skidding over dry nuggets of spilled dog biscuit. A considered plan. She had just caught some part of her breath but was still too weak to move when he ripped open her clothing with a couple of easy swipes like the paws of a bear, then tossed her up against the wall again, stabbing into her, retracting and stabbing again. No need to choke her now because any movement only involved her more in what was happening to her. The sensation was overpowering though couldn't otherwise be classified, though the screams she heard had to be her own.

She was faintly aware that her legs had wrapped around his back and she was howling both of them howling louder than the dogs outside and there was light now, several small piercing lights that were coupled with an electrical hum; the thin beams picked out detail she would rather not see and now she was down on her knees, choking again, gagging and trying to swallow as the cameras circled, now on her hands and knees

if you'd listened to that meth head you wouldn't have ever come in here

a lull in which she might have passed out, then the heavy hands flipped her over, limp as a filet of meat, hands bending her double so her ankles were pressed down by his shoulders. Kernels of dog biscuit crushed under her back. The light was more general now, daylight filtering in through some sort of fissure, so she could see the man's face, masklike, his eyes glazed over like the eyes of dogs fucking. This one wasn't Ultimo at all—she didn't know how many there were

she woke up again and lay quietly trying to assess her condition, the several raw punctures, how bad how serious but in a moment the hands had yanked her hair up out of the way to slip a chain choke collar around her neck. Voice-over: *once he's fucked you to death he's going to feed you to the dogs*

74

People have this stuff in their minds, Ultimo said. Or probably he didn't say that, because it didn't particularly fit the context of where they were now. Marissa raised a hand to touch the side of her neck. She was wearing a scarf but there were no bruises or tears underneath it. Her body was whole, intact. In this universe, the assault hadn't happened. Except, if it existed in her mind, it also had to exist in his. Didn't it?

The three of them were standing by the abandoned Harley, peering over the rim of the vast sinkhole. When Marissa looked down, her vision halted on the pattern of brightly colored specks expanding around the toes of her boots. She felt her breath catch in her throat. If this was some new wormhole opening in her brain she felt certain she didn't want to go into it. She went down on one knee to look more closely—to drag whatever it was back into some frame of ordinary reality. But the pattern blurred and she couldn't read it.

A shadow moved off of her shoulder. Ultimo hunkered down beside her, studying the pattern, then scooping up several bits of it into one hand. In his palm Marissa could now see ladybugs, a dozen or so, multicolored, polished and shiny, like Easter eggs or Christmas baubles. One had a pattern of yellow, black and white that momentarily resembled a tiny death's head. Another foolish trick of the mind.

"Well," Ultimo said, rising from the ground. "Sometimes. . . ."

Marissa stood up also. Ultimo was still looking at his

handful of colored beetles, his expression an odd fusion of childish delight and some sort of ancient sadness. Sometimes what? He sent a puff of air into his palm and the insects dispersed, each carapace opening a pair of minuscule wings. Jamal turned his head to follow their path out over the empty air above the pit, although as usual his bubble sunglasses made it hard to tell where he was really looking.

Five hours earlier, they'd come to the cliff where the rock-shelters were, but the opening there was impracticable. No way Ultimo could ever squeeze into it. Marissa might just have managed, but the thought made her cringe with claustrophobia, and even Jamal hadn't seemed too keen. It was he who pointed out that they had brought lights but no climbing equipment and that there was a considerable drop inside.

There has to be more than one way in, Ultimo said, and Jamal said that somebody else would have found it by now, and Ultimo said not if they weren't looking. Marissa suggested watching for bats, and Jamal said the bats wouldn't come out for eight hours at least, and Ultimo said, we've got all day, and plenty of water.

Since then they had been doing their best to circle the contours of the mesa—difficult to determine from ground level. Marissa wished her GPS would deliver a satellite photo, but in this area it barely showed the roads. Ultimo seemed to have a practiced eye, and it was he who suggested turns from his post overlooking the cab. Several times before they saw the buffalo he'd had them stop and scramble up to investigate a crevice between boulders, or just a swale in the ground where earth might have silted over an opening.

Jamal kept glancing at the motorcycle: he looked like he wanted to kick it over, but he didn't. Ultimo turned over the hand that had held the ladybugs, closed it, and stood with his fists cocked on his hips.

From the point where they stood, the sinkhole offered

a gentle slope down to the overhang of the cavern. A peculiar silence rose up from it, like smoke. Wings of a hawk flying overhead looked to Marissa like fins of a fish swimming, and everything had an oddly dampened quality as the three of them walked down. The caved-in earth on the sinkhole's floor was soft under their feet, scattered with fallen rock and knots of uprooted scrub.

Halfway to the overhang, Ultimo dropped to a crouch. There was an automatic pistol by his left foot but he didn't seem to notice it, staring instead at an enormous clawed pawprint. Marissa felt a shiver run over her, but she wouldn't exactly have called it fear. The fine hair on her forearms prickled up, the way it did when she was moved by music.

"Grizzly?" That was Jamal's voice.

"I never saw one that big," Ultimo said. "I never saw anything that big." He probed the pad of the print with his middle finger, which went down all the way to the knuckle. Then he flattened his huge hand into the print; his fingers didn't begin to reach the claw-marks.

Marissa backed up and looked around the rim of the sinkhole and saw nothing. On the ground there were buffalo hoof marks along with the bear tracks and (she thought) a set of boot prints not their own. The buffalo had run around a good deal and beyond that she could make no sense of it. She was no tracker. The bear tracks climbed to the spot where the buffalo had emerged, she could tell that much.

"He went thataway," Jamal said. Nobody laughed.

Jamal kicked at the pistol with his toe. Ultimo waved him back. With a bandanna he drew from his back pocket he picked up the pistol by the barrel, wound up and threw it, whirling end over end like a boomerang, out of the sinkhole altogether.

"What about the bike," Jamal said.

"What about it," Ultimo said, and then, over his shoulder as he walked down toward the cave, "Just don't touch it, that's all."

Just don't touch the bike, Marissa repeated to herself, like learning syllables of a foreign language by rote. By now all three of them had passed into the shade of the overhang.

"There's your bats," Ultimo said, looking up into the curve of the high dome.

"Some of them anyway," Jamal said. From croppings of the stone roof a couple of hundred bats were hanging in the shrouds of their folded wings, like shriveled fruit.

"Sound sleepers," Ultimo said, and turned to the rear wall. There were three openings, all about the same size. Ultimo looked at Jamal, who shrugged.

"I don't know if I was back this far," Jamal said.

"It would be pretty far," Ultimo said. He handed Jamal a two-foot-long mag lite. Jamal picked the middle entry.

Marissa couldn't measure how far they had gone, but it was only ten minutes or so before they came out of the passage into a much larger space, cathedral-size it seemed to her, though she felt it more than she could see it. The beams of their strong flashlights got lost in there, as if they were aiming them into the night sky.

"Okay," Jamal said. "I was here. I think. I'm pretty sure."

The bright circle of his flashlight's beam kept dragging along walls and ceiling, looking for something that wasn't there.

"This light's all wrong," Ultimo said. "Come back."

Marissa and Jamal stood under the overhang, blinking in the daylight while Ultimo fashioned a torch from a knot of greasewood that had fallen in with the other debris. This time Ultimo tied the end of a roll of twine to a stone before they went back into the passage, and handed the roll to Marissa, who went last, letting the line unspool behind her.

"Back off," Ultimo said, when they'd reached the cavernous space again. "Look up." He raised the torch above his head.

Now Marissa understood what he had meant about the light. The torchlight stroked, caressed the walls, instead of probing and splintering the way the flashlights had. Still, there was nothing on the rock but water stains. The images welled from inside her head.

75

I wondered when you'd come, he said. He folded the dog biscuit tin under one elbow and beckoned her through the gate.
Marissa stepped into the enclosure, watching the dogs, who
watched her with an equal care, without rising to approach.
The trailer door was shut, and she stopped at the step leading
up to it. Ultimo, she noticed, wrapped the chain around the
gate posts as it had been before, but didn't bother to snap the
padlock. As he walked toward her he switched the dog biscuit
tin from one hand to the other. She had the weird notion he
meant to offer her his arm, but that didn't happen. He reached
past her to open the door of the trailer, pushed it inward, and
waved her inside.

Instead of the room she had expected she was standing
in a sort of hallway, or maybe just a gap between two rooms.
The air smelled, not unpleasantly, of an animal musk, and it
was too dim for her to make any sense of the space, though
it didn't agree with her impression of the trailer from outside.
Through the doorway to her left was the colored flicker of
light from a screen, and sounds: hard breathing and a fleshy
slap. Ultimo turned from closing the door behind them and
pressed something on a remote that had appeared in his right
hand. The sound stopped and the light flicker with it. Surprised by the dark, Marissa touched her palm to the nearest
wall to orient herself. It felt like a totally flimsy partition; if
she put any weight on it, it might well collapse.

"Careful," Ultimo said. "There's some steps down." His

hand opened across the small of her back—huge as a bear's paw, but after the first uninterpretable thrill of the touch she understood it meant no harm. His other hand was under her elbow, in fact, using it like a rudder to guide her down a set of stairs into an even darker space, which smelled less of musk than cedar smoke.

"Just a second," his voice said. There was a tiny swirl of dizziness as his touch departed. She couldn't tell where he was in the dark—not near her. So long as she didn't move, though, she could still orient herself. It was a straight shot up the stairs behind her to the door of the trailer, and she remembered that he hadn't locked the chain around the gate.

Then a well of light opened and she saw him standing in the center of it, pushing a set of double doors open into the day outside. She was in some sort of half-basement with a field-stone wall the height of her heart. There was a fireplace full of ash and a lot of animal bones.

"Come on up."

Ultimo's jeans and boots were disappearing into the light at the far end of the room. Marissa followed, shading her eyes with one hand as she emerged onto a low wooden deck. She heard herself laugh in delighted surprise; it was like they'd come out on some other planet. A wide empty plain, white as salt, rolled out to a horizon toothed with the peaks of slate-blue mountains.

Ultimo motioned her toward two webbed deck chairs to the right of the double doors he had opened. On the other side was a battered blue cooler; he squatted beside it to lift off the lid.

"Beer? Pop?"

"Water?"

He straightened and walked over to her with a bottle dripping in his hand. He must have loosened the cap for her because it spun free when she opened it, bounced once on the deck floor and disappeared into a crack between two boards.

"Don't worry about it," Ultimo said. He settled into the

chair beside hers and twisted the top from a bottle of orange soda. Marissa took a long draft from her bottle. She was thirsty—her mouth dry. Maybe she'd been more apprehensive than she'd realized in the dark passage between there and here. She took a pair of sunglasses from her shirt pocket and put them on. Ultimo was wearing mirrored aviator shades. He set his pop bottle down on the boards and lowered the back of his chair, then stretched out with his face turned up to the blank sky.

Marissa felt an absence of expectation in him that she found reassuring. She might ask him anything, or nothing. It would be the same to him. Then she had a little stab of anxiety—if she had come ill-prepared the visit might after all be wasted. She took another long pull from the water bottle, noticing a faint acrid taste, like aspirin. The water was clear. Maybe the taste was in her mouth already. After all, there were three questions on her mind. Why had he firebombed the meth lab? But she couldn't very well imagine asking that one, and anyway the answer would be . . . not obvious, but in some way banal. People had died, though. She had seen them run out of the building streaming flame and afterward the news confirmed that they were dead. There hadn't been any news about the naked painted girl she'd seen him snatch out of the truck. Who was she? *Where* was she? Marissa was afraid of the answer to that one. She finished off her bottle of water. And what had Ultimo been doing that day out there in the desert? Performing some ritual—that much was clear—but what was its purpose? He had swung his boots up on the foot of the chair and now lay on his back in much the same posture as when he had collapsed that other day, though now he was clothed and his eyes masked by the mirror glasses. . . .

His face was turned straight up to the sky, but she still had the feeling that his eyes were watching her, studying and waiting for something.

"But you cut your own tires," she heard herself. The line

seemed to come from the middle of some discussion they hadn't even started yet. Ultimo didn't seem surprised of it.

"True," he said, without turning his head. "It's a form of commitment."

She had that forking feeling again in her brain, as if roots were prying apart the matter of her thought, but it didn't hurt this time.

"Same as you," Ultimo said dreamily.

"What?"

"You came here. Do you have a way back?"

She was too numb, as if anesthetized, to feel alarm at this proposition. Instead, an odd and rather pleasant lassitude was seeping all through her body; it no longer seemed important to keep on talking and in fact she probably couldn't have said any more because her tongue was too thick in her mouth. *Dosed.* The faint bitter taste. Rohypnol didn't have any taste but he might have put something else in the water. Even that stab of panic felt muffled, far away. She felt that she should get up and start running—anywhere, but her dense relaxation could not be overcome. There was no confinement here. No fence. She had come in through a fence but she wasn't inside one now—no obstacle between the deck and the horizon. The double doors they'd emerged from were made of plates of steel and must be immensely heavy, though Ultimo had pushed them up and open as easily as cardboard. She remembered now he hadn't locked the gate and maybe that was so other people could come in, strangers who intended her no good.

He had not moved toward her, only rolled his head in her direction, so that she saw two images of herself distorted in the mirrored teardrops. Those roots pulled her brain into several pieces and even

her fear was disintegrating

a feathery

tingle,

a separate orbit.

well

flood

gold light

aWomOnanimal

swirl into the opening coming

nearer—

not her.

The horned being

streaming into this small round

nowhere to be found.

fractured

pattern of

a spiral—eyes

But there was no difference between the inside and the outside of her head, Marissa wanted to say. Not here there wasn't. Here, again, in the cave. She wanted to say what she had seen, when the torchlight played over the water-stained stone, but the others were going on, into another passage. She followed, paying out the string behind her. When the string ran out, she called to Ultimo, who produced a second roll. They switched on a flashlight for long enough to knot the ends together before they went on. The torchlight seemed enclosed in itself. It was something to follow, but illuminated nothing.

"Stop a minute," Jamal said. He looked up, using both hands like blinkers to block the torchlight from his eyes. Marissa did the same. Above, she could see diffused gray daylight, indirect, as if it was coming around a corner or over a lip.

"Here's where she fell," Jamal said. "I'm sure of it."

Ultimo tilted the torch toward the wall.

"The bear was there," Jamal said. "Right there."

Ultimo looked at him through the firelight.

"There's nothing here," Jamal said.

"Just us," Ultimo said. It was odd how he didn't seem disappointed.

"Oh," Marissa said, in a sharp, shocked tone, almost a cry. "She's dreaming the whole thing."

76

"Careful," Ultimo said. "Step down here." He had set one large hand across the small of her back, while other grasped the point of her elbow, using it like a tiller to guide her down a set of stairs into an even darker space, which smelled less of musk than cedar smoke.

"Wait a second." Ultimo let go of her, once they'd reached a level floor. He moved away from her, into the dark ahead, and Marissa stood stock still, trying without success to make some sense of where she was. To her right was the reddish glow of embers from what must be some sort of hearth, and other than that she had no clue. Gooseflesh prickled hairs upright on her forearms and the back of her neck, but she couldn't interpret the sensation as either anticipation or fear. She'd been a fool to come here, maybe; this was a dangerous man. A shaft of light stabbed down into the dark, and after her eyes adjusted she saw that Ultimo had pushed up a pair of cantilevered doors at the far end of the space, opening a rectangle of cloudless blue sky in which there hung a fraying disc of daylight moon.

Now she could read the space she was in: a sort of half-basement with fieldstone walls as high as her chest, and a split-log superstructure, pole rafters under an A-frame roof. From outside, it must resemble an old-time spring house. There was the fireplace she had glimpsed in the dark, and a lot of animal bones. Into her mind came an image of Ultimo crouched on the floor by the hearth, his face streaked with

ash and tallow, splintering bones with his teeth for their mar-
row, but she shook it off and saw that most of the bones were
skulls—all sizes and kinds, and only a few she could recognize for certain. Collectible, even decorative, some might say.
A cloth couch and couple of worn leather armchairs were
draped with deer hides and buffalo robes. A slightly mangy
bearskin covered half the floor.

Ultimo was raking the coals with an iron poker, sending
a swirl of ash motes to spiral in the light slanting in from
outside. He motioned her toward one of the armchairs and
sat down himself in the other. With his huge scarred hands
folded below his navel, he fell into such a remarkable stillness
that Marissa felt fidgety by comparison, poised on the edge
of her seat. Fight or flight? But Ultimo's deep calm seemed
to emanate out of him across the room toward her. It lulled
her. She let herself sink into the chair, aware of the coarse
hair of a deer hide prickling the skin of her back through
her shirt.

"Okay," Ultimo said eventually. "Now is when you get
to ask me what you want."

The words forked into her brain like roots, dividing the
matter of her thought. She ran nonsensical variations: *Tell him
what I want. Ask for what I want.* Or maybe they weren't nonsensical. In spite of her unlikely sense of ease, she had the
feeling that terrible things had occurred here, in the past or
future, or even now.

"That stuff's not happening here," Ultimo said.

"What stuff?" Her throat was so dry she was almost
croaking.

"The stuff you're afraid of." Without warning, Ultimo
tossed her a bottle of water. She was surprised how adroitly
she caught it, in one hand.

"Thanks," she said.

"I owe you."

He was talking about the desert, she realized, and the
water Jamal had thought to leave with him. What in the hell

had been going on, then and there? But that wasn't the only thing she wanted to know.

Chaos, Ultimo said. It's our element.

No, he couldn't possibly have said that. But his naked eye was on her. An eye shared like a mirror.

"Things aren't always what they seem," he said. "Or they are but then again they're not. Example. . . ." He bent sideways to fossick in a cranny below the arm of his chair, and came up with a blue milk crate full of files. Something seemed incongruous about it; Marissa realized it was the only piece of plastic, or any artificial material, she could see anywhere in the room.

Ultimo was passing her a folder. She set down the water bottle to accept it. There was something unusually *good* about that water, like she could feel it expanding all the cells in her body. The file was full of photographs all featuring the same handsome, sometimes beautiful dark-haired girl, in her late teens or early twenties, sometimes alone and sometimes in company; there were prom pictures, family Christmas cards, a yearbook portrait, some casuals showing her rigged out for rock climbing or white-water rafting. And documents: *missing since . . . last seen in. . . .*

Marissa glanced at Ultimo but he had somehow withdrawn and she understood that he expected her to come to her conclusion. She looked through the pictures again, lingering on an eight-by-ten where the girl was wearing some sort of sheer wrap through which the naked energy of her young body glowed; here she had a half-feral gleam in her eye that Marissa abruptly recognized.

"She's the girl from the truck."

"Right," Ultimo said. "You saw me snatch her. And thought God knows what." He put the folder back in the crate and tucked the crate away. "Fact is, I'm a bounty hunter. Part time. Sometimes. I even have a license for it. Sometimes it's ugly, but this time I was working for the family. She's back with them now. No harm done. Or nothing permanent."

He reached to take down a skull from the stone ledge behind him. Marissa couldn't identify it; it seemed cat-shaped but much too big for a house cat—maybe a mountain lion.

"The people she was with, the junk she was taking. . . ." Ultimo rolled the skull between his hands. "She'd of looked like this, with a little skin on it, inside of eighteen months."

"You blew up that meth lab," Marissa heard herself blurt.

"You don't know that." Ultimo turned away from her to set the skull back where he'd found it. "You didn't see me that time. Just a vehicle that looked like mine."

The only one like it in a hundred-mile radius. Marissa didn't say it out loud.

"I know—people died," Ultimo was saying. "They weren't very nice people. In fact they dealt in godawful harm. Nobody'll miss them. Not much, anyway." He seemed to loom toward her, though he was only leaning a little forward in his chair, elbows braced on his knees. "But human beings still, you'll say. It's true—they are. You want to be careful how you call them animals."

He leaned back, closing his eyes for a moment. "Of course, whoever would have got paid by their enemies to do it. That's a fact too. You gotta get paid." His eyes rolled open again. "Sad thing—there's more people will pay to do harm than good."

The water bottle—that was plastic too, Marissa thought inanely.

"When bad things happen to bad people," Ultimo was saying, "sometimes I can help a thing like that on its way."

Well, that was a bit facile, Marissa thought, for justifying yourself as a hired assassin. Maybe it would be simpler just to go with it, though.

"But that's not what you're here for," Ultimo said, and raised an eyebrow at her. One of his scars went through the eyebrow, thick as a white worm.

"No," Marissa said. "It's not." Still, she didn't know how to frame the question she had wanted to ask.

"Savages," Ultimo said. "Savagery—is it the old ones dancing around a big kill or those drugged-out kids circling their cars around the town square all night long?"

She felt that forking sensation again in her brain. "I don't know," she said. Sometime previously she must have asked herself this question without knowing it. "Both. Neither? There's something the same in the pattern."

"Right," he said. "If you strike into a pattern there's something in you that wants to stick with it."

But all this talk was still obscure; he wasn't really telling her anything. In a burst of frustration—almost anger—she said, "Look, you had some reason for doing that thing out in the desert—digging a hole in the ground with your feet till you passed out from dehydration! Trapping yourself out there like that. You could have died."

"I could have," Ultimo said. He didn't go on. That cat-and-mouse thing. She was beginning to hate it, almost. Should she get up and leave (if he would let her), or keep trying to wind some thread of meaning out of all this elliptical talk?

"That headache you've got," Ultimo said. "It's the animal in you trying to come out. Trying to sprout its horns. Of course it's scary! That other stuff—"

"That's not happening here?" But she had the idea that stuff *was* happening somewhere, on parallel tracks, and it was just good luck that she happened to be on this track—the reasonably benign one. Or maybe somehow she'd had the power and good sense to choose it.

"Right," Ultimo said. "That's all about—you're afraid of losing your body. That your body would be taken from you. Or else you're afraid of losing your mind. And the risk is real—it can happen."

She saw a flash of the whites of his eyes as he rolled his head back against the cushion of his chair. Then he straightened up and looked at her again.

"I been scared plenty," he said. "If I look like the baddest thing on the block right now, it wasn't always that way. I lived

270

in New York for a spell, back in the day. Back when it was a dangerous place."

"Oh," Marissa said, realizing she'd meant to say *Why?* Her own experience of New York, came from movies, a couple of books and the TV news. She could hardly imagine herself there, much less Ultimo.

"I was a lot younger then," Ultimo said. "On my lonesome. I didn't belong to any of the local tribes. I had a crib in a slum on the Brooklyn waterfront and . . . there was no law around there back then. On the trains the same. Bad things happened all the time. Black Muslims rode the same train as me. It always felt safer when they turned up, even though I knew they had no use for me or anybody but themselves. But there was order in their lives. Just by being there they kept order on the trains. . . . And later on, when I went to prison, it was the same."

Ultimo leaned forward, his eyes returning to meet hers. "So I learned something—fear depends on your belief. And fear responds to your desire. Sometimes to get where you want to go you have to pass through it. And risk that you might not return."

"What are you talking about," Marissa said.

"I'm trying to answer your question." Ultimo covered his mouth with his hand for a moment, then took it away. "It's hard to talk about it, I guess. You know that animal person trying to tear its way out of your head? Well, what I think is that the old ones created the animals out of chaos. That's why I want to see the bear they painted on the rock. It's more real than the real one. It was there first."

"But what about Julie?" Marissa heard the hint of a choke in her voice, and realized her eyes had prickled with tears.

"I'm not out there to get your girl back. It's not like the other one. You didn't hire me. And I don't have what it would take for that."

"What was her name?" *What is her name?*

"Dunno—Melanie, I think." Ultimo glanced in the

direction of the hidden milk crate. "It's in the file if you need to know."

"It doesn't matter."

"Hey, there was nothing to that but bad drugs and bad company. Easy enough to claim her back." Ultimo paused. "The good thing is, in the end she was willing. Your girl now, she's making a choice to stay where she is."

"But why?"

"If something in this world frightened her, then maybe she feels safer on the other side. And more than likely there's something she has to work out there too." Ultimo shrugged. "But that's just guessing. Here's what I know."

He caught Marissa's eye and held it. "You're a pilgrim. She's a pilgrim. But you're more experienced than she is. You have a practice. I don't know what it is but I can tell that you have it. And she's the one who needs a guide. You've been with her there already, before now, haven't you? You're the one who can get there again—"

He's hypnotizing me . . . it was only a fleeting thought. A host of butterflies was rising in her throat, and she couldn't get unstuck from his gaze, which seemed to press on the fault lines of that headache. The pain was much worse, almost unbearable, and she felt a flash of real terror too. Ultimo was shaping something with spiral movements of his hands, as if the shadows of that cave-like space had taken on the density of clay and could be molded. He was still murmuring *I can only help you a little but I'll do what I can. . . .* Her jaw had dropped and with her mouth open it seemed that the pain in her head was diminished just slightly. How long had she been in that room? The shaft of daylight admitted through the double doors had perhaps been creeping toward her, toward of both of them, but now it was moving improbably fast, unless time had warped somehow, and the pressure in her head was truly unbearable. In the light shaft, motes of dust, or ash, kept swirling.

Then she was absorbed into the light and at the same

moment her skull cracked open and the antlers came out. The relief was so astonishing she could let her body relax completely; she was buoyed up in a warm sparkling fluid—an ascending helix whose glittering motes were now revealed as eyes of the animal persons, looking at her—thousands of eyes regarding her but benignly as if she was one of their own. Their horns fit comfortably on her brow.

It seemed to be a triple helix, and Ultimo, eyes sealed shut, was absorbed into a second funnel whose shining sparks closed about him like a cocoon. In the third spiral was Julie herself, eyes open and trained on Marissa, reaching out her hand. Marissa responded with the same gesture. She could feel the warmth of Julie's hand. Julie was ascending as Marissa was sinking. In passing their fingers grazed with the faintest feathery tingle of a touch.

Then there was nothing left but the bright well of light, with the powder blue sky at the top of the shaft, and the moon so frail and tattered—how could there be anything behind it?

77

The bison came into the dry gulch and stood for a long moment staring at the first bus in the caravan, which pulled to a quick stop, heeling over slightly from the unevenly distributed weight of its passengers. The animal's head lowered; it blew dust from the ground. It was big, and the horns looked bluish in the midday light. A buffalo was not a wholly uncommon sight hereabouts, but a cameraman got out of the KELO van and moved in, shooting steadily till the buffalo lifted its head with a snort, turned and went trotting away down the gulch.

From the edge where the buffalo had appeared the sinkhole offered a gentle slope down to the overhang of the cavern. Despite the considerable crowd unpacking itself from two buses and a good number of private trucks and cars, a peculiar silence rose up from it, like smoke. The caved-in earth on the sinkhole's floor appeared to be scattered with small yellow flowers, which struck Marissa as impossible, until, as more and more people poured in from the gulch, they uprooted themselves and took to the air; a saffron flight of butterflies. A general gasp went up from the crowd.

Where the butterflies had been thickest, Ultimo squatted on his heels, studying something on the ground. He wore brown clothes that matched the dirt, and nobody seemed to notice him except Marissa and Jamal, who slipped away from from the bus they'd come in and walked across the loosened earth to join him. Arms wrapped around his knees, Ultimo was looking into an enormous clawed paw-print. Marissa felt a shiver run over her, but she wouldn't exactly have called it fear. The fine hair on her forearms prickled up, the way it did when she was moved by music.

"Grizzly?" That was Jamal's voice.

"I never saw one that big," Ultimo said. "I never saw anything that big." He probed the pad of the print with his middle finger, which went down all the way to the knuckle. Then he flattened his huge hand into the print; his fingers didn't begin to reach the claw-marks.

Marissa backed up and looked around the rim of the sinkhole and saw nothing, other than a swell of people still pouring over the lowest lip. They were fast obliterating any tracks, and anyway she was no tracker.

The crowd was trying to coordinate itself. A famous anthropologist had come out with his coterie from Sioux Falls, and a team of archaeologists from the university in Iowa City. Each group was vying to be first in the cave; meanwhile Janice Rivington was already striding down toward the cavernous overhang. She was bigger than she looked on TV and wore a shiny silk suit that made sense for the studio, with a pair of blond Timberlands, which were doubtless not meant to appear in the shot.

Ultimo, Marissa, and Jamal had passed quietly into the shade of the overhang.

"There's your bats," Ultimo said, looking up into the curve of the high dome.

"Some of them anyway," Jamal said. From croppings of the stone roof a couple of hundred bats were hanging in the shrouds of their folded wings, like shriveled fruit. The KELO cameraman was craning back to shoot them.

"Sound sleepers," Ultimo said, and turned to the rear wall. There were three openings, all about the same size. Ultimo looked at Jamal, who shrugged.

"I don't know if I was back this far," Jamal said.

Janice Rivington was arguing something with the

famous anthropologist and the archaeological team, in front of the middle opening. Her blond hair tossed with the vigorous movement of her head. Then she turned from the others and called into the crowd: "Jamal? Jamal Bin Dajani? Jamal?"

Jamal didn't answer. The thicket of onlookers concealed him where he stood. Ultimo put his big hand on his shoulder for a moment, then took it away. The cameraman beckoned to Jamal's older brother, but Omar shook his head, pretending not to understand, while Ramin simply stared through him. Janice and her lighting men exchanged a couple of whispers and then the whole camera crew abruptly plunged into the middle opening. The famous anthropologist and the archaeology team were left gaping at each other for a moment, then began scrambling in after the TV group.

"All three of them come out in the same place," Jamal said. "I mean, I think they do."

With a grin, Ultimo handed Jamal a two-foot-long mag lite. "Wait a minute," he said, and walked back to collect a few branches from a knot of greasewood that appeared to have fallen out of the sky. He nodded to Jamal, who led their way into the passage nearest them. Marissa looked back once over her shoulder. Now that the crowd was all under the overhang, struggling to squeeze in after the experts and the TV crew, the butterflies were settling again: a yellow-orange carpet on the broken ground.

Marissa couldn't measure how far they had gone, but it was only ten minutes or so before they came out of the passage into a much larger space, cathedral-size it seemed to her, though she felt it more than she could see it. The beams of their strong flashlights got lost in there, as if they were aiming them into the night sky.

"Shut the lights," Ultimo hissed. When they had done so, the darkness seemed at first absolute, a black well of deep time.

Ahead and to their left a glow was building, then the first of the television lights emerged. Janice Rivington stepped into the open space, automatically striking a pose as her head moved snakelike, searching for the camera. The experts trickled out, and then the crowd began to pour, jostling and murmuring. Marissa thought of the bats they'd seen smoking out of the slit entrance on the cliff by the rock shelters a few days before, and she thought it was curious how all these people seemed only to be aware of themselves.

"Okay." Janice Rivington had raised her voice. "You think we could throw some light on that ceiling?"

In the shadows or inside her head Marissa thought a sound of drumming, warm broad hands slapping loose skins (skin maybe still growing on some animal's hollow flank, not yet stretched over the dug-out wooden round of a drum). And there was light in enormous quantities, as if the hands that drummed were fanning flames, like a river of pulsing fire away down to her left, illuminating the gallery wall to the right of her and above . . . and the gallery was big, enormously hollow, huge as a cathedral hall.

On the right wall and spreading up onto the ceiling above were bison, such a stampede of bison as she had never seen (even if she was really only seeing them projected on the lids of her closed eyes), magnificent in umber and ocher, humping their weighty shoulders out of the natural curve of the rock, bigger too it seemed to her than the ordinary buffalo they'd seen in the daylight not so much as an hour before. Among them too were antlers, not deer, she thought, but elk. And they looked at her in the same way as the bear had done before (where had the bear gone, then?). The eye of each animal person was upon her, as if it knew her. Even though there were so many of them in this procession, which seemed at times perfectly orderly, as if every animal person knew and followed the same purpose, or at times anarchic as though all of them were caught up in a flood.

"The lights are *too strong*." One of the archaeologists was the first to speak. "They'll damage the painting. At Lascaux—" Then someone apparently shut him up. A hush, and

the cavalcade of animals which seemed to have detached itself
from the stone and to be floating, flowing in midair. Marissa
heard a rushing sound, or felt a rushing in her ears.

a feathery tingle,
a separate orbit.

well

flood   *gold light*

aWomOnanimal

swirl into the opening coming

nearer—

not her.

The horned being
streaming into this small round

nowhere to be found.

fractured
pattern   *of*

a spiral—eyes

Janice Rivington and her crew had set up a shot, but
when the camera rolled the only sound that came out of
her was a sort of choked mouse-squeak. After about thirty
slow-moving seconds, the cameraman made a throat-slash
gesture and all the machines stopped whirring. Someone
handed Janice Harrington a plastic bottle of water, but when
she tried to drink most of it ran from the corners of her
mouth. Marissa could see her frightened face in the blaze
of the too-bright lights, the muscle in her long neck working, and she saw her beginning to compose herself, wiping
her mouth and dabbing the handkerchief at the spill on her
lapel. Although she didn't wait for the mic to swing in on
its boom or for the red light to glow on the camera, her

voice had regained the rich confident tone Marissa knew from the television.

My God. My God. Who where these people?

78

As the light faded the panorama fractured, into the pattern of brightly branching dots she'd seen before, though now and then she could still pick out a horn, an antler or a clear bright eye out of the vortex. She moved beside the stream, her bare heels (what had happened to her shoes?) sinking into heel prints made by others long ago in what had once been clay. She was hurrying, before the light would fail entirely, toward another narrow opening at the lower end of this great hall, into which the animal persons also seemed to swirl, but she felt somehow certain that on the other side of the slit portal there would be a human being sprouted with horns.

Behind her there came a crackling sound. Ultimo had struck fire to his greasewood torch. Enlarged by the yellow-red flickering light, Jamal's spindly shadow splayed over her.

Where had the animal persons gone? She had seen them all streaming through the opening into this small round chamber, but now they were nowhere to be found. Marissa's vision fractured, and the pattern of dots streamed in a spiral—she thought that the dots must be the eyes of the animal persons, who had lost their bodies but were still regarding her.

Then they were gone and her vision steadied. On the curving wall before her she did see a series of little horned heads—no, they were handprints, negative images, a black paint surrounding the pallor of the stone, so that the hands seemed to glow a little, like the phosphorescent plastic stars stuck to the ceiling above Julie's bed at home. One print seemed to attract her hand, magnetically, the left one. There was a tingle, a thrill in her palm. When she laid it there it fit so perfectly there was no line around it. Her left hand disappeared entirely into darkness, complete as the velvet black of a starless sky; it sank a little way into soft stone.

79

The stone was blue now, the color of turquoise, but soft like clay; she could move through it. She was aware of others near her, circling through the blue stone wall. Did she know them? They were shades. On one side the cave, the other the world. A pair of hands pressing symmetrically toward hers, from the other side of this giving surface.

Let me come out of this rock.

金雪灸雪 雹丌雹明創 昼臾 明問令

Beyond the surface was a cool, dim space, like an underwater cave. There were people there waiting, as if in a trance. A pair of hands reaching out toward hers.

The cave covered them like the dome of a tent. They were all looking down, as if waiting for something, or hoping for it. They were looking toward her, but they had not found her.

Her hands spread flat on a firm surface, solid though invisible. It wasn't stone, like a moment before. Maybe instead some sort of rock crystal.

In the cave the handprints were framed in black, and they fit her own hands to perfection. If she kept pressing she could come through, as she had come through the stone before; the stone had softened, like wet clay. She could come out of one cave into the other.

A bright white light bore down on her, piercing, like a laser or a diamond.

Julie, Julie. . . .

So the two halves made a whole: a squashed sphere like the gibbous moon. She was back to back with herself and facing both realms at the same time, curving outward into both realms, but falling or floating from one into the other. . . . So she raised her own hands, toward the other two hands that closed around hers. Now she did know those voices calling her name, which belonged to the ones she had loved, or was going to.